ONCE WICKED, ALWAYS DEAD

To Sandy
A lovely lady
Enjoy

By

T. Marie Benchley

T. Marie Benchley

Copyright ©2010, T. Marie Benchley

ISBN: 978-0-9844787-1-2

Library of Congress Control Number: 2010922577

Printed in the United States of America.

Published by
M.M.W.E. Publishing House
Tampa, Florida
MMWEPublish@aol.com

Dedication

I WOULD LIKE TO SAY "THANK YOU":

Mom and Dad, for teaching me to be tenacious and determined in whatever life dishes out, as well as giving me your gift of humor. You always make me laugh and because of you I never take myself too serious! I love you and will always be your little girl. Thank you for exposing me to the arts. I will always fondly remember our trips to the Dow gardens and library.

Yvonne, your grace and love touches me daily, and I so look forward to our Sunday brunches with you and Eddie. You both mean so much to me.

My Husband, you are my special ray of sunshine, and your love fills my heart! I could not imagine my life without you in it. You are my confidant, my best friend. You give me that gentle nudge when I need it the most. Thank you for your patience with me. I promise to never take you for granted.

I love you all so much.

10:35 pm
Atlanta, Georgia
September 1, 1985

THE DIMLY LIT ROOM WAS SPECIFICALLY DESIGNED TO CREATE A SOOTHING atmosphere for his patients. An illusion of safety and warmth was his mastermind. He was a Picasso when it came to the details of decorating his office. A large Mahogany bookcase became his backdrop and held the treasure chest of necessary books he would use to refer to in order to diagnose his most tormented patients. It was after hours and he sat in a supple, dark leather chair with his pad and pen upon the table beside him. The room was silent except for the ticking of the clock. The woman who lay upon the overstuffed couch was not one of his usual patients. She began caressing the opulent fabric while enjoying the scrumptious feel of it as it touched her skin.

"Thank you for letting me see you so late," she said softly, almost childlike. "I was pleasantly surprised when you called me and asked me to come in. Your office is beautiful. You have such an acquired taste, but I'm sure you have been told that before. I have always been curious, Doctor, how one develops such taste."

The attractive brunette raised her head allowing her long hair to fall upon her back while giving him a brief glance. "You

1

see, that has always been one of my problems," she continued. "I guess you could say that is why I'm here with you. I've been with so many men whose taste, well, how shall I say, is unique. Some men just have the strangest taste, wouldn't you say?"

She sat upright to adjust the strap of her candy apple red Stiletto. "I'm sure you personally know all about these kind of men, don't you, Doc?" Her soft childlike voice began to emerge into that of a confident woman. "I really enjoy showing these men how bad their taste is. I mean, someone has to. Wouldn't you agree? Let me give you an example of what I mean. I am specifically talking about their taste in sex."

With a seductive smirk on her face, she cocked her head and looked at the man who was silent in his chair. "Some men have very peculiar taste when it comes to sex. You know what I'm talking about, Doc. They like 'em young. You would be very surprised at how many men out there like the idea of having sex with very young girls."

As she continued to speak she rose from the couch, allowing her trench coat to fall open and reveal the red teddy that she wore beneath it. She turned to face the doctor and continued talking as she seductively walked toward him. "But Doctor, I don't have to tell you about these types of men, do I, when you personally know what I'm talking about, right?"

She now straddled the man, as she continued. "You can relate to these men, can't you Doc, because you like little girls." Bending over, she placed her mouth to the silent man's head and with her full lips planted a big red kiss upon the top of his forehead then laughed.

"You see Doc," she continued, "this is my calling, and this is what I was meant to do. Just call me your Super Hero, baby, because you know my motto: Once Wicked, Always Dead!"

With his body still warm, his ghastly hollow eyes stared into the dark abyss as the hypodermic needle protruded from the neck of his dead body. He was just another one of her many victims as she laughed hysterically at his expense.

Chapter One

1:30 pm
Tampa, Florida
July 25, 2009

MOLLY MADISON SAT AT THE LARGE ROUND MAHOGANY TABLE. SHE loved the fresh white linen tablecloths and the way the sun came through the window as it bounced off from her crystal water glass to create little rainbow prisms that danced upon the wall. Etched vases filled with fresh white magnolias sat in the middle of each table and the sweet smell of the South saturated the room. Each of the waiters looked as if they had been custom ordered. They were at least six feet tall, well tanned and wore crisp white shirts that complemented their muscular physique.

Palma Cia Country Club was first class by any standards. They certainly knew how to cater to women's needs. Any woman with money could come to the club and enjoy the finer things in life. Whether it was tennis lessons or relaxing and enjoying one of the many services that the spa had to offer, this was the place for a neglected wife to go.

Every week for the past twenty years, Molly sat at the same table across from her dear friend Leeza. They caught up on the weekly gossip of who was sleeping with whom, while Molly would watch Leeza stab at her spinach and raise it to her mouth. Leeza purposely tried to avoid touching her lips to her fork when she took a bite for fear that she might enjoy her food, lose all self-control and wind up looking like the repulsive Amberly Dent who sat at the table next to them. It was a well-known fact that Amberly married Dr. Dent when he was eighty and she was forty-two. He was her fourth husband, and although this time around she thought she had reeled in the big fish, she was gravely disappointed when she finally realized he came from an incredible gene pool and was as cheap as a Louis Vuitton knock-off. Years later, Amberly had gained thirty pounds due to frustration, and he was still kicking and demanding his daily tryst. Molly and Leeza could never figure out why the woman would ever want to be a member of such an exclusive country club and subject herself to the constant gossip and scrutiny from the other women.

Molly had just turned forty-five the week prior and, unlike some of the women who would be insulted if anyone asked their age, she was not. She was able to take great pride in how her body had matured from the young Montana girl she had been into the sophisticated woman who now sat at a table in this exclusive club. Time had been very kind to her over the years. The long golden hair of her youth was now cut to a more respectable shoulder length, and although she now made monthly trips to the salon to obtain the color of corn silk that had once come to her naturally, she was still stunning. Molly had the great fortune to be blessed with flawless skin, and although she now lived in the South with its intense heat, she always took great lengths to protect it.

The majority of women that belonged to the club would spend hours in the sun and bask their bodies in order to give themselves the bronze sex appeal that they so desired, only to have to eventually pay for their self abuse by spending large amounts of their husband's money to have regular Botox injections and mini face lifts. But not Molly; she never lay out amongst them. And whenever she did venture outside, she always lathered up her soft, supple skin with sunscreen so she could glorify in the results of not having a single wrinkle upon her flawless face. Yes, time had been very kind to Molly. Her eyes still looked just as blue and bright as they had twenty-five years ago.

As each year passed, Molly may have appeared fabulous, but on the inside she felt substandard and lost. For the past twenty years, Molly had always wrapped her life around her husband, his career and taking care of their only daughter, Savanna. Several years into her marriage, Phillip began keeping late hours and Molly had learned to ignore the emotional distance that grew between them. Savanna was married, had her own husband and was active in school. Molly was thankful in that staying busy volunteering and being an active member of the club did not give her much time to dwell upon her marital problems. Even though Savanna would call Molly daily to fill her in on the day's events or ask her mother for her advice, Molly still had a lot of extra time on her hands and she was finding it harder to fill the empty black hole growing inside of her.

Molly met Phillip while finishing her last year of law school at Harvard. Phillip was an absolutely dashing, true southern gentleman. Mutual friends introduced them and soon after they went on their first date to a poetry reading. Phillip was unlike any man Molly had known while growing up in the Big Sky country. He was tall, dark and extremely handsome, and Molly knew that he was very driven and would introduce her to the life that she had always dreamt of living.

A year later, Molly and Phillip were married. One year after that Phillip passed the Bar and was hired at Davis and Lynch, one of the largest law firms in Florida, employing two hundred attorneys. Phillip worked incredibly long hours and was determined to become a lead partner one day.

Molly stood out amongst the other wives and she was an incredible asset to Phillip. He knew that if he needed a small dinner for four or a large social event for four hundred, Molly would always pull it together with the utmost class. He could count on her to remember every face and name she met. When they were out together, people could not help but stare. Everyone wished to know and be seen with the attractive young couple.

Over the years, all of their hard work had paid off. Phillip became lead partner. Molly had assumed that once Phillip would become lead, he would relax a little more and maybe the two of them could become close again, but once Phillip had obtained his original goal, he had gained much greater aspirations: to pursue politics. Molly tried to be patient, standing on the sidelines waiting for whatever leftover affection Phillip could muster, praying that he would take an interest in their love life again, but to her disappointment, Phillip was always too tired. So, the lonely woman became an expert at pleasing herself, longing to feel Phillip's strong hands upon her and imagining that it was his hand pleasing her instead of her own.

"Molly, Molly, really you haven't been paying attention at all." Leeza said. "What the hell am I going to do if Jeff marries her? He's my only son for God's sake, and I know the bitch is only after him because he comes from money. He still has two more years of law school. To top it off what do you think she's getting her degree in? Would you believe Art History? Who the hell wastes four years to major in Art History?"

"Look Leeza, I know it's hard for you, but she isn't all that bad. At least she has an education and she went to school on a full scholarship to Princeton."

Molly knew Leeza did not like her son's girlfriend, and no matter how much she stuck up for the poor girl, Leeza would never be nice or accept her into her heart. The fact of the matter was that no one would be good enough for her baby boy.

"Okay, okay, I'm finished complaining," Leeza sighed. "I know that I just need to accept their love for each other and hope for the best." She leaned back in her chair and fixed her eyes upon the young stud that had been serving them.

"Really, where do they find them?" She purred with a devilish grin on her face as she ran her fingers through her short blond locks.

Even though Leeza was intolerable at times, Molly loved her and knew she could always count on her. Molly knew that Leeza would do anything for her.

Molly took one last drink of her glass of white wine. "Well sweetie, I'd love to sit here all day with you, but I really need to head home. Savanna and John are coming over for dinner this evening and Mommy and Daddy are driving down to spend a couple of weeks with us. Everyday they call me to let me know where they are so I know they're okay. I don't want to miss their call."

"Wow Molly, I can't believe your parents still want to make that drive all the way from Montana at their age. Why in heavens name won't they fly?"

"Oh Daddy takes the words of Alexander Chase to heart: 'Lovers of air travel find it exhilarating to hang poised between the illusion of immortality and the fact of death.' It's the death part that scares him. It's somewhat of a miracle that Momma was even able to tear him away from the ranch for three weeks to come for a visit. Quite a few years back, Daddy was out alone and had gotten kicked while trying to break in his new mare. It scared Momma to death, and she made him get some more men to help out. So he hired this ranch hand and made him foreman. Only now Daddy loves working with this man so much, Momma can't get him to go anywhere."

"Hmm, this cowboy has been around for years and you never mentioned him to me? So what does he look like?" Leeza cooed with delight.

"I don't know. I haven't been home in years. Is that all you think about? I believe Daddy thinks of him as the son he never had. God knows he certainly doesn't feel that way about Phillip. I think he's resented Phillip ever since we got married. He hates the fact that we're so far away from him and Momma. Daddy never felt that Tampa was the proper environment to raise their only granddaughter and that she needed to learn more about nature. They both hate cities and the people that live in them. Every time that Phillip tries to talk with Daddy about one of his cases, Daddy always responds by saying that Tampa is not a fitting place for his little girl and grandbaby. He then follows up by saying, 'You can't be suspicious of a tree or accuse a bird or squirrel of subversion.' Anyway, I love them so much and I know they mean well, but I just wish they could understand that we need to be here for Phillip and just accept it after all these years. I mean, look at Savanna. She's turned out just fine. I think they would be happy if I was still living with them, isolated on that ranch and cleaning the horse shit out of the barn."

Leeza took a drink of her water and laughed so hard she almost choked. "Please, what I wouldn't pay to see you with your fresh manicure trying to scrub the horseshit out from under your nails!" She giggled as a vivid picture ran across her mind.

Molly raised her slim body away from the table. "Well love, I suppose I'm just going to have to leave you with that wonderful picture of me in your head, because I really should go. When you talk to Jeff and Lilly tell them I send them both my love. Give me a kiss." She pecked her friend upon the cheek.

"OK, I'll call you later. Tell your mother and father I said hi. Maybe we can all get together while they're here." Leeza stayed seated and sucked upon a piece of ice while eyeing the young waiter as he refilled her water glass.

Molly strolled out of the club and handed a fat tip to the handsome valet who held the door open to her Bentley.

"Good day, Mrs. Madison."

Chapter Two

THE CITY LIGHTS CAST SHADOWS THAT STRETCHED ALONG THE BRICK WALLS upon the back of the buildings that lined the dingy alleyway. It reached up like bony fingers providing shade to mask the faces of those who wished to keep their dirty secrets from others. These people would walk down these alleys amongst the stench of garbage and vomit and paid little attention to the bums that lay in their own filth amongst the strewn bottles of poison that would become their demise. They could not contain their hidden desires and this was the price they paid for their dishonesty.

Phillip Madison was one of these people. Every Thursday night for the past ten years he came to this alley and walked to the back door of his hidden lifestyle. This one night of the week he would allow his secret passions to rise to the surface to fulfill his sexual cravings for male companionship. He would enter the back door of the popular gay nightclub wearing a baseball cap and sunglasses so as not to be recognized. Although he took great lengths to hide his identity, it was a common fact in the gay community that Phillip Madison led a double life.

While in high school, Phillip discovered that he was different from the other boys his age. His family was one of the richest and most powerful in the South and he had high standards to meet. But he had higher expectations and different passions. On the outside Phillip looked like he had it all, but on the inside he had dark, ugly secrets. Only he knew these feelings were not accepted by society's standards and he hid them well.

All the girls loved him. He was handsome, tall, and was always a true gentleman. He never tried to feel them up like all the other boys they went with. He would sit and listen to them talk for hours. He would notice their new shade of lipstick or tell them how he loved their shoes and notice how well matched they were with their outfit. The other boys never took the time to notice these things. They were only interested in sex and cars.

Phillip got along well with other boys in school. He was on the golf team, but he hung out with the football players. He went to all of their parties and games, he would offer them his support and they thought of him as one of their own. His appearance was always immaculate, but if they could look inside of him, they would have seen his hidden desires.

Phillip walked through the heavy metal door of the club and looked around. Everything was black and it was difficult to see, so he removed his sunglasses.

"Much better," he thought.

The electric voice of Donna Summer swirled in his head. He took great pleasure watching the sweat glisten from the men who simultaneously grinded their bodies together upon the dance floor and felt shivers of excitement run from the back of his neck all the way down to his groin. As he gazed around the club, he spotted his grand prize, Sloan. There he was in all his glory, grinning from ear to ear and waving franticly for Phillip to come and join him.

"Hey baby." Sloan grabbed the back of Phillip's head and slid his tongue into his mouth.

Although Phillip appreciated the passionate greeting, he gently pulled his mouth away. "Sloan, unfortunately we can't be long tonight, I really need to get home early. Molly has been getting a little suspicious." Phillip could feel Sloan tense up.

"Well maybe you better go now! I am just a little tired of being the other woman!" Sloan hissed at Phillip as he flung himself back like a small child and crossed his arms. He glared at his lover. "Look I'm tired of this. You know that you're not happy with Molly. Why the hell don't you just end the facade? You and I both know that I'm the one who makes you happy! And don't give me the excuse that you have a daughter. She's a grown woman. Why spend the rest of your life in an unhappy and sexless marriage?" Sloan's tone was almost whining.

Phillip's head began to hurt. He sat up straight. "Sloan this is it. This is all I have to give you. I will not leave my wife and ruin my career for my inner desires to be with you or any other man. I really thought you could understand that. I was honest with you from day one. My career means more to me than being happy. Molly is a very kind woman and I do love her. I never want to hurt her, so this is it. This is all our relationship is ever going to be. I can't offer any more of myself than a few moments together. I really wish it was more but I just can't."

Sloan reached over and pulled Phillip's hand into his. Neither one spoke. Time seemed to stand still as they let the same music in that filled their ears the first night they met.

Phillip had first laid his eyes upon Sloan at a fundraiser that Molly and he attended. Sloan had been working the party and, with a huge tray in hand, walked over and offered up various tempting morsels to Phillip. Phillip could see that Molly was busy working the room to help further his political stature, so he took the opportunity to get to know the young stud. When the night was over Phillip had slipped his business card inside of Sloan's pants pocket and let his hand linger while asking him to give him a ring the next morning.

Later that night after the last drunk had stumbled out the door and the last glass cleaned, Sloan went home to his loft apartment. It was small but very stylish and he loved how it always made him feel safe. Usually after catering big events like the one that night, he fell asleep before his head hit the pillow, but that particular night was different. He was too excited to sleep. He had a flutter in his stomach and every time he closed his eyes, he saw Phillip's face. He knew Phillip was one of the most high-powered attorneys in the South and he felt the man's eyes staring at his ass all night. He was everything that Sloan wanted in a man: power, money and best of all, Phillip was horny as hell.

"Yes," Sloan thought to himself. "This is just the right one and I've got him hooked. Only problem is his wife, but when have I ever let something like that stop me?" He assured himself. "I always liked a challenge!"

Sloan knew Phillip was just like any other gay gentleman from the South. He was extremely polished and appeared happily married with the perfect wife and daughter. He had been with these types of men a thousand times and he felt it his personal responsibility to help the poor saps step out of the closet and be true to themselves, which is just what he intended to do for Phillip Madison.

Sloan sat alongside of Phillip and listened to their song, remembering how they met. He was no longer the little waiter boy, as he now worked as Phillip's assistant. He would not say anything more to Phillip about Molly. He knew what he must do.

If Phillip would not take the first step for himself, then without a doubt, he would take care of the bitch himself. Sloan leaned over to Phillip and whispered gently into his ear. Rising in unison, the men walked out of the seedy establishment hand in hand and proceeded to Phillip's Bentley.

Chapter Three

Gavin and Addie O'Malley awoke before daybreak to get a jump on traffic. The air was thick with humidity and smelled like fish. Gavin hated the South. He loved the crisp clean air of Montana and could not understand why his daughter would ever want to live where perspiration bogged down the air. He loaded the trunk of their Lincoln with the luggage that was as old as they were.

"Bejesus Addie, I've been out here for five minutes and my shirt's already soaked clean through! I feel like I need to go back in and take another shower."

"Oh Gavin, quit your belly aching and get in the car. You can shower up as soon as we get to Molly's." Addie slid into her seat, happy that this was the last leg of their journey before they would see their little girl.

Gavin and Addie had left Montana four days ago and, due to Gavin's failing eyesight, they wanted to be at their daughter's by nightfall. It had been a long trip and their seventy-year-old legs were cramped from the hours spent in the car. Addie realized that her husband's mood had grown increasingly cankerous as the miles rolled along. Listening to his complaints, she had wished that flying was an option, but she had given up on trying to get Gavin on a plane years ago. She often joked with their friends that she was just happy he didn't make her go by horse and buggy.

Although she laughed about it, each year the journey to Molly's house seemed longer and they grew more tired with the long drive. The yearly trip always put Gavin in a sour mood, a reminder of how far away his daughter and granddaughter lived. He despised Phillip, and from his point of view, his daughter's husband wasn't much of a man. As he got older, Gavin worried more about his pansy-ass son-in-law getting his hands on his Ghost Bear Ranch. He knew that Phillip had absolutely no interest in living out West, let alone running the place, as it was a huge responsibility.

After many sleepless nights contemplating this dilemma, Gavin concluded that he would have to sit down and have a heart-to-heart with Molly. The only clear solution was to leave the Ghost Bear to Clayton, his ranch foreman. He would arrange to have Clayton make yearly payments to a trust that would be set up in his granddaughter's name. This way Phillip couldn't get his hands on the ranch or the money. The Ghost Bear was to be passed down to Molly, but Gavin knew that by giving Clayton control of the ranch the Ghost Bear would live on. This was the only way he wouldn't have to worry about Molly's husband stripping it apart and selling it off piece by piece to the highest bidders. Clayton would make sure the Ghost Bear would stay intact and prosper.

Gavin finished loading the luggage into the trunk and started the car. "Turn the air up Addie. It's going to be a hot one today."

Addie did as Gavin asked and then took out her new book, which she began to read as they entered on the ramp to Interstate I-75.

Chapter Four

Wanting to get a jump on things before her parents arrived, Molly set the alarm for seven a.m. When she awoke, she realized that Phillip once again had already left for work without even a kiss good-bye. He had worked late the night before and, tired of waiting for his arrival, she had put his dinner in the fridge and gone to bed.

Phillip was working longer hours and seemed to be coming home later and later. Molly noticed that he had grown more distant over the past few months. Any time she tried to bring up the subject, Phillip would quickly dismiss her concerns and tell her that he had been working on a big case and she was being paranoid. Although her intuition told her that there was something else going on, she chose to ignore her feelings. The last thing she wanted was any friction with Phillip while her parents were staying with them. Her daddy would surely pick up on it and he didn't need any more reasons not to like Phillip.

Molly climbed into the shower built for two and let the hot water cascade down her body. As she lathered herself, she tried to wash away all thoughts of Phillip and concentrate on the tasks that had to be finished before her parents' arrival. As Molly was finishing, the phone rang. She shut off the shower and grabbed the fluffy white towel, wrapping it around her body as she ran for the phone, trying not to slip on the wet marble floor. She managed to make it to the phone right on the last ring.

The voice of a young man was on the line. "Hello, Mrs. Madison?"

"Yes, this is she." Not use to receiving calls so early in the morning, she assumed it was another one of those obnoxious telemarketers.

"Mrs. Madison, this is Sloan Davis from your husband's office."

Molly instantly noticed the nervous energy in Sloan's voice and she began to worry. "Yes, Sloan I remember you. How are you? Is everything all right? Is Phillip okay?"

"Molly, Phillip is fine. I'm calling you because I would like to meet with you. I think there is something you should know, something that could be of great importance to you." Sloan's hands were cold and clammy as he tightly gripped the phone. He knew this would be the best thing for Phillip, even if he wasn't ready to admit it to himself. Since Sloan was a little boy, he never liked sharing his possessions, and as far as he was concerned, Phillip was his greatest possession.

MOLLY'S INTEREST WAS definitely piqued as to what was so important to cause this man from Phillip's office to call her. "Well, I'm really tied up today. Can't you just tell me over the phone?" She could hear Sloan's heavy breathing as she waited for him to answer. Just then, her phone beeped, letting her know that she had another caller on the line. "Sloan, I have another call coming in. Would it be alright to meet with you tomorrow?"

"That will be just fine. I will give you a call tomorrow morning," he replied reluctantly.

Sloan hung up the phone then looked in the mirror that hung upon the wall in front of him. He stared at his reflection and noticed the grotesque smile that covered his handsomely boyish face. For an instant, he thought it strange that he was smiling while knowing he was about to change this woman's conception of reality. He almost felt sorry for her.

"Almost," he thought as he walked out the door of his apartment, still grinning from ear to ear.

THE TRUCKER HAD been up for three days straight and running his rig hard on I-75. He had eaten his last handful of No-Doz the day before and now the urge to sleep was forcing itself upon him. He glanced at himself in the rearview mirror and noticed how his eyes resembled the road maps he used while on his nomadic journey. Over the years, truck stops across the country had become his home. While he fueled up his massive semi, he normally would shower, get a good meal, and watch a little TV before heading back out on the open road. This run had been different, as he had experienced mechanical problems in Amarillo and was way behind schedule. The shipping yard had been on his ass to get the load to Miami, so he didn't have time for such luxuries as a shower, and he became skilled at slapping a piece of cold bologna between two pieces of white bread all the while never taking his foot off the pedal. He made it through what seemed like another endless night of highway and now the morning sun began to bake the interior of the cab that imprisoned him. He noticed the pungency of his own body.

He took a deep breath and started to gag at his own stench. "Jesus, I smell like damn road kill."

He rolled down his window hoping a little fresh air would make him feel and smell better. The air swirled around the inside of his confinement; it blew through his hair and felt like a woman's hand caressing his long black curls. As he continued down the endless stretch of highway, the gentle humming of the engine soothed him like a lullaby and he felt his tense muscles begin to relax. The fragrance of the Gulf waters overpowered his subconscious mind and he started to have a succession of mental images of frolicking naked in the cool waters with the voluptuous blond in a red sports car he had passed by the day before. He envisioned the waves lapping over their sun-drenched bodies as they rolled, embraced in the sand. He could hear the seagulls laughing above their heads. As he was conjuring these mental images, his large blood shot eyes fell shut and soon his breathing became shallow. The machine he once dominated was now taking control of itself. His bulky shoe weighed heavy on the gas pedal, accelerating the massive weapon with impelling force. His nail bitten fingers were no longer on the leather steering wheel; they were now lying limp in his lap.

As he was in his somber state, the semi began its course of destructive action, hurling itself into the right lane in front of the shocked motorist beside him, starting a chain of unfortunate events. The driver awoke to the sound of metal tearing into metal. Cars were slamming into each other as if they were nothing but toys played with by small children. He slammed on his brakes to no avail, as the deadly machine skidded sideways wiping out everything in its path. Through the windshield, he could see the terrified expressions that became frozen upon the faces of one elderly couple, and within a blink of his eye, they were gone. The semi cut the Lincoln in half; flames erupted and now he could hear the hideous screams as their aged bodies melted into their seats. From that day forward, the trucker would never have lovely dreams of blue oceans, as his nights would be consumed with nightmares of the singed bodies on I-75.

AFTER AGREEING TO Sloan's request to meet up, Molly quickly attended to her other caller. She expected to hear the comfort of her father's voice calling to inform her that they would be arriving that night, only to be emotionally overthrown by the voice of a compassionate state trooper informing her of her parents' deadly accident.

Chapter Five

Molly was pained with guilt over the fact that she and Phillip were being pampered in first class along with her mother and father's charred remains that had been stuffed into body bags and placed in the cargo hold of the large airliner. She was knocking back her third Bloody Mary when Phillip reached over to remove the glass from her shaking hands.

"Honey, you better slow down. I realize that you're upset, but you don't want to be drunk before we land. There are many people we need to meet with and an awful lot of decisions to make. I don't want them to think I turned you into a lush."

Molly pulled Phillip's hand to her lips and kissed it gently. He had never done a day of physical labor in his life and his fingers were smooth as silk, resembling a woman's hand. As she held onto them, she could not help but notice the difference between Phillip's hands and her father's. Her father's hands had such strength and were thick and rugged, always there to pick her up when she fell. Now she would never have the support of his strong hands again.

"Thank you Phillip. I know you're right. I just can't stop thinking that if Daddy wouldn't have been so damn stubborn about getting on a plane instead of driving halfway across the country, they would still be alive. Well Dad, what do you think about flying now? How do you like being thrown down in the cargo hold?" As soon as the hateful words spewed from Molly's mouth, she began to sob uncontrollably.

Phillip watched helplessly as the tears flooded the face of his distressed wife. The attentive flight attendant, while serving another passenger, noticed the distraught Mrs. Madison and rushed to her aid.

"Mr. Madison, is there anything we can get your wife?"

"Yes, thank you. Bring her another Bloody Mary and hell, bring me one, too."

The alcohol Molly consumed finally cast its spell and she slept soundly with her cheek pressed against the cold window of the plane. As she lay passed out alongside Phillip, he felt as if she was a stranger and not the wife he had lived with all these years. Her blond hair appeared tousled upon her head. Her bright blue eyes were now swollen shut and her once-immaculate clothing now looked like rumpled rags.

As the plane neared their final destination, Phillip pondered over the business that lay ahead of him. Now with the death of both of his in-laws, Molly would be the sole heir of the 45,000-deeded acre ranch. Phillip could not believe his good fortune. He figured the sale of that land would net him a cool $100 million, and with bucks like that, he could have the kind of campaign that would make him a sure win for Congress. He could never understand why the old man would want to hang on to all that land when it was worth so much.

Well, his loss is my gain, Phillip thought to himself as he lovingly gazed down at his wife, covered with the new jacket that Sloan had given him as a gift. He watched in dismay as the drool leaked from the corner of her mouth and began to crust on the side of her face. He knew that manipulating her into selling off her family's estate would be easy because he knew that Molly's main goal in life had always been to make him happy.

The raspy voice of the unseen navigator boomed over the intercom. "Cross check for landing."

Phillip leaned over his wife and whispered gently in her ear. "Baby we're here, wake up. And don't worry, I promise everything will be just fine, Molly. I'll take care of everything, you have nothing to worry about."

Molly rose slowly out of her slumber and adjusted her seat in its upright position. She was extremely thankful for the skill of the pilot, as the landing gear came to rest gently upon the ground. As she waited to disembark, she felt lightheaded and knew she was still feeling the effects from her excessive drinking. There was no doubt that soon a hell of a hangover would follow.

Phillip led her by a steady hand to the door of the airplane. As she stepped off the plane, the mountain air slapped the inebriated woman square in the face and awoke her dulled senses. Molly Madison had finally come home.

Chapter Six

Wʜᴇɴ Cʟᴀʏᴛᴏɴ ʜᴇᴀʀᴅ ᴛʜᴇ ᴄʀᴜsʜɪɴɢ ɴᴇᴡs ᴏғ ᴛʜᴇ ᴅᴇᴀᴛʜ ᴏғ ʜɪs beloved boss and lovely wife, he felt as if his heart was ripped out of his well-developed chest. He became sick to his stomach, his muscular frame became heavy, his knees buckled beneath him, and he struck the ground with force. He had never experienced such extreme grief and sorrow until that dark horrifying day.

Gavin had personally handpicked Clayton to become head foreman to run every aspect of the 45,000-acre Ghost Bear Ranch. It was a huge responsibility for just one man to handle, but Clayton was more than capable and had never let Gavin down. He always knew how to treat the ranch hands fairly and had the gift to cool any hot tempers that rose up between the cowboys when their days had been too long and they had quenched their thirst with too much whiskey at night. Although Clayton had not extended his schooling beyond high school, he had more than enough hands-on experience and an uncanny sense when it

---

came to making a substantial profit for the Ghost Bear. Gavin had been more than pleased with Clayton's abilities.

Over the years, Gavin's and Clayton's relationship grew into something more than just employer and employee; a feeling of deep love and respect grew between the two men. Gavin treated Clayton as a beloved son and in return, Clayton viewed Gavin and Addie as the only family he had.

Slowly coming to grips with the horrific news, Clayton began to contemplate the outcome of the Ghost Bear. Although he had never met Gavin and Addie's daughter, Molly, he had seen pictures of her and her family. Gavin always talked fondly of his only daughter and grandchild, and often grumbled about his son-in-law. Clayton had known that it was a great worry to Gavin that if something ever happened to the both of them, Molly's husband would want to sell the family ranch.

Clayton knew this sacred land had been in Gavin's family for generations and was first homestead in the late 1800s. It was not only one of the largest spreads, but also one of the most pleasing to the eye. The rich land had been Gavin's piece of heaven with giant Ponderosa pines that reached out and gently caressed the grand blue sky. Trout swam in abundance amongst the ancient river rocks, while elk and mule deer filled their bellies with the cold sapphire currents of the mighty Yellowstone River, which flowed for miles across his spread. Even as Gavin aged into his ripe years, he still loved to punch cows with Clayton and his hired men. Together they had traveled endless miles straddling the saddles of their trusty steeds in order to gather up the heard of Black Angus cattle that roamed free to graze upon the green grass that lay as a blanket beneath their hoofs. As they drove the herd of cattle back to the ranch for winter, they would occasionally ride upon a carcass that wolves had ravaged or be lucky enough to spot an obscure mountain lion on the hunt.

Every stretch of the land had filled Clayton with intimate memories of Gavin and Addie. It made his skin crawl to think of anyone selling it to a greedy asshole whose only intention was to strip and sell the virgin timber and rape the land of its other natural resources. Gavin owned all the mineral rights to his Territory and Clayton knew that it would be worth a pretty penny to Molly's husband. For days, Clayton's stomach had been tied in knots with the anticipation of finding out if Molly's husband would push her to sell his beloved Ghost Bear and the history behind it. If that were the case, many men, including himself, would be out of a job and home.

Now with Molly and her husband flying in, the time had finally come. He waited anxiously as the assortment of passengers debarked from the aircraft, when suddenly he spotted the woman who had stared at him through photographs that sat upon Gavin's desk. Although he could see that Molly was in total disarray, her beauty instantly penetrated his soul.

"Miss Molly?" Clayton called out with his deep western voice.

Clayton took notice of a dark haired gentleman who had been supporting her up by her small arm. He was at least six feet tall, roughly the same height as Clayton, only on the thin side. As Clayton approached the man, he felt an unpleasant uneasiness. Phillips eyes were dark and slightly squinty, and when he spoke, he chose to avert his gaze. Clayton could hear the voice of Gavin in his head: "Don't ever trust a son of a bitch who won't look you square in the eyes."

Molly noticed the tall, brawny cowboy calling her name. She could not help but admire the thick blond hair that lay beneath his black cowboy hat or the way his tight fitting Wrangler jeans complimented his perfect ass. As Clayton approached them, Molly's swollen eyes spotted the silver rodeo belt buckle that rode just above the large bulge that filled out the front of his pants.

Clayton reached out, shook Phillip's hand and introduced himself. "My deepest condolences to the both of you. I'm so sorry for the death of your parents, Miss Molly. It was such a tragedy. Mr. Gavin and Miss Addie meant the world to all of us who worked for them and things have not been the same since their sudden departure."

Molly let go of Phillip's arm and reached out, wrapped her arms around Clayton and slurred into his ear. "Thank you, Clayton. Daddy talked so much about you. I know the two of you were very close and how terribly fond he was of you. This must have come as a shock to you and the rest of the men."

As she spoke, Clayton could smell the poignant stench of alcohol emerge from Molly's breath and he wondered how long she had been hitting the sauce.

Molly began to cry and an aggravated Phillip pried her arms loose from around Clayton's muscular frame. "Come on Molly, I'm taking you to the car just in case you pass out again. Clayton, I'm terribly sorry about this. Would you mind grabbing the luggage for us? As you can see, my grieving wife obviously had way too much to drink on the plane and I would very much like to get her to the ranch so she can have some black coffee and rest up."

"No problem, sir. There is a blue Dodge parked right in the front with the Ghost Bear Ranch on the side of the truck. I've also taken the liberty to retrieve Gavin and Addie's remains from the plane and instructed them to be taken straight to the funeral parlor."

Molly responded with complete clarity that made Clayton's blood run cold. "There's not much left of their bodies to bury after that damn accident burned them alive!"

No one dared to speak any further about the present state of Molly's parents. They proceeded to walk through the modestly small airport. Displayed throughout the airport was a wide assortment of Montana's wildlife housed inside glass cases. As they descended the stairs, a large mounted mountain lion appeared ready to pounce upon a spectacular white snow haired rabbit placed high above their heads upon a log. As they walked towards the outside entrance, on this particular day, Molly would not allow herself to take the leisure minute as she normally would have, to stop and admire the nine-foot grizzly towering upon its hind legs. It was in the same menacing position just as it appeared minutes before her father pumped it with lead, killed it and then donated it to the airport with a large sign that read: *Shot on the Ghost Bear Ranch, 1968.*

Gavin had told her it was to be displayed as a warning for all visitors to take heed and be watchful as they came to visit the wilderness, for they came not knowing the dangers that could lurk ahead. As she glanced at the giant monster she thought of her refined friends in Florida with whom she had shared hours of gossip and charity work, and she knew that they would find these displayed creatures with their blank stares offensive and vile.

Molly and Phillip found the truck parked exactly where Clayton had said it would be. They weren't waiting long before Molly spotted Clayton walking to the truck with his large biceps engorged from carrying the heavy luggage. He placed the bags in the back of the pickup, opened the truck door and slid in behind the wheel.

"Clayton, I'm sorry for what I said back there," Molly said with remorse in her voice and her head hanging low. "I didn't mean to bite your head off."

"I understand."

Those were the only words spoken, as the stress of the day had fallen upon all of them like a heavy rain cloud. They had a long drive ahead with much to do once they got there.

Chapter Seven

The household had been extremely busy in preparation for Molly's arrival and the events that would have to transpire over the next week. Rosa had always been Addie's right hand in making sure the working men had full bellies and that the inside of the house was wiped clean of any unwanted dust, and she had gone to great lengths to ensure everything was perfect for the arrival of Molly and her family. The weary housekeeper felt abandoned by the unexpected death of her employers and troubled over what would now befall upon her. She had arrived illegally from Mexico forty-five years ago, hungry and impoverished. Unable to find her family who had illegally crossed the border months earlier, Rosa, in dire desperation, had wandered up on the doorstep of Addie's house. She had only hoped for water and maybe some food to sustain her while she could figure out where to go and what to do. Fortunately, fate was on her side on that particular day as Addie and Gavin had provided her with much more than she could ever have dreamed.

Not only did Rosa feel blessed to have found a home, but Addie also realized that God had provided her with the female companionship that she had spent many nights praying for. She was tired of being the only woman on the ranch and longed for some help with looking after the cowboys. Over the years, Addie and Rosa had enriched each other's lives. Molly taught Rosa how to read and write, while Rosa helped with all household duties and raising Molly. Rosa even took great pride in teaching Molly to speak fluent Spanish. Everyone loved Rosa and Gavin himself took the time to teach Rosa to drive and provided her with an old truck so she was able to go to town when she needed to.

Rosa had been happy and light hearted for so many years, but now all of her old fears and insecurities came rushing over her like a huge wave. She felt as if she was treading water, not knowing if she would survive the heartache she felt. Once again, she was frightened as her days became dark and full of uncertainty. She longed for light at the end of the tunnel and hoped that Molly's arrival would be the glimmer that they all needed.

Rosa was deep in her thoughts when she heard Sedona, the ranch's beloved Bernese mountain dog, become excited and began to woof in her low deep voice. She looked out the window to see Clayton's truck pull up to the front of the house and the massive 150-pound mascot charging with her tail wagging and tongue hanging out.

As Molly stepped out from the dirty Dodge, she was unprepared for the massive dog that bore a strong resemblance to the black bears that roamed the land, and was nearly knocked over by her strength. Clayton caught Molly just in the nick of time and kept her on her feet.

"Sedona is a great girl, just so damn big." Clayton laughed as he rubbed the top of the loveable creature's head.

Rosa ran out the door to greet the child she had helped raise, who was now a beautiful woman. She could not help but notice the strong resemblance to Addie.

The next few days were a whirlwind. Phillip and Molly's daughter Savanna, her husband, and friend Leeza flew in and stayed in the main house with Molly and Phillip. Molly was grateful to her daughter and son-in-law for all of their love and support, and especially grateful for her friend's presence, as her humor and antics helped Molly smile.

The funeral was one of the largest the county had ever seen. Several hundred people came to pay their respects and offer their condolences to Molly's family. Although Molly had not been home for some time, she somehow connected the endless faces with their proper names. With the help of her daughter and husband, Molly had finally laid her mother and father to rest in the family plot, which was located on the Ghost Bear Ranch, amongst Molly's ancestors whom had previously loved and cared for the land before her parents. Now, with Phillip pushing her to rid her ties to the divine land, she feared the idea of dying and not being able to reside next to her beloved family for all of eternity, but instead being buried among a bunch of strangers.

With her parents put to rest Molly was finally able to sleep. She dreamt she was once again the little girl who would ride with her daddy upon the back of her painted horse named Sapphire who would carry them both effortlessly through the vast field of wild flowers. They would stop to devour the cucumber sandwiches that her mother had made for them and Molly would run amongst the array of butterflies that would land upon the alluring wild flowers in order to capture the sweet nectar. She would gather as many flowers as her little hands could hold and soon they would be back on their way to their sacred destination. When they had finally arrived, Molly spoke in a hushed whisper, as the sound of her voice seemed out of tune with the gentle breeze that sung through the trees. She would then proceed to scatter the palate of fresh flowers as an offering amongst the graves, and she would take deep breaths into her little lungs so she could savor the perfumed aroma from the clover that provided each grave with a pink blanket.

Then Gavin would tell stories to Molly about her family heritage. She would lie amongst the clover and close her eyes, as her daddy recanted to her the life lessons of those who now forever slept below them. He would remind her of the significance and sacrifices each family member had given to care for their homestead. Her father explained to her that each headstone was a trophy given to the dead to celebrate the accomplishments of their life, and the living must be thankful for what each person left behind for them. Molly would sit very still and be attentive while Gavin told the stories of each person's life. He would save Molly's favorite story for last where she loved to hear her father talk about how great-grandfather had ridden on horseback all the way from back east to find the most beautiful land he ever laid eyes on, abundant with elk and mule deer.

This spectacular land, located in Paradise Valley, had been where Molly's great-grandfather, Martin O'Malley, first laid down his spurs. He was one tough son of a bitch, who over the years had fought off many Indians and strung up several gangs of cattle rustlers who tried to steal what was rightfully his. He believed in hard work, hard play, and most importantly, providing for his family. He expected nothing less from anyone who wished to be his friend.

The Indians claimed that when they passed through the sacred land a Great White Grizzly Bear would appear from out of nowhere. They named this white bear The Great Spirit of the Ghost Bear, and Martin O'Malley kept the original name of this land.

Over generations, great tales were told of the day Martin O'Malley was riding horseback across his land and came face to face with the Great Grizzly. His horse had charged back to the corral without him. Everyone searched for him to no avail only to wake the next morning and find Martin passed out by the front steps of the house, his bruised body covered with scratches and blood. He never did tell anyone what had happened to him, but after that unfortunate day, his full head of blond hair had turned the color of polished silver.

As Molly awoke, the sun was just presenting itself in the sky. She shook off her childhood dream and carefully climbed out from beside Phillip, so as not to wake him. She grabbed her jeans, shirt and boots and dressed without making a sound, then went down the stairs where Rosa was in the kitchen. The intoxicating aroma of fresh brewed coffee was inviting.

Molly walked up behind Rosa and embraced the heavy woman in her arms. "Thank you, Rosa, for all your help."

Molly kissed the woman upon her plump cheek and felt the residue of leftover tears. Turning Rosa to face her, she saw the dark circles that now outlined the dear woman's brown eyes. Molly realized that the poor woman had spent the last week in her own anguish over the loss of Molly's parents.

"Rosa, I know you're worrying yourself sick over the outcome of this tragedy, but please don't worry. I will never let you be alone. You will always be with me and we can take care of each other, just like you and Momma. I love you Rosa. It doesn't matter where we live as long as you are with us."

Rosa was relieved to hear Molly's reassurance. "Thank you, my sweet girl. I will go with you and help you. Every night in my prayers, I promise your Momma and Poppa that I will take care of you. It just makes me so sad to leave this place. It has been my home for so long. And Molly, this is your home too. Please don't let that selfish man who sleeps in your bed make you sell your home, Molly. This is where you belong!"

Molly promised Rosa that she would not do anything rash, and reminded her she was Gavin O'Malley's daughter and the only heir to the Ghost Bear. No one would make up her mind for her. She would come to a decision by herself. After spending the time and speaking the comforting words to the old woman, she asked Rosa for a Thermos of coffee, then informed her that she was going to go for a morning ride upon one of her father's mares to contemplate the decisions of what to do.

"You're a good girl, Molly O'Malley!" Rosa's pudgy mouth turned up into a smile.

Molly left the kitchen and went out the back door. The morning air was clean, crisp and around forty-five degrees. A northern breeze blew against her face. As she stepped out onto the back porch, Sedona raised her head and appeared to smile at Molly, then rose tiredly, stretching the aches from her body and waddled to the door, looking as if she was waiting for someone else to appear before her.

Molly knelt, put her arms around the gentle dog's neck and kissed her on the head. "I know Sedona, you are expecting Daddy. Well big girl, he won't be coming out that door. I don't have the slightest clue what I'm going to do with you. Phillip is allergic to you and it just doesn't seem right making you live in the city in the Florida heat."

As Molly loved upon her father's best friend, a deep voice, spoke out. "I suppose you're right, ma'am. It just doesn't seem like the right thing to do to the old girl. This ranch and these mountains are all she's ever known. With your permission I sure would like to take her off your hands." Clayton's voice startled Molly, as she had not seen him walking towards her.

"Clayton, I can't think of anyone else who Sedona would want to be with. Thank you."

Clayton began to take a stronger interest in the woman who now stood beside him. She was a different woman than the one he first met at the airport. As she stood in front of him dressed in her worn jeans and dusty boots, she looked like her father's daughter. He could see some of that O'Malley grit in her. Maybe, just maybe, he thought to himself, that with a little coaxing more would emerge from this lady. He admired how she had pulled herself out of the pit of sorrow in which she had so deeply wallowed in.

Over the past week, Clayton could not help but notice how Phillip was always pushing his opinions upon Molly, always in control over his beautiful wife and that she always seemed to bow down to his obnoxious bullying behavior. Clayton observed in disdain and disbelief as Phillip would contemptuously belittle his wife as if she was a young, stupid child, making mocking comments about what he thought were the ignorant people who lived in this part of the country. Clayton would bite his tongue and stand with clenched fists as he would listen to the arrogant bastard objurgate comments about Clayton's fellow ranch hands, in his annoying southern drawl. He had a strong dislike for Molly's husband and could not understand how she ever wound up with the likes of him.

Now that Molly was finally alone and not in the grips of Phillip's company, Clayton could see the inner strength that had lain dormant within her. She no longer looked meek and scared. Something was brewing inside this woman and Clayton knew she was ready to let it pour out.

Molly asked Clayton which one of the mares he might suggest she take, telling him that she wished to go for a ride and that she had some final decisions to ponder over. Clayton quickly suggested her father's horse and offered to saddle the mare for her, but Molly politely refused his offer and saddled up the golden palomino herself.

Molly took off on the horse just as she had when she was a child. The mare seemed to have the ability to read her thoughts, and without any prodding, proceeded to carry her to their destination. She rode effortlessly amongst the trees, breathing the deep scent of the evergreen pines when her attention came upon a herd of surprised mule deer. She watched awestruck as the herd bounced off with their large rabbit like ears and fluffy white butts. She continued on to the open field of wild flowers, still moist with the morning dew then dismounted staying only long enough to gather as many of the delicate colors that she was able to hold. Her gentle beast waited patiently for her to remount so they could continue their journey.

They rode through the clover fields where the bees had already begun their day's work, going from one to the other retrieving the sweet nectar that lay waiting. While she crossed the river, she observed the cutthroat trout dancing in and out amongst the colorful rocks.

She continued her journey until she arrived at her final destination, her parents' burial site. She knew her father had visited the same spot frequently, as the horse that she now rode upon had known the way well. She stared down at the two freshly dug graves and knelt down to place the wild flowers upon her Momma and Daddy. She was surprised to feel the fresh tears fall from her eyes and drench her cheek, as she thought that she had run dry.

"Damn it, Daddy! I just don't know what to do! Phillip is putting such pressure on me to sign the papers. How am I supposed to tell all those men who have worked for you and made this ranch their home, thanks for your service now hit the road. I'm selling the only thing they care about. It kills me to think of some greedy selfish developer mutilating our land into little pieces just so he can build ugly tract houses that all look alike."

She knew that Phillip hated the ranch and his southern city mentality did not sit well with the men who worked upon it. She knew the sale of the ranch would help with his political campaign, and he expected her support, but this time he was demanding an awful lot. This land meant so much more to Molly and she felt that she could never put a price tag on it. This was who she was. Just as the giant trees rose from this ground, so did her family. How could she turn her back on it?

The wind began to blow gently through the treetops and she could hear the whispers of her ancestors speaking to her and the calm voice of her father. She knew what she must do. She mounted her horse to ride back to the house. She knew Phillip would not be happy with her decision.

Over the past week, Phillip had been diligent with making preparations for the future sale of the Ghost Bear and was now waiting for Molly to sign the papers so they could sell it to the lead developer in town, go home and get on with their lives. He was tired of being stuck in this God forsaken cow country. He could not get past the feeling that Gavin's spirit was now peering at him in complete revulsion and he could feel Gavin's testosterone oozing out from the chink amongst the cabin's log walls. He was tired of walking down the long staircase lined with photographs of all the past cowboys who lived and worked on the land. These men had always made him feel inadequate. It was time to tie up all the loose ends and head back to Florida.

Since their arrival, Phillip could not help but notice how flush his wife's face would become whenever she was near her daddy's ranch manager, and to his surprise, it was beginning to piss him off. After all, Molly was still his wife and they had been married for a long time. He was not stupid. He knew these men viewed him as weak and he felt their hostility.

Phillip desperately missed his life in Florida and longed for Sloan's companionship. Spending so much time with his wife and daughter, he was becoming increasingly plagued with guilt over deceiving them. A part of him had become so codependent on his wife and he was becoming increasingly scared of losing her before he was ready to let her go. He knew his secret relationship with Sloan was becoming riskier everyday and the sexual feelings he felt for this man could eventually lead to his downfall.

As Phillip pondered over his troublesome thoughts, he aimlessly wandered inside to what had once been Gavin's study. The room was of great magnitude, with walls made from enormous ponderosa pines that had been harvested from the land that the ranch now sat on. Mahogany bookcases lined the walls, rising up from the hardwood floors to almost touch the planked ceiling. Grossly neglected leather-bound books overflowed from its shelves.

As he looked around, his nostrils were filled with the aromatic scent of cherry tobacco that still lingered thick in the air. He spied Gavin's expansive collection of assorted pipes sitting on the large hand carved desk as if anticipating his arrival to be puffed upon once more. A massive fireplace made out of Ancient River rocks, which had once been painstaking hand selected and gathered specifically for their color, emerged from the floor to fill the corner of the room.

Phillip sat down in the tattered wingback chair and stared at the photographs taken of his family in happier times. He was in a somber mood and felt a twang of guilt as he gazed into the faces of his loved ones as they smiled back at him, unsuspecting of his treacherous actions. He opened up the desk drawer and reached in to remove the manila folder that contained the final documents requiring Molly's signature. He then picked up the telephone to dial the number he knew so well. He waited patiently as the phone rang, only to hear Sloan's voice on his answering machine telling him to leave a message.

"Sloan, it's me. This whole thing shouldn't take much longer and I hope to be home in a day or two. Why don't you make a reservation at Burns Steak House for Friday night. I know how you like the desert room. And speaking of rooms, I made a reservation at the Ritz for that night as well. You and me babe all night!"

Phillip looked at Gavin's portrait peering at him with scrutiny as he placed the receiver back where it belonged. He was so engrossed with thoughts of Sloan he had failed to hear his wife walk into the room.

Molly had hurried back from her ride to tell Phillip of her decision. She cleared her voice so as not to startle him. She could see he was in deep thought and figured it had something to do with work.

"Hey, honey."

Phillip turned to face his stunning wife. "I was just going to hunt you down. Did you have a nice ride?" He spoke sweetly, not knowing how long she had been standing there.

Molly noticed her husband appeared flustered. "It was great. I've forgotten how much I love going for a ride in the mornings." She plopped herself down on the opposite side of her father's desk. It seemed a little strange for her to see Phillip sitting in her father's favorite chair. "Phillip, was that someone from the firm on the phone? Is everything okay?"

"Well sweetie, I really need to head home. I've been gone longer than I probably should have. I have the papers right here for you to sign, and the attorneys will take care of everything else." Phillip spoke in his usual pushy tone.

Molly looked into her husband's eyes and took a deep breath. "Phillip, I've been giving this a lot of thought and I've decided it would not be wise for me to sign anything at this time." She watched the smile on his face slowly turn into a scowl of contempt. "Please, Phillip, try to understand that this is not easy for me. I just don't want to make any rash decisions. There are a lot of people whose lives are dependent upon this ranch."

The strength in Molly's voice took Phillip by surprise. "For God's sake, Molly, you and I both know these guys can get a job at any ranch down the road. It's time to let it go and be sensible. You're living in a pipe dream if you think you're capable of running this place, especially from Florida!"

Clayton had walked in downstairs and could hear Phillip bellowing from above in Gavin's study. He knew Molly was in the room with him and he could hear the arrogant son of a bitch once again running over her. He knew he should just stay out of it, but his blood was boiling and his head began to feel like a pressure cooker that was ready to blow. He'd had enough. He ran up the stairs to Gavin's office and barged into the room to see Molly pinned up against her father's desk and Phillip shrieking in her face. Clayton grabbed a hold of Phillip's shoulder and swung him around with force in order to face him.

"What the hell is wrong with you?" Clayton roared. "For God's sake, your wife just lost both her parents!" Clayton screamed at Phillip, with a clenched fist, ready to pound upon the weasel now held tightly in his grasp.

Molly reacted quickly, knowing that if Clayton struck her husband, Phillip would certainly demand his removal from the ranch. "Clayton, please, it's okay. Phillip has just been under a lot of stress at home and being here is not helping."

Phillip felt Clayton loosen his grasp and pulled himself back from his hold. He smoothed his now-wrinkled shirt and rubbed the spasm out of his shoulder with his hands.

"Molly, I owe you an apology." Phillip said to his wife all the while glaring at Clayton with immense loathing. "If you feel that strongly, then I'll allow you one month before you have to sign the papers. As for you Clayton, don't you ever lay your grimy hands on me again. Gavin's not here to protect you and I'll have you shoveling pig shit!"

Phillip then grabbed his wife around the waist, kissed her hard upon her lips, and stormed out of the room. Molly and Clayton stood staring at each other in disbelief.

"Jesus Molly, something is really wrong with him."

Molly lowered her head. "I know."

Chapter Eight

UPON THEIR RETURN TO FLORIDA, THEIR LIVES HAD RESUMED TO THEIR natural state. Phillip had a weekend business trip. When he returned his mood was much better and he chose not to mention their heated argument before he left. He spent the majority of time at work and Molly had once again found herself sitting in her kitchen and eating dinner alone. As the dutiful wife she was, she prepared dinner for Phillip each night, only to once again place the plate in the refrigerator for his return.

As she sat alone with only a flicker of the candle to illuminate the room, she was alone with her thoughts. As she retraced the events of the past month she could not shake the feeling that she had forgotten something. "What the heck is it?" She thought. When suddenly it hit her, the day she received the phone call informing her of her parents' accident, Sloan, Phillip's assistant, had asked to meet her. She recalled how strange Sloan had sounded and her curiosity was once again piqued. Molly looked across the room at the clock on the wall and decided it wasn't too late to give him a call.

Phillip and Sloan had been inseparable since Phillip's return. They had spent a weekend together full of lovemaking and room service. The following week, they worked side by side to prepare the cases that Phillip was behind on while they enjoyed late-night dinners together. It was a wonderful time for Phillip, as he did not have to worry about Molly; she expected he would be so far behind in his work and would have to work late in order to catch up.

One day after they had worked hard Phillip suggested the two of them grab a bite to eat at one of their favorite Italian hot spots. They had just finished their dinner when Sloan's cell rang. He glanced at his phone and saw Phillip's home number appear on the caller ID.

Shit, bad timing, Sloan thought as he turned the phone off. He smiled at Phillip who was sitting across from him. "Just my mother. I'll call her back later," Sloan lied.

The waiter delivered their luscious deserts. As Sloan devoured his chocolate treat, his thoughts wandered to his future meeting with Phillip's wife, which made his dessert taste even better.

Disappointed that she was unable to talk to Sloan, Molly left a message on his voice mail asking him to give her a call and that she would like to meet with him as he'd requested.

She was tired of waiting for her husband and went to sleep alone. That night, while Molly had erotic dreams of a stately cowboy, wrapping her in his arms and laying her down upon a blanket of hay, Phillip and Sloan's bodies were in tempo together as they performed a sexual duet upon Sloan's bed. After their performance, Phillip left.

As Sloan shut off the light, he whispered softly into the darkness, "You'll be back, Phillip, and next time you'll stay."

Sloan rose early with the vehement enthusiasm of a malicious child. He had spoken with Molly and they planned to meet at ten a.m. at a nearby café. He purposely picked that time of day just in case Molly would lose her cool and freak out.

He took great care in choosing his attire and primped the thick red locks that fell from his head and framed his feminine face. "God, I am so hot!" He spoke adoringly to his image. He blew himself a kiss, grabbed his keys and pranced joyfully down the stairs to his awaiting blue BMW.

Yes, Sloan was as proud as a peacock as he drove to his meeting. He was well aware that spilling the beans to Molly would undoubtedly destroy her sense of reality and he felt confident that she would no longer wish to tolerate Phillip's deceitful behavior.

He glanced at himself in the rearview mirror and said out loud, "What? She'll eventually get over it! It's time for all this shit to be out in the open!"

Sloan pulled his car into the sparse parking lot. He turned off the car, stepped out, slammed the door shut and took a deep breath.

"Ah, at last the final finale!" Yes, it was time for the final curtain call; time for this drama to come to a close.

Sloan's hands felt clammy and his skin was tingling from the mixture of nerves and excitement, as he was ready to bring down the show. He approached the glass doors of the stylish coffee house and he was able to see Molly sitting near the window. The sunlight stretched through the pane of glass and touched her lightly upon her golden blond hair to make it glisten.

Molly spotted Sloan instantly and offered up a smile and a wave. "Sloan, so nice to see you. I'm sorry that we were unable to meet sooner." As Molly removed her hand from his she noticed the leftover residue of his perspiration upon her. She coyly wiped the palm of her hand beneath the table upon her napkin. "This can't be good," she thought to herself.

Wasting no time, Sloan cut to the chase and began to tell Molly everything, painting a very vivid picture of the type of relationship that he had with her husband. With every word he spoke, the precise details of the two men played out inside her mind. As he spewed the poisonous words from his lips Molly sat very still, feeling her stomach become ranted as it began to churn. Not only did the son of a bitch describe the acts of passion, he was able to back their lovemaking sessions with dates and times that Molly knew Phillip was unaccounted for.

All these years, she had tried to figure out why Phillip always seemed so distant, beating herself up emotionally and trying to make some sense of their relationship. Now this man was offering her the true explanation and never in her wildest dreams would she have figured it out on her own. She didn't speak a word nor moved a single tense muscle. She was transfixed by the man in front of her.

Sloan finished up by professing his love for Phillip, and with extreme arrogance stated his last words to his opponent. "So, the bottom line is Phillip loves me and I love him. I figured you would want to know the truth, and I'm finished playing this game. All the cards are on the table, and Molly, I would have to say, I won this hand."

Finally, he was finished. It was over. They both stared at each other, Molly in utter disbelief and Sloan in explosive thrill. The air became extremely heavy with tension.

She took a deep breath to fill her lungs and to give her strength then began to speak with precision and calm. "You enjoyed that didn't you?" Her face was empty of emotion. "It must have been very hard for you to keep the passionate details of your relationship with my husband silent for so long. Why Sloan, you seem to have a look of relief on your face. Do you feel better?"

Sloan could feel the wind blown from his sails. He cautiously observed Molly, as she did not emit any feelings, and this disappointed him. "Yes, Molly I do feel better. It has been terribly excruciating for Phillip and me to hide our feelings for each other." He smiled at her, mockingly.

With her large coffee in hand, she slowly lifted her body from the table. "Well Sloan, now that you have informed me of my husband's extracurricular activities, I must be going."

She slid out from the table and for one short and deserving moment she stood over Sloan before beginning to speak. Just as he looked up at Molly, she poured her hot, Venti Café Mocha upon the top of the maggot's red curls.

"Go fuck yourself! You're one of the most pansy ass sons of bitches that I have ever met! You know what I think is more troubling than my husband being gay? Knowing that he lost his fucking mind, because out of all the men out there he could be with, he slept with you! You see Sloan, I've known plenty of men like you and you're all the same, little bitches!"

Sloan jumped to his feet, while Molly, satisfied with her action, walked out of the café knowing she would never again return to the spot that had changed her life forever.

Chapter Nine

As she waited for the arrival of her next John, she couldn't believe her incredible good fortune of being present in the exact location and time of the two people who were enthralled in such turmoil. She sat back, stretching her long, sensual legs under the table, placing her bright red stilettos comfortably upon the seat of the black leather booth. She was unafraid of being recognized, as she had become an expert at pinning her own locks up under the long amber wig that she wore as her disguise. Just in case one of them should happen to turn around and make eye contact with her she chose to leave on the dark shades that hid her eyes.

"No need to take stupid chances," she thought.

Feeling confident, she sat back and enjoyed the show as the openly gay man ousted the woman's promiscuous husband.

"Damn, this day is turning out better than I could have expected!" She thought.

She glanced at her watch, hoping her next victim would not show up and interrupt the entertainment that had been bestowed upon her. She admired how the ostentatious loafer spoke with such giddy malevolence while the woman appeared to be impenetrable. To her disappointment, the conversation ended. In a blink of an eye, the attractive woman walked out, leaving the reprehensible clown, screaming profanities while her hot coffee scalded his freckled skin. The server ran to the enraged man and began wiping him down with a damp rag, only to infuriate him further.

"Get the hell away from me you little twit!" He bellowed.

He then promptly removed himself from the establishment, threw open the door, nearly knocking over the old man who was walking through, who also unknowingly happened to be her next prey. As the red-headed man plowed through the old man, his reflexes kicked in overdrive and stopped what would have been an embarrassing fall.

The old man quickly gained composure, patted down his comb-over and spotted his vivacious, bombshell. He felt himself get an instant rise due to the Viagra that he had taken earlier in preparation for his little tryst. She quickly focused her attention on the little fly now walking excitedly towards her.

She had enjoyed her time in Atlanta—the shopping, the spas and the therapy session at the doctor. "It was all desperately needed and time well spent, it took her back many years to the last time she had seen a doctor in Atlanta. Although there had been many victims between then and now. None had taken her back to her sexually abused childhood like the doc did. Her soul felt cleansed," she thought as she watched her little man hustle towards her.

"Hey baby," she cooed. "You look real good."

The dirty old man slid in beside her, reached under her short skirt and touched the special spot between her legs.

"I see you were a good little girl and did as you were told," he whispered in her ear, as he withdrew his hand and sucked upon his wrinkled finger.

"Let's go, Big Daddy, I know you can't wait to see your little girl in her school uniform. I've been so naughty and I need a good spanking."

As she licked the side of his pruned face, she thought how repugnant the old bastard was. The old man instantly stood at attention and couldn't get out of the coffee shop fast enough.

"You can follow me in your car, Daddy, I know a real private spot and I am sure you want to teach your little girl a good lesson."

Damn this whore is good, he thought.

He normally preferred the real thing, little girls twelve and under, but the last one he had preyed upon had threatened to tell her mommy and his wife was becoming suspicious of his interest in children.

She drove quickly to the remote destination with his car following. Within a short time, she led him to her secret spot. She turned down a deserted dirt road that was no bigger than a path and parked the car amongst the cypress trees that grew thick, near an old swamp. She turned off her engine and jumped out of the car to see him walking towards her.

She spoke in her little girl voice. "Daddy, you wait right here while I change and get ready for school."

As she reached for the duffel bag that she had placed in the back seat of her car, she let her short skirt ride up so her naked ass could peek out at him.

"Hurry up you little slut," he hissed.

She ran around the tree and changed, reached into her little bag of surprises and closed her dainty hand around the extra special treat she had in store for him.

"Minxie, come on. Daddy doesn't know how much longer he can wait," he hissed at her in an evil voice.

As she walked out from behind the giant cypress, she found him standing in all of his naked shriveled glory, waiting for her to rock his world. She skipped over to him never breaking her role.

"Daddy, I want some of your candy. What do you have for me?" She whined.

"I want you to suck on this, you little brat!" He reached for her head and shoved it down. Within that very instant, she snapped open the switchblade she had concealed in her hand and sliced off his erect member.

He instantly fell to his knees, his ugly old face contorted. A chilling, unnatural animalistic sound arouse from deep within the old geezer. His mouth wide open in terror, he stared in utter disbelief at his manhood that she now held in her hands, and without missing a beat, she stuffed his member into his contorted mouth. Tears streamed down the old man's face, his own blood squirting out covering him like a warm blanket, as he lay helpless. She knelt beside him sneering as she waited for the life to drain from his hideous face. His vision became blurred and soon all he could see were the little faces of the young, innocent victims that he had molested over his lifetime, more than he could even remember. His tears flowed heavily from the corners of his closing eyes to form small pools amongst his wrinkles. He felt nothing and he knew his miserable life was over.

"Well that's one less pervert that anyone has to worry about."

She worked fast and grabbed the feet of her conquest, dragging him over to the gator-infested swamp water. She quickly ran back, took a tree branch, brushed away all of their tracks and covered the blood-stained forest floor with dirt and leaves. She could hear splashes coming from the swamp where she had just dumped her victim and was quite amazed at how fast the hungry beasts reacted. She happily thought to herself that very soon there would be nothing left of him. She then grabbed her bag and made sure she left nothing behind.

As she drove off, she began humming a song her mother had taught her when she was a small child and she felt really good.

Chapter Ten

Molly could not control the emotions that were beginning to
well up inside of her. She put on a brave front while Sloan explained in graphic detail his relationship with her husband. But
as soon as she drove her car from that café, she broke down. Tears
flooded her like a massive tsunami. She pulled the Mercedes that
Phillip had given her on her last birthday to a halt on the side of
the road. As the traffic rushed past her, she sat with her head in
her hands and cried.

Memories of Phillip's past behavior came forward from the
dim recess of her subconscious mind. She knew deep within her
soul that every ugly word Sloan had told her was the absolute
truth. It all made sense. Phillip always appeared mentally preoccupied and distant; the late hours he kept and all the dinners
she'd had to sit and eat alone; the weeks he chose to be absent
from her and telling her that he was sorry but he knew she understood. She'd wasted her youth on him. While their marriage

had always been wrapped around his needs it was all based upon utter deception.

As these thoughts swept across the frontal lobe of her mind, she struck the helpless steering wheel with several hard blows. She screamed while calling her husband obscenities that would have made even a sailor blush. She hated him, but worst of all she hated herself for choosing to ignore all the signs that had presented themselves over the years. She had chosen to stick her head in the sand and pretend that their life was perfect. She had chosen to let the goals and dreams that she had once cherished as a young woman fade as if they never existed. She had always put what Phillip wanted first, as he always made her feel that his career was far more important than anything she would like to do. She had always been available for him, never letting him down and in return she received the ultimate betrayal. Phillip was a homosexual; he loved men and felt more physically connected to the jackass who worked for him than his own wife.

After what seemed to be hours of kicking herself in the ass for not figuring out about Phillip's betrayal sooner, Molly started her car, wiped the tears from her eyes and pulled back on to the busy street. She had things to do and she was finished wasting her time.

First things first, she thought to herself as she drove her gifted Mercedes Benz into the local Ford dealership. She saw the eager grin upon the face of the car salesman who was practically tripping over his own feet to be the first to greet her. She hated car salesmen, but she hated being in the car that Phillip had bestowed on her.

"I would like to trade this car in for a new F350 diesel with dullies. Oh and by the way, make it red; I always liked the color red and my husband hates it. You will find a clean title in the glove box. Make it an even trade." She then proceeded to walk inside the dealership, leaving the stunned salesman staring at her and her pristine Mercedes in disbelief. "Well I don't have all day!" Molly spoke in annoyance.

After the paperwork was finished, Molly removed all of her possessions from her old car and transferred them into her brand new, bright red, pick-up truck. She jumped up into the Ford and then drove out of the parking lot, leaving the bewildered salesman unsure of what had just happened.

From here on out, she was prepared to make some big changes. She now knew who she was and what she wanted. Even though it had taken this tragedy to open her eyes, she was ready to fix her mistakes and prepared to start over.

With her hands on the steering wheel, she looked through the windshield and up at the sky. "Daddy, I always did have to learn the hard way. Just give me the strength to do what I know is right," she spoke to her father's spirit, hoping he was smiling down on her.

Molly knew that she needed to get a jump on her soon-to-be ex-husband and that the rest of her day would be crammed filled with unpleasant events.

After the major purchase of her new truck, her next stop was to visit one of the best divorce attorneys in the state where she hired him on the spot. After recounting everything to her new attorney, she was shocked to learn that he had been familiar with the rumors about her husband's secret passions.

"I guess the old cliché is true. The wife is always the last to know," she said.

After leaving the law firm, she drove straight to the free clinic. She knew that there could be a chance that Phillip had contracted AIDS. Now with her eyes wide open to her husband's years of reckless behavior, she could not count on him using condoms and partaking in safe sex.

She hated sitting in the free clinic but she did not want to take the chance of running into anyone she knew by going to her personal physician. While she sat in the small chair she stared at the crying babies, the homeless, and promiscuous teens who were looking to receive free birth control without their parent's knowledge.

The waiting had been the hardest part. Time seemed suspended as she silently prayed that the results of the test would come back negative. The anger that was building up inside took over any emotions of hurt that she might have felt earlier. Never in her wildest dreams had she imagined she would be going through anything like this at this age or time in her life. She was callously told that the results would not be available for a week and she should call the clinic to receive them. More unbearable waiting.

She walked out of the clinic feeling dirty and ashamed as if she had done something wrong and she was now uncertain of her future. By the time she left the clinic she was running out of steam. She knew her final task for the day was to confront Phillip.

Sloan knew he would have to tell Phillip that he had spilled everything to Molly; he wouldn't want Phillip to be unprepared when Molly confronted him with the news. He wasn't quite sure how Molly would react. Would she choose to end their marriage or have an open relationship? He knew that Phillip would be angry with him, but he felt confident that no matter how upset Phillip would become, his lover could never deny the love that they felt for each other. He drove to the office.

Phillip greeted him warmly. "Sloan, come on in." They walked into Phillip's office and Sloan closed the door behind them.

"Hey, what a surprise. I thought I wouldn't get to see you today!" Phillip seductively grinned.

Sloan stepped back from Phillip, keeping the chair between them.

"Phillip, I have something to tell you, and I know that you're going to be angry with me, so I'm just going to say it. I met with Molly and I told her everything."

"What do you mean, you told her everything?"

Sloan saw Phillip's seductive grin begin to turn downward and watched as the color quickly drained from his face, leaving it pasty white.

"Sloan, what the hell did you do?" Phillip could feel his anger rising, ready to boil over.

"I told her everything about us, Phillip. Our love for each other, our passion, who you really are and what you want." He spoke slowly, his eyes pleading for Phillip to understand.

"Who in the fuck do you think you are? You made the decision to tell my wife that I'm a fucking queer. How could you be so damn stupid? Don't you have any idea what you've just done to my life and my career? I can't even imagine what my poor wife must be feeling right now! Get the fuck out of here before I smash in your righteous face!"

"Phillip, it was for your own good. You know that you can't keep this lie up! You're pissed right now but after you get through all of this, you're going to be a lot happier. We can be happier. Let it go Phillip." Sloan turned and left the room, leaving Phillip betrayed and motionless.

Phillip gave himself a few minutes to gather his composure. He knew that he needed to go home and confront the devastation that his lover had caused. He had absolutely no idea what he was going to say to Molly and he felt a sense of horror to have to confront her about the truth behind their marriage. He told his secretary to cancel all of his meetings; he had an emergency and he would be gone for the rest of the day.

He drove home in silence, debating whether he should fight to save his marriage or let it go. It was not just about coming out to his wife; it was about being honest and coming out to the world. Everyone would soon find out. His parents would be devastated. And what about his daughter! Even though she was grown and married he didn't want to have to look her in the face and reveal his secret. He was so ashamed and he knew he would be a disappointment to everyone.

It was dreadful to him that his wife of all those years had learned the truth in this way. How could he have been so damn stupid and gotten messed up with Sloan. If only he could have been different, controlled his urges, be the man his wife expected him to be.

Phillip pulled into his garage and noticed Molly's car was gone. He walked into the barren house they shared. He had become so accustomed to her consistency. He threw his jacket over the couch and fixed himself a Grey Goose on the rocks. He plopped himself down upon the overstuffed chair that had been strategically placed in the great room and began to cry.

When Molly arrived home, she noticed the lights were on. With Phillip's car parked in the garage, she left her new truck parked in the drive. The door to her house was unlocked. She took a deep breath as she entered through the side door. She could hear heavy sobbing coming from the great room and found Phillip with his head in his hands and his body trembling.

"Don't you think I should be the one crying?" She spoke as she entered the room.

Phillip was startled and jumped up, wiping the wetness from his eyes. "I didn't hear you come in."

"Well by the way you're acting I guess I don't need to tell you who I spoke with today and the devastating news I was told." Molly walked over and sat next to Phillip.

She took only a short breath while continuing with what she needed to say. "Phillip, we have been married for so long. We have both wasted our youth on each other. We have built the foundation of our lives upon the lies that you have created, and now the trust and love that I thought we shared has turned to rubble. How could you be so damn selfish? You married me for appearances and stayed with me to further your career. Fuck you, Phillip. We had a child together. Every time we had sex it must have been disgusting for you!" Molly gasped for breath with her fists clenched, keeping them by her side so she would not strike blows to the pathetic man who was sitting next to her.

"No Molly, it wasn't like that! I wanted this marriage and I never wanted this to happen. It's been so hard for me. I love you so much. You're my life partner. You and Savanna mean so much to me. Please believe me. I wish to God that I had never given in to those feelings. I never wanted to hurt you. I'm so deeply sorry."

Throughout the day, Molly's emotions had been flowing through her like turbulent waters. Waves of anger, pity, sadness and loneliness kept pounding the shores of her heart. She didn't recognize the man who now sat before her.

Molly took her husband's face in her hands, making him look directly into her eyes. "How long Phillip? How long have you known that you were gay?"

Phillip spoke truthfully, knowing the words he was about to speak would throw another undeserving blow to his wife. "Since high school," he spoke in shame. "I knew back then that I didn't have the type of feelings a young man should have for a woman. Honestly Molly, I never thought I would ever marry, but then you came along. You were spectacular. You made me feel something I had never felt with any other woman. I was faithful to you for years. Then, over time…"

Phillip continued with his confession as if a guilty child with his head hung low. "I don't know what happened. My old urges, they just seemed to creep into the corners of my mind and grab hold, and they wouldn't let go. I couldn't shake them! The fantasies started getting stronger until I told myself just this once. Just one time I would allow myself to give in, you know, so I could get it out of my system. But then that one time led to another and it felt so good, so I allowed myself another. Jesus, when I say it out loud it sounds so dirty, so deceptive! Finally, I don't know, I gave up and stopped fighting the temptation."

Molly was silent as she let Phillip confess his sin.

Then it was her turn to speak. "Phillip, I'm sorry. I'm sorry for you and I'm sorry for our daughter and myself. You have been a real asshole for a long time. I knew that things had not been good between us for some time. Because you were unable to be truthful to yourself and to me, you have brought this shame upon our family. I can't forgive you. I'm leaving you. I've had enough. I'm going back home, back to my roots. You can keep this house, the contents and the lies you created. For the sake of our daughter, we need to tell her everything before it becomes public and she reads about it in the newspaper. I already called her and told her we would meet with her tomorrow. I think she needs to hear this from you. I'm leaving to drive back to Montana at the end of the week. I already filed the divorce papers with the attorney and I don't want you in the house until after I leave. And one last thing; I went for an AIDS test today and I'm not sure if I can ever forgive you for that."

Leaving Phillip stunned, Molly walked from the living room into her bedroom, shut the door and locked it. She lit the candles, put on Nora Jones and drew herself a long-deserved bath.

A heavy-hearted Phillip left with only the clothes that he had worn, nothing else. He would find a hotel for the night. He needed to be by himself. He knew that his life had just changed. He wasn't sure if it was for the better, but he knew he was about to find out.

Chapter Eleven

It had only been a week since the troubled woman took her vengeance on her last victim. Her inner voice told her that it was way too soon and she should let more time lapse, but as soon as she heard the bad news, her compulsion became too overwhelming. She did not hate all men. She had a son whom she loved with all of her heart and for whom she would sacrifice her life. She just despised the perverts, the evil men who preyed upon the good and innocence of others; the evil types that she craved to rid from the world. She relished in making them suffer, just as they had made others suffer; the ghastly, vulgar men who consciously thought they could destroy other people's lives without any consequence for their actions and she made sure they received their just punishment.

"Today justice will be served," she spoke as she sat before her computer. She signed on as Cindy, a thirteen-year-old schoolgirl and hoped the sick asshole she had been in contact with earlier would respond.

She began to type. "Hey, are you there? I skipped school today and thought we could meet up?" Her fingers flew across the keyboard. She waited for the fly to step into her web.

The words she wanted to see magically appeared across her screen. "Great. Let's have some fun today! How about the town center parking lot? Meet me at ten a.m. I'll be your teacher today and give you a few lessons in sex education."

As she watched his words appear on the screen, she pictured the stupid dildo sitting in front of his computer drooling with anticipation.

"Cool. My girlfriend told me her first time hurt like hell."

"Don't worry. You're going to love it and wonder why you waited this long."

"Gotcha, you sick son of a bitch," she spoke to herself as her fingers flew across the keyboard typing with excitement and precision.

"Okay. See you at ten. What kind of ride do you have?"

"It's a blue Honda. I'll be right out front."

She could picture the smirk upon the asshole's face. She shut down her computer. She knew she had to work fast as she had only one hour to get everything ready and she wanted to be at the mall before he arrived. She would have her revenge today; something extra special for this little fly. She reached into the nearby aquarium, placed her gloved hands inside, and gently picked up the poisonous dart frog. She admired the outstanding colors of the tiny little creature and gently pricked the frog with the tip of her darts. She quickly gathered up all the necessary goodies to complete her plan.

With no time to waste, she wanted to arrive before her predator. She drove furiously to the mall, only to find that the impatient asshole had the same idea and was already waiting in his shitty little car. She decided to park a few spaces behind him.

"Oh well, no problem," she thought.

She observed him for a minute then got out of her car.

The middle aged man rolled down his window and was hungrily looking for his naïve schoolgirl. She approached him from behind and, with efficient speed and accuracy, reached into the open window and pricked his neck with her dart. As quickly as she had arrived, she was gone.

"Hey, what the hell! Jesus Christ!" He reached for his neck and looked in his rearview mirror while trying to figure out what had just happened. The poison swarmed promptly through his bloodstream, paralyzing his heart and just like that, he was dead.

She was back in her car in a matter of seconds.

"Finite. End of the line for one more slime ball." She spoke to herself in a hushed whisper as if someone nearby might hear.

She sat watching the car that had now held the remains of the dead man.

"Hmm, I feel a little unsatisfied."

She pulled away slowly, feeling that the kill had been too fast to suit her taste. She always took personal pleasure in watching their faces when they realized that they were dying. She liked to savor the terror in their eyes before the blank stare washed over them as they gasped for their last breath.

As she drove off, she pulled her grocery list out of her purse. Her husband had invited a few friends over for dinner and she needed to stop at the store and pick up a few things.

Chapter Twelve

By week's end, Molly had survived all the turmoil. With a heavy heart and tearful dialogue, Phillip and Molly divulged his transgressions to their daughter. Molly was very proud, as her daughter had put on a brave face. She knew that Savanna had ignored her own emotions, setting them aside for concern over her mother. After several unsuccessful attempts to apologize to his only daughter and feeling large amounts of guilt, Phillip aborted quickly, leaving the two women to console each other over the wreckage that he had twisted amongst their lives.

Molly stayed with her daughter that night. They stayed up until the break of dawn talking about Molly's future and reminiscing over their past. After long talks and tears, both mother and daughter's anger and self-pity had dissipated into a newfound understanding of the turmoil that Phillip must have felt over the years.

The next morning, Molly gave her daughter one last loving hug and kiss and promised to call her daughter every night during her journey back to the safety of her Montana home.

The rest of the week had flown by with a blink of an eye. After all of her preparations were complete and meetings with friends were finished, Molly finally found herself with her truck packed and her small shaking hands upon its leather steering wheel ready to head down the new road in her life.

The first day, she drove in silence with her own uncertainties. By the second morning, clarity slowly formed out from the mist that had clouded her head. She arose from the staleness with a renewed sense of spirit; she was driving her truck and leaving the comfort of her entire world behind. She needed to pick up the pieces, allow herself to reminisce about her childhood, and start a new life filled with a purpose and self worth of her own. She spent the rest of the week driving, listening to her music, reflecting and enjoying the scenery.

As she left the miles behind her, the humid air grew crisp and cool. Her thoughts, recollections and desires around Phillip dissipated, while new images of the cowboy Clayton Leatherbe began to tickle the back of her mind.

After the fifth day, her vision filled with the glorious Montana skies and massive mountains, she felt transformed. She didn't need the help of her Garmin or a map to find her way in this country. She knew these roads like the back of her hand. She rolled her windows down and took in a deep breath of the salubrious air.

By late afternoon, she pulled her Ford off from the smooth ride of the pavement and onto the dusty gravel road that led to the entrance of her Ghost Bear Ranch. She stepped out of the truck to open the gate.

To her sensual pleasure, Clayton was standing near the gate. He embraced her, his smile wide and gleaming. "Howdy, boss!"

Molly was grateful for his kindness. "Clayton, you're a sight for my tired eyes!" She kissed the side of his stubble and could taste the salt on his skin that had formed while working in the heat of day. "Would you like a ride to the house?" She asked.

"Thank you, but I really need to finish checking the fence posts. We want to move some of the cattle up here for a little grazing, but I sure do appreciate the offer. I'll see you tonight at dinner. Rosa has been in that kitchen all day fixing up something real special for your homecoming. The boys have been running around here in such high spirits ever since they heard that you were back for good. You've been long missed, Miss Molly!"

"Thank you, Clayton. It sure is nice to be somewhere I'm wanted. I'll see you tonight."

She left Clayton to finish with his work. As she drove up that long drive to her renewed home, she couldn't deny herself the pleasure of sneaking one last peek at Clayton Leatherbe.

Chapter Thirteen

Sᴌᴏᴀɴ ᴡᴀs ᴅᴇʟɪɢʜᴛᴇᴅ ʙʏ Mᴏʟʟʏ's ʀᴇᴀᴄᴛɪᴏɴ ᴏᴠᴇʀ ʜɪᴍ ʟᴇᴛᴛɪɴɢ ᴛʜᴇ ᴄᴀᴛ out of the bag and honestly surprised by how quickly she reacted to the whole torrid thing. He knew Phillip was pissed at him and would not return his phone calls. He put Sloan on a leave without salary, but Sloan really wasn't that concerned. Since he hadn't been terminated, Sloan figured that with enough time, Phillip would cool down, call him and be back in his bed, even though it was still unpleasant not being able to talk to or see his lover.

Sloan was a high maintenance kind of man and he was used to Phillip taking care of his desires. He did fairly well for the first week, but by the end of the second week of not having Phillip popping around to entertain him, boredom had nudged at him.

"Oh for God's sake, I can only shop so much and get so many facials." Boredom had now become self-pity. "That's it I'm calling." He picked up the phone and dialed Phillip's cell.

After the fourth ring, Sloan was startled at the sound of Phillip's familiar voice when he answered. "I would fire your ass if I didn't have to worry about you going public with this!" Phillip spat the venomous words that struck Sloan hard. "Don't call me and don't bother showing your faggot face around my office, you little prick!"

Just like that, the phone went dead. Sloan stood in his living room, dismayed, his words stuck in his wide-open mouth and phone hanging in his hand. "What the hell was that?"

He stomped his foot and threw the receiver angrily against his wall. His blood began to boil causing his veins to explode from his neck, while his face slowly turned devil red.

"Who in the fuck is he calling a faggot? That ungrateful closet freak bitch! He should be kissing my prick in thanks for giving him a way out of his bullshit life! That's it I'm out of here. I'm not going to sit here and wait for that ass to come to his senses!"

Sloan stomped out of his condo, slamming his door like a fitful child. He was ready to hit the scene, have a little fun and make up for some lost time.

AFTER HIS TIRADE against Sloan, Phillip poured himself another glass of booze. Molly had been gone for a week and he had remained in a constant drunken stupor. He chose the safe confinement of his large home, striking up a friendship with Mr. Jack Daniels. He would say hello to his new found friend early in the morning by spiking his coffee and would end his day passed out in the bed with his arms wrapped tightly around the neck of the bottle. He hadn't shaved and cared even less about showering. His breath stank from the thick layer of unpleasant grime that had developed upon his teeth and tongue.

When his housekeeper had returned later in the week, she found him wandering around wearing the same clothes that she left him in four days earlier. His words were unintelligible garble and she knew it was time to take action.

"Phillip, you need to snap out of it and stop feeling sorry for yourself!" She spoke in a harsh tone. She didn't feel any sympathy for the drunk as she went around picking up empty bottles that he had strewn about the house. She then called his daughter to hurry over and take control of the situation.

Within the hour, Savanna arrived to find a man who was barely recognizable as her father. She cleaned him up, shoved black coffee down his throat and brought a little life back to his broken self. It took hours of constant babysitting before Phillip finally started coming to his senses.

She spent the time talking with him and letting him know that she was disappointed in his actions over the past years. He was her father, she loved him and this was his chance to be who he needed to be.

Savanna was the cure for Phillip and he felt much better knowing he still had her love. He replaced the liquid comfort with the comfort of her words. He would pull it together and he would continue. Things would be better.

He still wasn't sure if he wanted Sloan to be a part of his new life. He thought that it might be time to start over with a new lover. He could take his time and find a partner whom he could trust. Sloan was no longer that partner and Savanna validated his concerns.

Savanna left her father after making him eat the dinner she'd prepared for him. A new understanding developed between them and once again, Phillip felt good about his relationship with his daughter.

Chapter Fourteen

O<small>NCE</small> M<small>OLLY</small> <small>SETTLED IN, SHE QUICKLY STARTED TO REACQUAINT HERSELF</small> with all the working and financial aspects of the ranch. It took her a few days with the accountant to familiarize herself with everything. Even though she had grown up on the ranch, running the day-to-day business was something she never had to trouble herself with before. Her biggest challenge would be the fact that she was a woman and that for years she had lived her life as a privileged housewife. She was now ready to show not only the skeptic accountant who sat before her, but also the fellow ranch owners who were some of the toughest, roughest, cowboys in this country that she was here to stay and ready to step up. She would earn their respect and play in their game. She was an O'Malley and she was electrified at the challenge. Blessed and honored to have been born into this family, she was determined to live up to her name. She gave up her designer dresses and shoes and now wore boots, jeans and a cowboy hat.

After going through the books and seeing everything was financially in order, she sat back and took a deep breath. It was all about to begin and from here on out, good or bad, it was her responsibility.

As long as Molly could remember, Abe Hackathorn had been the Ghost Bear Ranch's accountant. He was a small man who wore boots with lifts and large Stetson hats in hopes of appearing taller. His sparse white hair was coarse and would pop out of the sides of his hat, resembling barbwire. Molly could not help but stare at the long handlebar mustache that reached out endlessly across the front of the man's face. She would observe with interest, as he would work the numbers at hand and unconsciously played with the tip of his mustache, twirling it between his stubby little fingers. Although Molly found him to be interesting, she also found him somewhat unpleasant.

Abe stretched, leaning as far back in his chair as he could without falling over. He plopped his cockroach stompers upon the top of his desk and tried to pierce her with his little eyes. "Look Molly, I'm going to be straight with you." He spoke in a typical long western drawl. "Honey, you're not cut of the same cloth as your daddy was. I frankly don't know what you're thinking by leaving your husband and coming back out here. I want you to know, little girl, that an offer was presented to me by someone who is very interested in your ranch."

He took his feet from the comfort of the desktop and leaned across furthering an attempt to intimidate Molly, who sat across from him. "It's a real good offer and I advise you to take it and go back to being a housewife."

Molly could feel the anger rise like an active volcano, ready to spill its lava all over him.

She rose out of her chair, standing at full attention. "Abe, you and I have a serious problem. First of all, your lack of respect for me is unacceptable. Second, you may decline the offer on my behalf. I will not be selling to anyone. And don't ever, I mean ever come to me again and make any suggestions of me ever selling my ranch."

She then walked around the desk, bent down and placed her face inches from the coward's face. "And last but not least, you old fuck. If you ever call me a little girl, honey or anything else besides Miss O'Malley, I will personally have the shit kicked out of you!"

Abe could feel her breath was as hot as a dragon's. She left his office slamming the door with such force it knocked his framed degree to the floor, shattering his accomplishments. Stunned and shaken, he responded to himself, "Goddamn, she is an O'Malley after all."

Molly stormed out of Abe's office and marched to her pick-up truck, spitting obscenities under her breath.

While she was in the cab of her truck, she screamed to an unusual extent of vengeance and punched at her leather steering wheel. "Jesus, what is up with men? Are they all a bunch of mother fuckers? I should have slapped that chicken shit senseless!"

She picked up her cell phone to call her attorney. After giving him firm instructions to hire a new accountant, she came to the realization that she liked the woman she had become. She was finished taking shit from anybody. She was ready to be the one to dish it out. This would be her life, played by her rules, and fuck anyone who would stand against her!

Gravel flew from the tires as she drove with fierce momentum back to her ranch. She flew into the driveway and threw her truck to a dead stop.

The majority of the ranch hands were near the bunkhouse as she yelled at them with authority. "Men, round everyone up. It's time for a meeting!"

After her talk with Abe, she knew there was a severe storm brewing and she had better prepare her ranch hands to keep their eyes open and hunker down for a hell of a fight.

Her boots echoed across the wooden porch as she ran into the house, slamming the screen door behind her. "Rosa, I need you. Where are you?"

Hearing the urgency in Molly's voice, the woman came scampering out of the kitchen with her hands full of flour. "What, what is it?" Her voice with filled with motherly concern.

"The men are all coming in the house. Could you gather up some beer for them? I need to have a meeting. I have some concerns over this ranch!"

She could hear the men approaching as they scraped their boots off by the front porch. She opened the large doors and invited them in. There were twenty-three men in total and they seemed to be in pretty good spirits. Each walked through the wooden double doors, taking their hats off in respect to their lady boss.

True cowboys, she thought to herself as she greeted each one.

She shook each man's hand firmly while looking each square in the eyes; all of them, that is, except for Clayton. She found it extremely hard to look directly at his deep blue eyes, as she knew heat would rise from her and make her face turn beet red.

Rosa appeared from the kitchen and offered each one of the cowhands an ice-cold long neck, which they happily accepted.

Molly began to speak. "Men, I really want to thank you for stopping in the middle of your work and coming up here. I know that there are still a few of you who I've known for years and there are a lot of you who my father hired since I've been gone. I realize that you probably are concerned over my gender and taking charge of the Ghost Bear. I want to tell you that this ranch is my legacy and I plan on staying and doing what is expected of me. This ranch will stay intact and with your help we will make sure it continues to be one of the largest working ranches in the state of Montana!"

As Molly spoke, she was very careful with her dictation, so as not to let any of her southern drawl emerge from her voice. "Mr. Leatherbe, whom you all know and admire, will still be acting ranch foreman. If you have any concerns or problems you will address them to him. He will continue working alongside of you just as he always has. Now, for those of you who might have a problem with having a lady as your boss, I'm going to ask you to please step forward and I will be happy to give you a great compensation package and ask you to pack your bags, put on your spurs and remove yourself from the premise by tonight."

She looked around the room at the dirt covered faces. Everyone was silent.

"Okay, then I'll take it that everyone is happy here and is willing to have orders coming from me."

The men looked at each other and nodded their heads in agreement.

"Great. Since everyone is staying on, I would like to say that I really appreciate your confidence and trust in me. I know how hard you men work and I know that there wouldn't be a ranch if it weren't for all of you. So, in return for all of your past and present loyalty, I will give each man here a bonus based on a percentage of the net profits from the Ghost Bear. Now let's drink on it!"

Molly popped open one of the ice cold Moose Drools and took a long swig just as if she was one of the men.

"Holy shit!" They yelled. They clanked their bottles to each other's and slapped their large callused hands upon each other's backs. As they laughed and hooted it up, Molly could see a new sense of spirit arise from the worn men.

"Now finish up your beer, men, and get back to work, we all have a lot to do."

"Yes ma'am!" They shouted. They gathered up their hats as they thanked her profusely for her generosity then walked with a new bounce in their old steps out the front door.

"Clayton," Molly called out. She wanted to catch him before he went back to work with his fellow workers.

Turning his head to face her, he looked down at her with his sexy blue eyes and spoke. "Ma'am, what you just did by giving that bonus out to those men, well I just want to say you just did more for those boys than anyone else in their lives."

"Thank you, Clayton. Just to let you know, I will be doubling your bonus. I'm grateful to you, and I trust with your help I know that we can make this ranch even greater."

"Now Miss Molly, that's just way too much. You really don't need to do that."

"Clayton, I won't hear another word. This is something that is important to me. But you could do one thing for me."

Clayton peered at Molly quizzing, narrowing his eyes.

"Take me to dinner tonight. After today I could use a shot of whiskey and a T-bone steak." She smiled widely showing her perfectly white teeth.

"I knew there would be a catch," he laughed. "I know just the place. I'll pick you up at 6:30."

Clayton tipped his hat at Rosa, and as he walked towards the door, Molly stared at the perfectly formed ass that was hiding inside his Wranglers.

"Damn, he's fine," she muttered to herself as she took one last swig and finished her beer.

Rosa raised an eyebrow at Molly and gave her a loving grin. "Those jeans do fit him rather nice." She chuckled and walked back into her domain to finish her preparations for dinner. She had many happy hungry men's bellies to fill and she knew that they would be in the mood to celebrate.

After the meeting, everyone who lived on the ranch was full of enthusiasm and eagerness as they performed their duties.

Unfortunately, no one had taken notice of two underhanded, questionable men lurking inside the unknown Chevy that had crept around the massive acres of Molly's private ranch. They spoke amongst themselves while taking notes and plotting the future demise of the Ghost Bear Ranch.

Chapter Fifteen

Molly was full of great cheer and looking forward to a night out. Halfway up the log staircase, she yelled at Rosa that she was heading up to her room to get ready for her date with Clayton. As soon as she heard her own words leave her mouth, she stopped dead in her tracks.

"Oh my God, what the hell am I doing? I haven't been on a date with a man besides Phillip in how long?" As she pondered this terrifying thought, her hands became clammy, her chest tightened and she felt as if she was on the verge of one of those panic attacks that she had heard about. "Pull it together Molly! For God's sakes, just take a long deep breath."

Her inner voice spoke with such strength that she almost thought someone else was standing right next to her. She was still getting accustomed to the person whom she was becoming. Surprising herself such as now, she would revert back to the woman whom she no longer wished to be.

She wrapped her small hand tightly around the banister and commanded her feet to move her up the staircase and onward to her private quarters. She was going to allow herself plenty of time to get ready for this man who had a way of making her feel like a teenager.

She pulled herself together and then began to get down to business. She drew herself a hot bath, putting lavender and rosemary oil in the steaming water and allowed her body to soak up the fragrance. She put her makeup on with a steady hand and precision to accent her natural beauty and not to appear overly done. She decided to leave her hair down, shaking it out so it would be full and sexy. Last but not least, she chose to dress somewhat casually, but with as much sex appeal, as she could muster. She squeezed her slender frame into a new pair of tight fitting jeans that lifted her ass up and took ten years off. She pulled on a long sleeve, button down snake print top while purposely leaving several buttons undone to let her cleavage out for a breath of fresh air. Then with great contemplation, she decided to wear the gold chain that securely held her large diamond cross, knowing it would be the perfect length and nestle down between her large breasts. She had hoped that the sparkle of the diamonds would catch Clayton's eye and help him take notice of her better assets.

Just as she was pulling on her cowboy boots that matched her top and wrapping a rhinestone belt around her waist, she heard Clayton's voice from downstairs. She walked out of her room to spot the wrangler standing at the bottom of the stairs talking with one of the other hands. As she proceeded down, she caught Clayton glancing up towards her, causing him to lose his place in the conversation and become noticeably flustered.

Her beauty left him breathless. "Hi Molly. Are you all set?"

"I sure am, and you look great!" She spoke with such giddiness that she surprised herself.

"Great. Let's get out of here I have a surprise for you. It will take us about an hour to get to dinner."

"An hour? Where are we going and are we riding by horseback?" She joked.

Clayton held the door for her and she jumped into his truck. "Well no, just by plane." He gave her a playful grin and grabbed her by the knee.

Sure enough, within fifteen minutes of leaving the massive log gate of the Ghost Bear, they arrived at a small hanger that held a small single-engine Cessna. Molly looked at Clayton in astonishment when he jumped from the truck

"Let's go," he said

"You're really serious about this? Who's going to fly this thing?"

"Well boss, that would be me."

He strapped her in tightly, gave her a pair of headphones with a mike attached and told her to put them over her ears and hold on.

He amazed her more each day. "Jesus Clayton, I didn't know that you could fly. You're full of surprises!"

"My daddy was a very busy man, but in his spare time, he loved to take me up. I've been flying for a long time but that's another story for another day. These days, the ranch keeps me busy and I don't have a lot of time, but I still try to get up when I can. It's a better view up here than sitting on the back of a horse."

The take off was smooth. Clayton felt just as comfortable flying the plane in the big sky as he did straddled in a saddle and riding amongst the Montana mountains. It was a perfect summer evening; seven o'clock and still plenty of light out, as it didn't get dark until ten in mid-summer. Molly wasn't sure which view was better, the majestic mountains scattered down below or Clayton Leatherbe sitting beside her. But she was taking them both in and they were both a sight to be seen.

Clayton put Trace Adkins into his CD player and his deep country voice streamed through the headphones and filled their ears.

"Clayton, where are we flying to?" Molly asked, cutting off Trace in the middle of his serenade.

"Well, I thought I would take you to Seeley Lake. We're going to eat in an old schoolhouse." Molly knew that Clayton was only willing to tell her enough to further pique her interest.

"Clayton Leatherbe, you're such a tease." She smiled, turned her head and went back to relish in the moment.

About an hour later, Molly spotted a small logging town that was centered between a cluster of alpine lakes and a chain of mountains that were part of the Bob Marshall wilderness. Clayton landed the plane with precision onto the small grass landing strip and geared it gently towards the hanger.

"Well here we are. And it looks like Vicky personally came to greet us!"

Molly could see a raven-haired beauty waving as she ran over to give Clayton a warm greeting. Clayton helped Molly down from her seat to solid ground. He then turned and wrapped Vicky in his large muscular arms making her little frame disappear, as he twirled her around giving her a big bear hug.

"Oh put me down, you old cow hand and introduce me to your lady!" Vicky giggled as she wiped the remains of her rose lipstick away from Clayton's cheek.

Molly watched as the two old friends interacted and she felt a twinge of jealousy. She could only imagine what it would feel like, having his arms wrapped around her and she knew they must have known each other for sometime.

"Vicky, this is the owner of the Ghost Bear Ranch and my boss, Miss Molly Madison, formerly Miss O'Malley." Clayton was grinning from ear to ear.

"Clayton, just a reminder, I prefer O'Malley," Molly replied.

And with that statement Clayton tipped his Stetson at Molly O'Malley and continued his conversation with Vicky. "As I was saying, Miss O'Malley and I are celebrating and we really appreciate you taking my reservation in such short notice. I know you're a little tight on space and the summer is pretty busy in these parts. I really didn't expect you to take the time yourself to pick us up."

"Well Molly, it's so nice to meet you!" Said Vicky. "I almost fell over when my girls told me Clayton was flying in and bringing along a special female guest. I figured I better come out here myself just so I could lay out the red carpet." Vicky gave Molly a big hug and nudged her two guests towards her truck. "Now, come on. I know the two of you are ready for a nice meal."

Clayton suddenly turned and ran back to the plane. "I almost forgot the wine." He pulled out from behind the seat of the plane a beautiful bottle of Cabernet from the Cake Bread Winery. "We can't have a nice dinner without a little vino."

As they drove to dinner, Clayton proceeded to tell Molly that Vicky was one of the best chef's in the state. Before she had settled in Seeley, she was the owner of one of the finest restaurants in Jackson, Wyoming. After a number of years and watching the beloved small quaint town and its good hearted people become overrun by a high hat, inflated, narcissistic group of outsiders who had too much money to know what to do with, she had had enough. So she closed up her establishment and moved to Seeley Lake, Montana.

"That's right, the millionaires moved out and the billionaires moved in," said Vicky. "Seeley Lake may be a small town, but it has a big heart and good people. I found a quaint little two-room schoolhouse, and with a little help from some friends, converted it over to a restaurant/art gallery. Winters are tough, but the summers more than make up for it."

Vicky pulled up to one of the quaintest establishments Molly had ever seen. The sign on the building said "Little Bird School House", and with all the little yellow birds flying around, she certainly understood why Vicky had chosen that name. The vintage wooden building sat in the middle of a park-like setting with grass that was so green, it produced a strong desire to take your boots off and tickle your bare feet in it. Café tables and chairs were placed in soothing comfort around the lush grounds for customers to reside upon while butterflies and dragon flies playfully danced amongst the colorful variety of summer flowers that were planted firmly in the window boxes. Towards the back of the building, Vicky had a lovely garden filled with herbs and vegetables that she personally grew by hand. She cut her herbs fresh and harvested the vegetables, using them in her nightly divine dishes, making the meal irresistible and hungrily devoured by her customers.

Once inside the dimly lit room, floorboards creaking beneath their feet, they were led to a small room which held five wooden tables pre-set with fine china. Lavender had been freshly cut and placed within mason jars as centerpieces. As they were seated at a table for two, Molly thought of how the schoolhouse, which once held the aroma of leather books and freshly washed children, was now saturated with lavender and the aromatic mixture of roast duck, along with other scrumptious meals.

Molly reached across the table and lightly touched Clayton's hand. "Clayton, this is absolutely perfect."

"I'm really glad you like it. This has been my secret little get away for some time and you're the only person I've ever brought here." Clayton's smile was warm and genuine. "Now have a glass of wine and let's take our time. I made arrangements for us to stay at a friend's cabin tonight. I have an extra set of keys to the place and when I fly in, Kirk likes me to pop in and make sure everything is in good shape. You probably have heard of the place: the Borealis Lodge."

Molly had heard of the place, which was well known for its beauty and view. When the private home was under construction people came from all over just to stand on its decks and stare at the mountains as they rose up to touch the sky. It faced due north and was the perfect place to observe the Aura Borealis, hence the name. Although Molly would have loved to see the remarkable log home, the cowboy's liberty surprised her and she opened her mouth in protest.

Clayton stopped her before the words could leave her lips. "I can't drink and fly. There are plenty of bedrooms and we each can have our own suite. We'll head back at first light."

Molly looked into Clayton's blue eyes, swallowing the lump inside her throat, and nodded her head in agreement.

They filled the rest of the night with wine and laughter, and between bites of their meals, exchanged ideas, stories, hopes and dreams. To their surprise and sadness, the hours slipped by, the sun descended down in the sky, and Vicky was at their table taking away their desert plates and presenting them with the check.

The night had passed too quickly for both of them and they now found themselves each standing by the door that led to their own private rooms. They anxiously stared at one another, not knowing how to act on their feelings. In Clayton's mind, he could see himself sweeping Molly into his arms and laying her onto the bed, removing her clothes and feeling her warm body under his; but instead of acting on his impulse, he gently spoke.

"Goodnight ma'am, and thank you for giving me the opportunity to spend some time with you, I had one of the best nights of my life."

And with those words Clayton opened his door, took off his clothes and crawled into the large four-poster bed. He stared out his window at the full moon that hung alone in the black sky and thought of the extraordinary goddess that lay sleeping in the room next door.

Chapter Sixteen

It had been several months and Phillip had not heard Molly's voice or been in her presence. He had been served with divorce papers and it looked as if the only thing Molly had wanted from him was her freedom. She was willing to give him everything that they had accumulated together over the course of their marriage in exchange for him to just sign the papers and let her go. Although most men in their right mind would be jumping for joy, Phillip was not like most men, and asking this of him was easier said than done. His aspirations of optimizing his career by becoming a congressman had quickly become a distant memory when Molly walked out on him.

Soon after Molly left, Phillip's sexual preference quickly leaked out and his face was plastered all over the papers with torrid details about how he hired his male lover to be his personal assistant at his law firm and paid him an inflated salary for his nonexistent qualifications. The firm asked him to step down from his position as lead partner but he refused, threatening them with a discrimination lawsuit. They backed down, as he knew they would.

Phillip's parents learned about his scandal by reading the Sunday paper while they ate their brunch. They called to tell him that he was a huge embarrassment and they no longer wished to have any association with him; he was no longer their son and would be cut out of any inheritance.

His friends would have nothing to do with him and his social life was non-existent. He had cut off all relations with Sloan and there wasn't a man straight or gay that wished to be seen with him. Everyday he left his house was a struggle of pride and he tried to forget all about his current problems by immersing himself in the few cases he had with the clients that hadn't dropped him.

Even though Molly just wanted him to sign the divorce papers, he couldn't do it. Just her leaving took everything away from him. It's true that he was having a hard time letting her go, but now that his career was up in the air and his parents had written him off, he needed the money from that ranch. The assets they had accumulated together didn't even come close to the net worth of the Ghost Bear.

After a month had passed without a word from Molly, Phillip called one of the ranch hands he had befriended the last time he was there. He explained to José that he was still in love with his wife and was able to persuade the feeble-minded man to feel sorry for him. Phillip offered to give him some compensation in exchange for a detailed report of Molly's whereabouts and actions. José would call Phillip with his weekly reports about how Molly was taking a strong hold of things at the Ghost Bear. Then one week, while giving his usual news on Molly, José's voice sounded different. Phillip listened with interest and when José was finished he asked the man sternly if he was sure that he wasn't leaving anything else out. That was when José spilled the beans on Miss Molly and Clayton, the ranch foreman.

José told Phillip how Molly had offered every man a bonus and how Clayton had taken her to dinner, and they hadn't come home until the next morning. This infuriated Phillip; was it jealousy he felt or just pride? Trying to sort out his feelings, the voice in his head told him that he had absolutely no right to be angry. She was a wonderful woman who deserved to be with a man who wanted her mind, body and spirit.

"Oh shut the fuck up," he told his inner voice. "I know that I don't want her sexually, but I sure as hell need her for everything else in my life. I'm fucking falling apart and I'm not about to let some ass clown take advantage of her when she is vulnerable because of the shit I put her through. I'll beg her back and tell her I was wrong. I'll change. I know she'll come back.

"No, she won't and you know it." That damn inner voice just wouldn't shut up. "Sign the papers and let her move on. For once in your life do the right thing and think of someone else besides yourself." The battle raged inside his head as he stared blankly at the legal documents. "Today is not the day," he silently thought and he put the papers away in his desk.

Chapter Seventeen

SHE WAS TRYING TO KEEP THE RAGE THAT HAD BEEN SLOWLY BUILDING tucked deep into the pit of her stomach. Her mood towards her husband and friends was becoming increasingly foul. They weren't accustomed to seeing her in such a bad manner. So when she snapped at their simple questions, she would apologize sweetly and tell them she was not feeling well and had a terrible migraine. This was somewhat true, as she wasn't feeling great and the throbbing in her head was becoming stronger and stronger.

In all these years, she had never had to wait so long to take a victim. Killing was a release for her. Some people cut themselves to release the pain inside. In the beginning when she was a young girl, she tried this but after a few times she thought, *Why the hell am I hurting myself, when I really want to hurt the son of bitch who is to blame for my pain.*

She was just fourteen and she knew exactly how she would kill the molester who was her mother's husband. His name was

Ted. He was fat, his hair was long and greasy and his hands were always dirty from working on cars. When she was a small child, her mother drank large amounts of alcohol, passing out and leaving her to fend for herself. When she would see her mother start to drink she would run and hide, cowering in different parts of the house knowing it was just a matter of time before her mother's stinky husband would come looking for her, calling her name, wanting her to come to him and do the bad things that he had taught her. It didn't matter where she hid; he always found her. So eventually she stopped hiding and would wait naked in her dark room, praying that he would be quick about it and not pass out on top of her.

For years she dealt with the abuse by cutting at her own flesh with a steak knife, hoping her mother would notice the self-inflicted wounds on her arms and just once ask her daughter about it; but she never did.

The destructive behavior continued until the young girl's fourteenth birthday, when for some reason someone upstairs had finally heard her prayers and gave her the sign and strength to make a change. On this particular day her mother stayed sober and made her a chocolate birthday cake, and on top of the cake she lit fourteen candles. It was the best day of her life and the first birthday cake she ever had. When she blew out the candles, instead of making a foolish wish, she made a promise to herself that she would never let any man ever get away with hurting her again.

That night after everyone was asleep, she went out to her stepfather's beat up old Dodge and cut the brake lines. This was not difficult, as she knew exactly how to do this. On several occasions, when he worked on his car, he would make her stand above him holding his tools, wearing the only dress she owned, with no panties. He loved threatening her by telling her that if she ever told anyone about what he did to her, he would cut her mother's throat, so he could do whatever he wanted to her anytime of the day. Then just for effect, he would take out his switchblade and show her the sharpness of the knife.

The next morning when he left for work, he hit an ice patch and flew right off the mountain. No one ever suspected a thing. At the funeral when her mother was bawling her eyes out, the young girl was laughing to herself, secretly thanking the dead man for teaching her about cars.

Two months after they buried the fat slob her pathetic mother found herself a new bum and brought him home. Realizing that she couldn't knock off this new guy, as people might get suspicious; she packed her bags and jumped out her window, hitching a ride South, killing any old man who tried to have his way with her.

Killing felt so good that she became increasingly addicted to it. She viewed herself as a super hero, ridding the world of the undesirables who preyed upon the innocent. Now, she wasn't a dummy and she had watched enough Superman movies to know that every true superhero had to have a double life, so that is what she did; her past was hers and hers alone.

Her husband was a good provider and a very busy man. This suited her just fine, as she needed her own private time to do her good deeds, which in turn kept her headaches at bay.

Usually she chose her prey and quickly devised a perfect plot for his demise, never having to wait long in between killings. But this time she had a very special man in mind. His punishment was taking a lot of planning and effort on her part, and she did not want to rush his death.

This particular man she had bore witness to him destroying the life of a married woman. Granted, he wasn't the usual victim she would normally go after, but she truly disliked his arrogance and lack of compassion. This man was a challenge and she would make sure that the rest of his living years would consist of misery and agony. She knew that even though he would eventually become aware of the affliction she was about to bestow upon him, he would not want to be alone in his suffering, so he would selfishly spread his deadly disease, sharing it with other men who were foolish enough to be with him. This was no concern of hers; in fact, contaminating this particular menacing prick would procure the demise of hundreds of assholes, and the thought of this made her jubilant. She took great pride in her past creativity, but this one would take the cake.

"Here is to my next poor, sap. Let's drink to him," she giggled, as she mixed herself up a whiskey sour and threw it back, letting the whiskey burn the back of her throat. "Hell, I might as well have a second. Here's to Mom for making me into the woman I am today!"

She only had to wait one more day and then she could carry out her plan.

"Fuck it, what's one more day?" She thought.

She felt the pain in her frontal lobe start to fade and she suddenly realized that she had lost track of time. She had better start dinner; her husband would be home soon.

Chapter Eighteen

Sloan was sick of Phillip's behavior and he decided he wasn't going to wait around any more. As far as he was concerned, Phillip had brought all of this on himself. Everything was his fault and if Phillip didn't want to be with him and be happy, he could just wallow in his pathetic misery by himself, because he was not into pitying anyone … except maybe himself. Sure, Sloan may not have gotten the man of his dreams, but he did get a lot of attention and he was ready to take it all right to the bank.

Attorneys had been calling Sloan trying their best to entice him into filing a lawsuit for the loss of his job and the paparazzi was following him everywhere. He was like a kid in a candy store. He loved waking up in the morning and primping himself to make sure he looked his best, knowing there would be a mob of hunky men fighting over each other just to shoot his picture. They would always yell at him asking for details of Phillip's and his relationship, and Sloan would slyly tantalize them with small amount details, making them want to follow him around to find out more. They were like puppies on leashes and Sloan was leading them on.

As soon as the succulent story got out, and filled the pages of the local papers, he ran to the nearest newsstand and bought several copies. He kept them all lovingly in a large box with pink tissue paper between each one. His friends told him he was ridiculous to save them; well most of them. He burned the papers that wanted to make him look bad and showed pity to Molly.

It pissed him off every time he even thought of her, let alone that day she poured her hot coffee over his head. "The stupid bitch. She ruined my favorite shirt and I had to wash my hair three times to get the fucking mocha smell out of it."

But he didn't care. After all, isn't it the little things in life that make us happy? And reading about himself and playing the victim did just that. He was enjoying all the attention. But he knew that just like all good stories, it would eventually end and he wasn't really sure what he was going to do with himself when that happened. This was a huge dilemma; after all the excitement the thought of things returning to his hum drum life, was well, shall we say, less than appealing.

Then there was also the little problem of finding a nice guy who would even want to have a serious relationship with him. The pickings had become sparse. As soon as Sloan introduced himself to someone he found enticing they fled in the other direction, not wanting anything to do with him. He blamed Phillip for this as well. If Phillip had just come out on his own, he wouldn't be going through this.

After hours of feeling sorry for himself, Sloan decided that he didn't have any other choice than to somehow get Phillip alone and convince him how sorry he was, even though he really wasn't sorry at all. If he could accomplish this task, he was sure he could use his magnetic charm to his favor and Phillip would be his forever. Sure, life with Phillip might be a little boring, but at least he would have someone to snuggle with at night and give him the attention he craved.

Sloan thought long and hard, putting a plan together and after diligent thinking, he came up with the perfect scheme. As he looked out his window, winking and blowing kisses at the men who were now going crazy with their cameras, he thought first things first, he needed to ditch the cameramen who were staked outside his complex. He called his friend Angel who worked as a drag queen down in Ybor and asked him to bring some stuff over. Within no time, Angel came flying over like a gay knight to the rescue.

Angel drove up and walked with his bag full of disguises right past the paparazzi. Sloan opened the door as he came joyfully skipping through, excited over the fact that he was able to participate in the game.

They worked fast, and by the time they had finished, Sloan was transformed into a brunette that any straight woman would pay thousands to look like. After looking in the mirror, satisfied with his transformation, Sloan began to work on his friend. He had Angel strip off his clothes and Sloan gave him the pants and shirt that he previously had on. He then put on a wig, similar in color to that of Sloan's own hair and put it on Angel. He quickly chopped at the fake hair, cutting it into a similar style as his own.

"Hmm. You're not as good looking as me, but I think we can pass you off," Sloan said as he made Angel stand in front of the window.

"You're such a bitch!" Angel spat, as he started waving at the men who once again began flashing their cameras.

"Now, just keep their attention long enough so I can walk by them and get in your car," Sloan said, admiring how he was really getting into his part. "Where are your keys?"

"They're over there on the table. Don't forget to take your purse. Hey, you walk pretty well in those heels. Have you been doing something on the side that I don't know about? If you don't get your job back, I might be able to work you into the club. You would make a great Demi Moore."

"Thanks. I'll keep that in mind." Sloan appreciated the compliment from his friend. As a last minute thought, he grabbed some of his normal street clothes along with a pair of shoes and crammed them into his oversized purse.

"It might not be a good idea for Phillip to come home and find me dressed in drag," Sloan spoke to his friend. "He might think I really lost my mind."

Sloan knew that Phillip would be pissed at him when he found out he had broken in, but he hoped he would give him a few minutes and listen to what he had to say before calling the police.

"I'll call you later," Sloan said to Angel as he ran out the door. "Help yourself to what's in the fridge."

"No problem. Good luck!" Angel yelled back while still putting on a show for the people camped outside.

The disguise worked perfectly; no one gave him a second glance as he walked out the front doors of the condominium complex. He strutted right past the unsuspecting photographers and looked up at Angel, who was now bending over and looking between his legs in order for the photographers to get a good shot of his ass.

Sloan rolled his eyes and thought, "Jesus they must all be gay."

Sloan drove out of the parking lot with Angel's pink VW and headed straight to Phillip's house. He made one stop at a nearby gas station so he could change his clothes and wipe the makeup off his face.

He arrived in record time and Sloan knew that Phillip had a key that hung on a nail inside the trunk of a large orange tree that grew in his backyard. There had been several times when Sloan was with Phillip and he had forgotten his key and had to use this particular one to get into the house. As he hid the car around the corner from Phillip's estate, he walked to the back yard hoping that the key would still be there. *It would sure make things a lot easier,* he thought, while not wanting to have to break a window and have Phillip pissed off at him even more. He reached up into the tree stretching and rubbing his girlish like hand against the inside of its trunk.

"Bingo!" He said, quite pleased with his luck and the way the day was heading.

Sloan went to the side door. Not wanting a nosy neighbor to spot him, he unlocked it and let himself into his lover's home. It was the first time that Sloan had actually been inside of Phillip's house. He admired the large rooms filled with warm lavish furnishings. As he looked around he thought, *this will do quite nicely.* He could see himself living here with Phillip and being very comfortable. He pictured himself cooking Phillip's dinner in the extravagant kitchen. He looked inside Phillip's fridge to happily find an untouched twelve-inch Philly with cheese. Figuring Phillip wouldn't mind in the least and it was well after lunch, Sloan took the sandwich out and warmed it in the microwave. Taking a large bite of his sandwich, Sloan resumed to his fantasies while continuing his inspection of each room, when suddenly he heard a strange noise that abruptly brought him back to reality.

"Shit!" He panicked.

Darting his eyes around the room he began to look for options. The terrifying thought of Phillip's housekeeper walking in and finding him standing in Phillip's house would not be good. She would surely recognize his face, as it has been in every paper for the last few weeks, and call the cops on him.

His thoughts were racing through his head like cars in the last turn at the Daytona 500. Just when he was ready to turn and bolt back through the door that he came in he heard the sound again, but this time he could tell it definitely wasn't Phillip's housekeeper. It sounded more like an animal.

"Did Philip get a dog?" Sloan thought to himself as he followed the animalistic noises coming from the hall towards the back of the ranch style home. He knew that Phillip really wasn't into animals, let alone a dog that he would have to take care of by himself, but as he now stood in front of a closed door, he listened to the sounds coming from behind it. The sound heightened, sounding more like moans and groans. He placed his hand on the handle of the door and slowly pushed it open.

"Oh hell no!"

Sloan's face turned deep crimson, his blood boiled over with anger, as he screamed a stream of profanity into the well lit room.

Chapter Nineteen

Earlier that morning Phillip awoke, showered and sat down for his breakfast. He picked up the *Times*, only to be disgusted once again as Sloan's face was staring back at him, while his written words were divulging their most intimate moments for the rest of the world's entertainment.

"Jesus, will he just let it rest! He's such a media whore!" Phillip's scream echoed off his empty kitchen.

Suddenly, having lost his appetite, he placed his uneaten breakfast into the kitchen sink, grabbed his keys and headed out the door. He quickly scanned his yard for any unwanted paparazzi. Not seeing anyone who might give him suspicion, he jumped into his car and headed for the office. Cranking up his stereo and feeling the sun beating down upon his face, he began to calm; for the moment, the storm inside him was dissipating. Starbucks was within a short distance from his office, so looking at his watch, he decided he had time to go in his favorite

establishment and enjoy his coffee. Once inside and having purchased his Columbian roast, he spied an empty table, sat down,
opened his laptop and proceeded to look over some of the briefs
he had prepared earlier in the week.

A few minutes had gone by when, after taking a long
sip from his java, he looked around the coffeehouse and
noticed a handsome gentleman close to his own age staring
at him. Not thinking anything of it and figuring that the man
had recognized him, Phillip smiled politely and returned
his attention to his work. Within a moment and much to
Phillip surprise, the man walked over and sat himself down
at Phillip's table.

Phillip lifted his gaze from his work and asked the man,
"Excuse me, is there a problem?"

"I'm sorry to bother you, but are you Phillip Madison?" The
man asked with a deep French accent.

"Look, if you're a reporter, please just cut me a break and
let me enjoy my coffee," Phillip spoke with pleading eyes, while
looking extremely beat down.

"No, no, I'm not a reporter. I just recognized you. I would
normally never do this, but I wanted to tell you, it's going to be
okay." The stranger had concern and sympathy in his voice, and
kindness upon his face. "Give everything a little time. You'll soon
be old news and not so interesting. I know coming out is hard
enough, let alone having someone else decide for you when that
time should be."

Phillip admired the man's handsome European features.
"Thank you. That is really nice of you to come over and tell me
that. I think that was the nicest thing anyone has said to me in
weeks. What's your name?"

"Oh, I'm sorry, I didn't introduce myself. My name is Jacques
Adur, but you can call me Jack. I see that you're busy and I don't

want to interrupt you. I just wanted to give you a little support. It was a pleasure to meet you."

Jack started to stand, when Phillip quickly responded. "No, please don't go. Sit."

"Well, if you're sure I'm not taking up your time."

Jack sat in the empty chair across from Phillip. The two men began talking as if they were old friends, letting the hours pass. Neither one wanted to leave the other and the two men spent the rest of the morning enjoying each other's company.

Jack had confided in Phillip, telling him that he also had been in a marriage and denial of who he was. He understood Phillip's pain and the pain he caused his wife, child and all those from whom he hid his secret. Phillip listened, letting Jack's words of comfort warm his insides. They both were surprised at how comfortable they felt with each other and how easy it was to communicate and share their honest thoughts and feelings.

"Jack, I feel so comfortable with you." said Phillip. "I know this is going to seem forward, but I think if we stay here any longer they might kick us out. Would you like to follow me back to my place?" Phillip held his breath awaiting Jack's answer.

Jack looked into Phillip's eyes, and reached across the table lightly touching Phillip's hand. "I hope you don't think I'm forward by saying I thought you'd never ask!"

Jack followed Phillip to his house and he asked him to put his car in the garage, as Philip did not want to feed his neighbors with any new gossip for their neighborhood watch sessions. They walked side by side into the house.

"Hey, I don't know about you, but I'm starving. What do you say I whip us up something to eat?" Phillip led the handsome French man into his kitchen.

"Only if you let me pick the wine."

Jack gave Phillip a wink and the two men soon began to prepare a cheese board with various selections that they found in the
fridge, along with cut up apples and a bottle of Phillip's favorite
French wine.

As they drank their wine and shared the delectable morsels,
Philip could not help but be impressed with Jack's wit and charm.
Throughout their intimate talks, Phillip discovered that Jack had
come from a prominent European family, and like Phillip's family, they had been very disapproving of his life style. He had been
in a three-year relationship with another man, for whom he had
left his wife. This man was the first man that Jack had allowed
himself to be physical with, and when he came to the realization
that in order for him to be happy with his life, he would have to
be who he was, not the person everyone wanted him to be. This
decision had crushed his wife and his only son, who to this day,
refused to talk to him, let alone see him.

Phillip listened attentively to Jack as he shared his story of
heartache. Not wanting to ruin the moment by asking this remarkable man if he was still involved with his lover, he knew
he must. "Jack, what happened to this man that you fell in love
with?"

With a look of anguish, Jack whispered the words. "He's
dead."

To Phillip's secret relief and a sense of sadness for his new
friend, he kept his ears opened as Jack reveled to him the sorrow-
ful ending of his love story.

"I had lived with him blissfully for two and a half years. We
were so in love. I had been driving back from the airport. We had
just come back from a romantic Tahitian vacation. He was asleep
in the passenger seat. I remember he looked like an angel." Jack
reflected as he looked down at his hands that were placed in his
lap. "It all happened so fast. A young kid, he was drunk, ran the

red light and slammed his SUV into the side of our car. He died instantly."

Phillip was speechless. Not knowing what to say, he wrapped his arms around the strong man and held him. In return, Jack held onto Phillip. The two men held each other tightly and what seemed as natural to them as breathing, they touched their lips gently together.

What started out as a gentle kiss soon erupted into frenzied passion. Phillip took Jack by his hand and led him down the long hall that led to his bedroom. Neither man spoke a word as their hands worked feverishly at the task of removing each other's clothing, only to stop and caress each other, making their manhood grow to great lengths.

Phillip's arousal was more than anything he ever felt with Sloan. He was oblivious to anything else around him, as his only desire was to pleasure Jack, this wonderful man who had come when Phillip needed him the most. Each hungry thrust brought him closer to a state of ecstasy as their moans turned into a unison song. As their bodies moved together, neither of them noticed the figure coming through the unlocked door.

Chapter Twenty

It took a minute for Sloan's brain to distinguish the mingled forms that thrashed in front of his eyes. But then like a huge bolt of lighting, he realized what he was seeing and it struck him. Phillip was fucking another man just a few feet away from where he was standing, their passion so heated that neither of them noticed the uninvited guest who was boldly peering at them with contempt.

Full of fury and unable to think rationally, Sloan picked up the largest object that was closest to him, which happened to be a lamp. He then threw it with surprising force while screaming like a banshee, hurling his body through the air, landing on them both, creating a three-gay pile up.

With the Philly Cheese Steak sandwich still in hand, Sloan began to beat the shocked men and screamed, "If you want something up your ass, take this."

Creating a flying carnage of meat and cheese, he then began to tear at Phillip's hair while punching at Jack, landing him square in the eye.

"Sloan, damn it, stop!" Phillip yelled

Sloan was now kicking violently at the naked men. As he rolled back on top of Phillip to further beat him with his fist, Jack seized the opportunity and landed a blow against Sloan that sent him flying backwards off the bed and crashing unconscious onto the floor.

Jack jumped off the bed, down onto the floor and looked at Sloan. "Shit, I hope I didn't kill him. I've never hit a single person in my life!"

Phillip bent down and felt Sloan's pulse. "Don't worry; we could only be so lucky. The little prick is only knocked out."

The two men dressed in a hurry, wanting to be fully clothed by the time Sloan awoke.

Phillip slapped Sloan in the face to wake him. "Sloan, get the hell out of here before I call the cops!" He narrowed his eyes in contempt. "I don't ever want to see your face around here again!"

"Fuck you, Phillip and your little whore! This is the thanks I get? This is how you repay me by giving you a life, giving you the opportunity to be happy?"

Sloan's voice became highly pitched as he started to cry. He leapt from the floor and ran out of the house yelling, "This is not over, Phillip Madison! It will never be over until I want it to be. Do you understand?"

Sloan slammed the door and ran as fast as he could while sobbing and cutting back through Phillip's yard to the safety of his car.

After Sloan ran out the back, Phillip looked at Jack and could see his eye was beginning to swell shut. "My God, Jack I am so sorry. I have not talked to or seen that man in weeks. I don't even know how he got in here."

Phillip walked from the bedroom down the hall and retrieved a large piece of steak he had planned to grill for dinner that night. He quickly returned and handed Jack the prime cut of beef. "Put this on your eye."

Grateful for his gesture of kindness and feeling a twinge of guilt for engaging in sex with a man he hardly knew, Jack said, "Phillip, it's not your fault. I should never have come home with you. I knew that you were in the middle of so much shit. The last thing you need right now is for me to make things more complicated for you. I'm going to give you my card, and when you get your life sorted out call me. Who knows, maybe I'll still be around and then we can pick up where we left off."

Jack kissed Phillip on the cheek and left. Phillip was alone once more.

Chapter Twenty One

SHE HAD BEEN STAKING OUT HER NEXT TARGET, OBSERVING, WATCHING, and learning all of the details of his daily fucked up life. The newspapers made her job easy. Her husband had left for a conference two days earlier and would not be home for a week, so she had plenty of time to plan every detail to perfection. She sat in her car as she watched the circus of men parading outside.

"How the hell am I going to ever get this man alone while he has this much attention?" She thought to herself. She knew it could be disastrous for her if some cheesy little photographer took her picture with this man.

Her car was parked close enough to observe everything, but far enough away that no one would pay her any attention. She pondered her dilemma as she watched this man play with the photographers from his window. Suddenly she noticed a woman leave the building from the side door and she watched as the strange woman walked right by the preoccupied pushovers armed with cameras.

"There's something very odd about her," she thought.

The strange looking woman walked extremely fast to a car that just moments ago a man had emerged from. She slumped down in her seat. As the woman unlocked the car and slid inside, she was able to get a good look at the woman's face. She was not a woman at all; she was a man; her target!

As the man peeled out of the drive she knew that this was her opportunity to follow him. She stayed behind him a few car lengths away as she didn't want to alarm him. He made one quick stop and to her amusement, she watched him walk into the building as a woman, and out as a man. She admired his cleverness and was excited to have such a worthy opponent. As she continued to follow him, she was very curious to see what the sneaky little devil had up his sleeve.

"Oh, you little bastard!" She spoke aloud, as she couldn't believe what she was seeing.

He ran from his car, into the backyard and grabbed something out of a tree. She watched as he approached the back door and then went inside the house.

Once again, she found herself waiting, not knowing how long. He would eventually come out and she would follow him, waiting for the right time to make her move.

She looked over at the Styrofoam container sitting beside her that held a vile mix of venereal cocktail. It had been easy for her to obtain the tainted samples of blood. Her husband was on the board of Tampa General. Twice a month she volunteered her services, which enabled her to swipe the blood samples. She enjoyed mixing the deadly concoction herself; safely, of course. A shot of Hep B, a shot of Hep C and a chaser of AIDS. Shaken, not stirred, and that should do it.

She placed her infectious mixture along with a needle carefully into the covered container that now rested beside her. She knew that she only had four days to administer the ghastly disease for it to be fully effective, and she was hoping that tonight would be the night.

Suddenly, the man came flying out of the house, nearly tripping over his own feet. His face stained with tears, he was obviously in extreme distress. Once inside his car, he screeched his tires leaving behind the black marks of his departure. She had to work fast to keep up with him, and she was concerned that his erratic driving would call attention to an unsuspecting officer of the law.

She let him get far enough ahead of her, but still kept him in her sights. She followed him as he led her from the affluent part of town into the seedier section well known for its gay establishments. She became elicit when he pulled into the parking spaces at one of the bars. She would allow the deplorable man some alone time inside the bar so as to have a head start on his alcoholic consumption.

After about a half an hour, she walked into the dimly lit, smoke filled tavern. She spotted her red-haired devil pounding shots of whisky and lining the bar with remnants of empty glasses. Various gay men were coupled up and hung onto each other in dim corners and booths scattered around the bar. Knowing how out of place she looked, she walked over to her pathetic loner and plopped down on the stool next to him.

Half sprawled out on the top of the bar and waiting for his next shot, he looked up at the attractive woman and slurred, "You know this is a gay bar?"

"Then I guess I don't have to worry about some asshole trying to pick me up, when all I want is a shot of whisky."

She smiled at him, reached over to grab the bottle from behind the bar and poured the little sludge another shot to numb his pain. She then poured herself one and raised the glass at the bartender who was now giving her a dirty look.

She clanked her glass to the man sitting at the bar and said, "Thanks. Here's to the dumb ass men who don't know a good thing when they got it."

"Oh, by the way my name is Sloan," he sputtered at her.

"Nice to meet you, Sloan. Have another; you look like you need it."

Once again she filled his glass. She yelled down at the bartender, who was now preoccupied in flirting with an attractive muscular black man dressed in gym clothes, to start her a tab and add the bottle. Not wanting to be interrupted in his frivolous flirting, the bartender gave her a nod and turned his attention back to the handsome man.

She sat with Sloan for an hour, keeping his glass full and listening to his whining. When he could no longer keep his ass planted upon his bar stool, she told him he'd had enough and she would drive him home.

Her skinned crawled with disgust as he leaned on her for support as they walked out to her car. She shoved him into the front seat and buckled his seat belt around his skinny torso. Being that he was unconscious, she knew he wouldn't remember much the next day, so she drove straight to his house and pulled into his parking lot. She carefully sized up the area, scouting for any straggling paparazzi. After close observation that all was clear she took her prized concoction out of its cooler and placed the deadly syringe into her purse. She then opened the passenger door and roughly pulled Sloan to his feet. After much work, they were standing at his door.

"Okay, Sloan, I need your keys," she spoke as she put her hand inside the pocket of his tight fitting jeans.

"This is a first. A girl putting her hands in my pants." He giggled uncontrollably. "I kind of like it."

She rolled her eyes, found his keys and while still hanging onto him with one hand, she unlocked the door and led him inside. She quickly looked around and noticed the scribbled note left behind from his friend who had helped him with his escape, informing him that he would be back tomorrow to retrieve his car and couldn't wait to hear all the juicy details.

"I'm sure you will have a lot to tell him," she spoke while still supporting and escorting him to his bed.

He fell upon his bed like a dead weight. She took his shoes off and placed his legs on top, not bothering to cover him up. Working quickly, she pulled the syringe from her purse. Her hands began to feel clammy, and for the first time in all of her heroic deeds, she felt nervous. She didn't like being in his house and it made her very anxious. She took a hold of his scrawny arm and pricked the bare skin with the needle. She watched his face as she inserted the deadly venereal mixture into his blood stream. He didn't even flinch. She then told him to have sweet dreams as she left him soundly sleeping and completely oblivious to his future, which would entail great suffering and possible death.

The next morning, still fully dressed in clothes from the day before, Sloan awoke with an incredible headache and a distant memory of a kind woman who had driven him home. He pulled himself from bed and scuffled into his bathroom. When he reached up to open the glass door to retrieve the bottle of Tylenol that he kept in the medicine cabinet for such occasions, he felt a stiff soreness in his right arm.

"Damn," he spoke aloud while looking into the mirror to investigate where the pain was coming from. To his surprise, the top of his upper arm was bruised, and under the skin was a lump and what looked like a needle mark. "What the fuck?"

He questioned his disheveled reflection. Unable to recall the events of the previous night and knowing there was nothing he could do about it, he undressed and went back to bed, hoping to feel better when he awoke later.

Chapter Twenty Two

Within a couple of months, the ranch was running like a well greased machine. The hands were happy and they felt that their future was solid, Clayton was in high spirits, and even the cattle and horses seemed to appear calmer, almost lulled by the positive energy that blew across their land.

They lived and worked in their own happy world, oblivious to the evil that lurked beyond their gate that hid itself within a small group of vicious greedy land developers. Their mouths were watering like a pack of wild dogs at the thought of taking control of Molly's prime land and placing hundreds of wells across it to pump the oil and gas that hid beneath the soil.

Evin Murdock was their leader. He was ruthless, malicious and didn't have any scruples when it came to making dirty deals. While Gavin was alive, Evin would never even consider going after the ranch. So when news spread about the death of the old man, Evin saw the opportunity of a lifetime.

He went to work right away. Abe Hackthorn was the Ghost Bear's accountant, and as luck would have it, he was Evin's as well. He had known Abe for twenty years and Abe had always been loose tongued when it came to talking about the affairs of the Ghost Bear. Abe often spoke to Evin of how foolish Gavin was not to put the wells on his land, as he had a huge fortune just waiting to be made. The big boys that ran the huge oil and gas companies had been after him for years and he always refused their offers.

Abe was loyal to Gavin and in return, Gavin paid him well for his services. But luck was now on Evin's side as Abe's loyalty for the Ghost Bear was laid to rest when they buried Gavin O'Malley. Abe was of the old school. He thought a woman should stay in the kitchen and raise kids. She didn't have any business running a ranch, even if she was Gavin O'Malley's daughter.

Evin made Abe an offer he couldn't refuse and the two men calculated a plan. They had it all worked out and things were going great. Abe had proven to be very useful in brokering the deal between Phillip Madison and himself before the wrench that was Molly came into the mix. Evin's luck turned sour when Molly filed for divorce and decided to be a damn Annie Oakley and take over the ranch.

After Molly moved back she fired Abe wherein the ranch became extremely profitable. Since she had decided not to sell, Evin had kept close contact with her soon-to-be ex-husband. Phillip had informed him that he had someone on the inside providing him with information. But unfortunately, things were not running as smoothly as he liked. The informant was growing a stronger conscience and Phillip felt he had become unreliable. Evin felt that even Phillip himself was becoming softer around the edges and was starting to have a change of heart. And as if Molly wasn't a big enough problem, Evin would also have to take care of Clayton, who had been Gavin's right arm.

Talk had it that the sly cowboy was getting pretty chummy with Miss Molly. He knew that if their relationship became stronger it would be harder to squeeze Molly out of her ownership. So Evin had to act quickly as he knew he was running out of time. The longer Molly stayed, the more settled she would become. He had to make her life on that ranch unbearable, make her feel like a failure, so he could sweep in and offer her a low ball price, take the problem off her hands and save the day. But how was he going to do that?

Evin knew that it was time to get dirty and he loved playing in the mud. He would call in a few favors to some of those men that wouldn't mind roughing up her tail feathers. He kicked back his boots and watched the sales assistants running around in the outer office like worker bees.

"You know, Molly is pretty fine looking," Evin thought to himself. "Maybe I could put a little charm on her myself. I wouldn't mind having a little taste of that fine thing. I'm sure she gets a little lonely at night and it can get pretty cold sleeping all by herself. I think I'll go pay her a visit and introduce myself this evening so I can check things out."

He stood to full attention, grabbed his cowboy hat and shouted orders to his disgruntled staff on the way out the door.

MOLLY HAD CURLED up in her chair with a good book with Sedona sprawled out upon the sheepskin rug that lay at her feet. The dog's heavy breathing was hypnotic and shadows of the fire were performing ritual dances upon the walls to the soothing sounds of larch logs cracking and popping. Days that had once been bogged down with endless boredom were now saturated with hard work, leaving her feeling tired and content at night. As she read, her eyes grew heavy, and she felt warm and secure wrapped up in the old quilt that her grandmother had made. Occasionally she would lift her head from the words that she was reading to look out at the flickering lights of the bunkhouses. Having the men out there made her feel safe and protected. Deep in her own thoughts, Sedona's harsh growl brought Molly abruptly back to reality as her loyal pet jumped up and ran to the entry, barking madly at the double doors.

"Quiet Sedona." Molly could see the faint lights of someone driving slowly up her drive. "I wonder who that could be. It's okay." She spoke softly to the gentle giant who was now looking questionably at Molly, unwilling to give up her guard post.

The outside lights lit the truck up to reveal an attractive man who was roughly around her age. He stepped out of the truck, and she opened the front door while holding onto the dog, who was not pleased with this visitor.

"Howdy ma'am, I assume that you are Molly Madison?"

"I am." She spoke in a guarded voice.

"My name is Evin Murdock."

Before Evin could even finish his sentence, Molly stopped him in his tracks. "I know who and what you are, sir. Please turn right around, get in your truck and drive back to where you came from."

"Look, there is no need to be rude." Evin spoke trying to keep his temper in check. *Who the hell does this bitch think she is?* "I just wanted to come out here and offer ..."

"I don't want to hear your offer. I'm not selling! You already know this and you coming out here and trying to present me an offer yourself will do you no good! Stop wasting your time, Mr. Murdock."

Molly was hanging tightly onto the 150-pound dog's collar, as Sedona was now curling her lips threatening and exposing her large canine teeth at the menace.

"I can't hold her back much longer, so you better get in your truck!"

Evin gave Molly a look that sent shivers down her spine. "Fine. I'll leave, but when you're ready to sell and believe me you will sell, my offer won't be as generous!" With those words he went back to his vehicle and left.

As Molly turned to go back inside, she caught a glimpse of Clayton standing in the front of his window with shotgun in hand. She closed the door behind her and this time securely locked and dead bolted the door, not feeling as safe and secure as she had just moments before.

Before Evin even got to the gate, he was already on the phone. "Hey, it's me. She's a big pain in the ass. I want you to let things cool off, wait a few weeks then start with the plan. And one more thing. The first thing I want you to do is kill her damn dog."

Chapter Twenty Three

A COUPLE OF WEEKS HAD GONE BY SINCE SLOAN HAD CONTEMPTUOUSLY attacked Phillip and his lover and he couldn't stop thinking of that humiliating day. He also regretted getting so drunk that for the life of him he could not remember much of that night, or anything about the woman who had brought him home. He strained his mind trying to remember why he had the track mark on his arm, but the large amounts of consumed whisky killed too many of his brain cells and his memory was wiped clean. Since he was unable to recall the events of that night, he decided to go back to the scene of his inebriation and ask the bartender if he knew of the woman.

"Unfortunately, honey, I really didn't pay much attention," said the bartender. "I was shamelessly flirting with one of my regulars, but I know I have never seen her before."

"Well at least give me a description of her."

"Well, pretty generic. Maybe 5-5, red hair, but it kind of looked like a wig. Other than that, nothing special. Oh, I do remember one thing. She had this kind of irritating laugh, almost like a cackle. Dude, you were pretty fucked up when she helped you out."

After listening for several minutes to the bartender ramble on, Sloan concluded that the woman would remain an unsolved mystery and he should just forget about the unfortunate event.

No matter how much he didn't want to, he was being forced to move on with his life. He needed a new job, a new man and on top of all of that, he had the flu and felt incapable of doing either, let alone leaving his bed.

After a week of progressively getting worse, Sloan knew he would have to go see a doctor. Undeniably weak, he pulled himself together and put on the rumpled clothing that were scattered on his floor.

Without much regard to his outward appearance, he drove himself to the nearest clinic. He looked bedraggled, unrecognizable and instead of his usual vanity, he could care less.

The wait seemed exceedingly long as he sat in the frigid room shivering uncontrollably, while trying his best to ignore the little boy who now stood directly in front of him staring with snot spewing like a spigot from his tiny red nose. He hadn't the energy to lash out at the receptionist who sat protectively behind her glass window, so he stayed planted in his seat silently wishing he could just pass out and finally see a doctor. After another excruciating twenty minutes, some relief was in sight, as a heavyset nurse came to his rescue. She called his name, and with a significant struggle, he lifted his aching body from his seat and sluggishly followed her.

"You look like you're really not feeling well." For as large as the woman was, she spoke in a soft sympathetic voice. "Step on the scale so we can get your weight. How long have you felt like this?"

Pondering her question, Sloan responded in a quivering voice. "It started the beginning of last week and just gradually got worse. I feel like shit. Sorry."

"Hey no problem. I've heard worse." She gave him a gentle smile and looked at his chart. "You've lost quite a bit of weight from the last time you were here."

"Really? I think it's probably been in the last couple of weeks. I've lost my appetite and what I do eat, I can't keep down."

She took Sloan by the arm, wrapped his muscle within the cuff and allowed it to constrict so as to get an accurate reading of his blood pressure. Not offering him the results, she led him down the hall and into a private exam room.

"The doctor will be right with you." She walked out of the room and closed the door behind her.

A few seconds after the nurse left, the physician walked in smiling widely. "Hi Sloan. Long time no see. What's going on with you?"

Not happy to have to repeat himself again, Sloan gave a long description to the doctor of his symptoms. "Body aches, muscle soreness, fever, chills, diarrhea, I think it's the flu, but I just can't shake it."

While Sloan was speaking, the diligent doctor began prodding upon Sloan's body. "Your glands appear swollen and you have a temp of 101. Sloan, you probably do just have the flu, but I would like to take some blood just to make sure that nothing else is going on in there." The doctor turned his back to Sloan and washed his hands thoroughly in the stainless steel sink. "I'm sending the nurse back in to take some blood. I'll be back."

No sooner did Sloan's physician leave, when the pleasantly, plump nurse, came back into the room. She pulled out her needle and began to fill the empty vials with Sloan's blood. "Why don't you lie down and relax. It will take a few minutes for the results to come back."

Sloan didn't need any coaxing. He allowed his upper body to fall backwards, allowing his head to lie upon the paper pillow barley attached to the table and instantly dozed off.

The doctor returned and gently woke him. "Sloan, are you awake?"

"Yeah. Sorry Doc. I can't keep my eyes open."

"Sloan, I don't want to scare you, but we have a serious problem." The elderly physician was no longer smiling as he had when he had first seen Sloan. Instead, he had a look of concern.

"What the hell do you mean?"

"The test came back as positive for Hep B, Hep C and HIV. I've never seen anything like this. I want to admit you to Tampa General right away and run more tests to make sure we're not getting a false reading. If the test still comes back positive, you need to be started on treatment right away."

Sloan felt his heart pounding as he panicked over the devastating news. "How could you get the results back that quickly? Doesn't this usually take weeks?"

"Not any more. We've progressed medically over the last twenty years."

"I don't understand! I haven't been with anyone but Phillip since my last test. Something must be wrong!"

"Well, let's retake the test at the hospital and hope something is wrong with my equipment. But Sloan, I want you to prepare yourself for the worst. Even though you didn't sleep with anyone else, how do you know who Phillip slept with? And don't forget Phillip's wife."

Sloan was stunned and totally speechless. He was unable to have a rational response to his doctor's statement. "Doc, could I get a ride to the hospital, I don't think I can drive myself."

As he rode to the hospital he was in disbelief as to what was happening, knowing that over the last couple of weeks his life had changed forever.

Chapter Twenty Four

Several weeks had passed and Phillip's days were once again retaining a certain normalcy. He hadn't heard from or seen Sloan since the day he ran from his home. The unwanted public attention had dissipated and he felt his moral qualities were finally becoming solid. He had nothing to hide and he felt good not having to lie or make excuses. He was who he was and he was okay with that. He immersed himself with work and had joined a gym, not just for the physical reward but also for the social aspects.

Once a week he would have dinner with his daughter and her husband and they would chat about current affairs and family topics, staying clear of any discussion about Molly. Phillip knew that his daughter found it a little odd that he never asked about the wellbeing of her mother.

What his daughter didn't know was that he had been secretly keeping tabs on Molly's actions. Although his motives had changed since he originally started the scrupulous inquiry into her life, and now with his new sense of guilt, he felt compelled to protect her. He knew that Molly was playing the lead role that her father always wanted her to play and that she had bonded with the ranch hands, especially one in particular. He also knew that she would never sell that ranch.

Phillip had received several phone calls from the uncultivated money hungry SOB Evin, who was foolishly attempting to force Molly into selling. Phillip took this man's calls and played along with his devious plan, feeling that was the only way he could help the woman he had once brazenly betrayed.

The more communication he had with Evin, the more he disliked the man. He was extremely arrogant and lacked any type of moral sense. It also angered Phillip the way this man talked down to him. But he would allow this belittling behavior in order to give the imperious man a sense of false authority just so he could obtain as much information on the man's intent.

Remaining quiet and submissive to Evin was a difficult task for Phillip. But he knew that in the end, he would redeem himself by crushing this man and his well thought out plans. Evin's biggest mistake was that he thought that he could play to Phillip's greed, and Phillip knew that this simple misjudgment of character would become the pompous developer's deserving downfall.

Phillip was well aware not to trust the man and covering his own ass was well in order. So over the course of their monthly phone conversations, Phillip recorded all communication. He also had one of the detectives, employed by his firm, run a background check on the developer. This man had so many dirty dealings and affairs that in comparison, Phillip's life looked like a Disney movie. He was well aware of Evin's dangerous abilities. And even though he knew Molly was tougher than he had ever given her credit, he wasn't sure that she could handle this by herself. He also knew that at this point in time Molly would never listen, let alone believe anything that he would tell her, and if she ever found out that he was keeping tabs on her, God help him. He had to tread lightly, and stay behind the scenes.

Phillip had been sitting at his desk thinking this matter over when the familiar voice came from the speaker on his desk. "Mr. Madison, you have a phone call. It's a Dr. Evens on the line."

Phillip picked up the receiver. "This is Phillip Madison."

"Mr. Madison, this is Dr. Evens. I'm sorry to bother you, but I need to inform you that I have a patient who had tested positive for several sexually transmitted diseases including AIDS, and he had listed you as his sexual partner. I strongly suggest that you come to Tampa General as soon as you can. You need to be tested."

"Is this a joke? Did Sloan put you up to this? Because let me tell you, this time that little son of a bitch has gone too far, and if I find …"

The man on the other line interrupted. "Let me assure you, Mr. Madison, I don't play jokes on anyone. I don't make my living as a stand-up and believe me when I tell you that I would never call you, if I didn't feel positive that there is a very strong chance that you have been infected."

Phillip still did not believe the stranger that he was talking to, figuring that Sloan was playing one of his sick little games and he wasn't about to fall for it. "Okay, I'll tell you what, why don't you give me your number at the hospital and I'll call you back. You said your name was Dr. Evens?"

"Yes, that is correct and you may call me back." Dr. Evens gave Phillip his number at the hospital.

Phillip wasted no time calling the number he had jotted down. Expecting to hear Sloan's voice, he was horrified to be greeted by a woman running the switchboard at Tampa General. He wearily asked for Dr. Evens and the woman connected him.

"This is Dr. Evens."

"Dr. Evens, this is Phillip Madison. When can I come down?"

"I will have to put my receptionist on with you. She can set the appointment and we will try to get you in as soon as possible."

"Doctor, may I ask you, where is Sloan?"

"We admitted him today. He's here at Tampa General."

What felt like another blow to his gut, Phillip made his appointment for the next day, then quickly ran into the bathroom to upchuck his lunch.

The rest of the day was a blur, and his night was a fit of sleeplessness. The room that had been shadowed with darkness was now filled with the dawn of a new day, though Phillip still faced a new nightmare. He knew that Molly's test had come back negative and he hadn't been with Sloan since she left him. He could only hope that his test would come back negative as well.

Phillip resentfully arrived for his test and held his breath as the young nurse wearing protective gloves and a mask stuck him to retrieve vials of possibly tainted blood. He was so angry with Sloan that he was surprised his blood wasn't boiling as she removed it from his forearm.

"We're all set, Mr. Madison. I'll take this right over to the lab and the doctor will come back shortly with the results." As the nurse spoke, she stepped back away from him and removed her mask.

"You know, AIDS is not airborne," Phillip snidely remarked to the young woman as she left his room.

As he sat in the stark room alone, he thought of Molly. He thought of how she must have felt when she heard the news of his own infidelities and went alone to be tested. He mentally began to prepare himself for the news that would change the course of his life. He knew that he had gambled with reckless behavior, but he never allowed himself to consider that it could lead to this. He never cared enough at the time to stop it. The voice in his head told him that he couldn't put all of the blame on Sloan. It was his actions, his body, and his responsibility to care enough about himself to be more cautious with his partners and use protection.

Time slipped away from him as he came to grips with the idea of living with the disease. He told himself that it wasn't a death sentence, as it would have been ten years back.

Phillip was giving himself a verbal pep talk when the doctor walked in. His face turned red. "Don't send me away to the funny farm, Doc. I'm just giving myself a little moral support."

"Well Phillip, I think you can put that conversation with yourself on the back burner. Your tests came back negative. You are completely clean. But I might suggest that you come back in three months just to be safe. Sometimes these things can take a little while to show up."

Phillip felt as if he had just been handed a gift from God. "Thank you, Dr. Evens, I will definitely do that."

As Phillip left the hospital, he thought about Sloan. He could picture him lying alone in a bed somewhere inside the large hospital. He felt sad for the man, but he couldn't bring himself to go see him.

Chapter Twenty Five

THE SUN SPARKLED THROUGH THE GOLDEN TAMARACKS TO DAZZLE THE eyes of the men riding their horses. They rode in single file snaking around the steep mountain as the autumn air cooled their bodies. The horses were sure footed, as they had made this trek many times, checking on the small herd of five hundred. This time Clayton rode amongst them, enjoying the time he spent with his fellow wranglers. The men needed to round up their cattle that grazed freely, fattening their engorged bellies with the thick grasses that covered the other side of the high grounds. They would gather the large beasts and their young and lead them down safely to a lower altitude to join other cattle that were already at their winter home.

All of the Black Angus that roamed upon the Ghost Bear were organic prime beef and sold for top dollar. It would take the men a full week to ride and gather up all of the cattle that summered up here. They would share stories during the days and sleep by the protection of a warm fire under the stars.

A cowboy's life for these men was the same now as it had been a century before, plus a few modern devices that made things easier, and Clayton loved every minute of it. As the men rode near where the herd would be scattered the smell of something dead drifted towards them and they could hear the cry of some of the younger calves.

"Hey Clay, do you smell that?" Tom, who was in the lead, pulled his bandana over his nose and turned in his saddle to face Clayton whose mare was close behind.

"Yeah. Something's not right! Do you hear those calves?"

Clayton's horse flew past the man at full gallop. The men kicked their fillies into gear, galloping wildly, ducking through the trees, when they came upon the large pasture and a sight that ran the men's blood cold. The decaying bodies of what was roughly one hundred head where scattered across the ground. The pungent smell of rotten meat was unbearable and flies swarmed around while the young calves cried amongst them. The rugged men were stunned and sickened.

"What the hell happened?" One of the men yelled.

Thinking quickly, Clayton yelled for the men. "Check the water and keep the rest of the herd away."

One of the hands, Buck, yelled back and confirmed Clayton's fears. "It's bad, Clayton, real bad. Someone or something poisoned the water!"

"I need you men to round up these cows and head 'em on out of here. I need six of you to stay here with me. We need to burn the dead."

Clayton took control ordering the men around like a chief detective at a crime scene. The ranch had a total of ten thousand head. They were lucky; they had five hundred that grazed up here, and he knew it could have been much worse.

The men worked together like the true grit cowboys they were. As the majority gathered up what was left of the herd the other six men began roping the dead and dragging them to a pile to be burned. Clayton emptied out his canteen and filled it with the poisonous water to take and have it tested. He knew that someone had done this and this could just be the beginning.

Concerned for Molly's wellbeing, he pulled out his cell phone and dialed the main house.

"Molly, is everything OK down there?"

"Well, as far as I know. Why?" Molly could tell by the tone of Clayton's voice that it wasn't going to be good.

"I want you to send a few men to ride out and check on the rest of the herd. Have 'em check the watering holes and the river. Someone poisoned the water up here. We lost roughly a hundred head. The men are gathering up the remaining cows and they will start heading down. I'll be a day behind. We have to take care of this mess."

"I'm on it. And Clayton?"

"Yeah?"

"Watch your back up there. They could still be around. I can replace the cattle. I can't replace you."

"Don't worry about me. You just make sure you keep those doors locked and keep your eyes and ears open."

"Hey don't worry. I have my guard dog. Sedona's here and she'll let me know if anyone is anywhere near this place."

By the time Molly hung up the receiver, her Irish temper had exploded. She had an idea who was behind this, but she also knew proving it would not be easy. She went outside and gathered up the men who were in the barn and told them what happened. She sent them out with their side arms to check the rest of the livestock.

Molly turned towards the large dog that had followed her. "Okay girl, you need to keep an eye out for anyone you don't know!"

The intimidating creature stood at attention and let out one deep bark. Molly then went back to the house to check on Rosa.

No need to scare her. I'm sure the son of a bitch who did this wouldn't dare show his face, she thought as she went through the side door and into the kitchen.

"Hi Rosa." Molly walked over to the fridge, pulled out a Coke and went over to where the woman stood near the sink busy preparing the pork loin that would eventually become their dinner.

"Hi baby girl." Rosa looked over at the young woman who was nervously staring out the window. "Okay, what's going on? I saw you run out to the barn and the boys take off on their nags." Living all the years that Rosa had on the ranch, she was use to seeing the men getting their tail feathers in an uproar. "What is it, mountain lion or griz?" Cocking her eye at Molly, she waited for a response.

Knowing she had better come clean, Molly spoke calmly. "Neither. Clayton had the men up top." She nodded her head towards one of the mountains outside the window. "They were going to bring down the five hundred head that were still up there and when they got there, they discovered that someone had poisoned the water. We lost a hundred head. I sent the boys out to check on the rest of the herds."

Rosa's anger became visible. "It's these damn old ranchers. They're not happy having to compete with a woman. After your daddy died they were like a pack of hungry hyenas, all of 'em thinking they could gobble up pieces of the Ghost Bear. Girl, if your daddy was still alive he would whip their ass!"

"Rosa!" Molly chuckled out load, as she had never heard Rosa flare her temper to the point of cursing. "Well, don't even worry about it. He's right here inside of me, and believe me, I'm about ready to do a little ass kicking myself. I have a strong suspicion who it is."

Rosa laughed at the pretty and petite girl who stood beside her talking so tough.

The phone rang, startling both women. Molly answered and as soon as she heard the voice on the other end, she wished she hadn't.

"Molly?" It was Phillip.

"What Phillip? This really isn't a good time for me right now. I've got some stuff going on over here." Molly couldn't help sounding perturbed, as his voice was the last thing she wanted to hear.

"Is there something I can do?" Phillip asked although he knew that her pride would never accept anything from him.

"I think you've done enough. I don't need or want anything that you might have to offer."

"Ouch, I could feel that blow clear across the lines! But I suppose I deserve it. Okay, just call me back when you think you can talk rationally." Phillip spoke while keeping his cool.

"Fuck you, Phillip. I am rational. I just don't want to talk to you." Molly slammed the phone down hard, stinging Phillip's ears then looked over at her old friend and smiled. "That felt good."

THE TWO MEN had, without any conscience, done the job they'd been hired to do and were now sitting in front of Evin anxiously awaiting payment. The tall blond-headed developer reached inside his desk and pulled out ten crisp one-hundred-dollar bills. He counted out five for both men and laid them down in front of them. They greedily grabbed at the cash and stuffed it into the front pocket of their western shirts. Evin then led the two men out the door of his office.

"Don't forget! Keep your big mouths shut! I don't want you two getting shit faced at the Hard Saddle and running your big mouths."

The two delinquents mumbled their agreement and left.

Chapter Twenty Six

Phillip's ear was still ringing after Molly hung up. He knew that something must have been going on. His concern for his wife deepened, so he jumped back on the phone and dialed José.

José filled Phillip in with all the details and soon Phillip had a clear picture of why Molly had been exceptionally moody. He contemplated her situation and knew that the outcome could have been a lot worse. For the time being, Phillip decided, no matter how much he wanted to, he shouldn't intervene. Molly and her men were on the right track with their suspicions and he would give her a chance to handle the problem on her own. He also concluded that he better not mention anything about Sloan. He wasn't infected, so why scare Molly or piss her off any more. Keeping quiet for now was the right thing to do, even though he didn't feel good about it.

He went to the gym. Working out cleared his mind and spirit, and he needed both. He pushed his body hard, and increasing his reps, he maintained focus until his mind was clear.

"One more!" He yelled at himself as he lay on his back, lifting the heavy weights over his head.

"Hey Phillip, is that you?"

Phillip instantly recognized the woman's voice.

Shit! He thought as he dropped the extremely heavy weights down on the bar. She was the last person he wanted to see. *God, do you enjoy torturing me?* he thought. He sat up and looked up at the chunky woman who stood in front of him.

"Oh my God, Phillip Madison it is you! I never thought I'd see you here. You're looking great; good enough to eat! Coming out of the closet really agrees with you."

Amberly spoke loud enough for the striking man who had been working on the machine next to them to quickly change his mind and move to a machine that was farther away.

"Thanks for the backward compliment. Do you think you could have said that a little louder?" Phillip stood up, taking the towel that he brought from home, and soaked up the sweat that covered his face.

Ignoring his obvious irritability, she proceeded. "So, last week I spoke with Leeza at the club, and she told me Molly moved out and headed back out to Montana to run some big ranch or something. Of course, that was just about the silliest thing I ever heard. It's too bad she moved so damn far away, but I guess I understand why, I mean with the embarrassment and all. The ladies at the club won't shut up about what happened to her. How devastating! I can't imagine being married all those years and finding out that you really didn't know your spouse at all!"

Amberly brushed a piece of her dark hair away from her face and gave Phillip a smirk.

"You know, I might take a trip out there to see some family. I'll have to look her up. It's too bad she moved so damn far away, but I guess I understand why."

Towering over the nasty woman, Phillip responded with contempt. "Well, if I was you I wouldn't bother. She never did like you or half of those bitches at that haughty club." He moved on to the next machine and wished that someone would drop a dumbbell on top of the woman's head.

"Yea, maybe you're right. I guess she wasn't one of my favorites either. Anyway, the word on the street is that your lover caught a little something. Funny how things work out." She kept her eyes fixed on Phillip's expression. She enjoyed shocking him.

"How the hell did you hear that?" He was seriously considered throwing one of the weights at her.

"Oh you know women. We have our ways. Oh wait. Maybe you don't know us very well, I mean being gay and all." And with speaking those words she let out one of her most annoying laughs.

"Okay you stupid bitch, get the fuck out of here before I get someone. I don't need your snide remarks. I'm not one of your fellow bitches from the country club!"

Content that she was able to get under his skin, she happily turned to leave. But not being able to contain herself, she got in one more dig. "Be careful Phillip. We all have a penance to pay and yours might be coming due."

That was enough. Leaving the wretched woman and his uncompleted workout, Phillip headed for the locker rooms. Provoked over the dowdy woman, he took some of his hostility out by smashing his fist into the door.

"It really isn't the locker's fault."

Phillip's heart melted as he recognized the familiar voice of his favorite Frenchman.

"Hey, what are you doing here?" Phillip gave Jack a big hug. He was extremely happy to see him.

"Oh, I've been thinking about joining, you know, checking the place out."

Phillip loved Jack's thick French accent. "Yeah, well it's a great club; lots to offer. I just joined and I'm hooked." Phillip grinned irresistibly at Jack.

"Well, I don't know about that! It looked as if you were having a problem with your locker."

Phillip smiled. "Oh that. It was nothing. So listen, if you're free tonight, what do you say we get something to eat?"

"That depends. Are we going to have any surprise guests?"

"I don't think you have anything to worry about. I was thinking maybe the Lobster Pot over on Madera Beach?"

"Okay, sure." Jack scribbled his address down on a piece of paper and handed it to Phillip, lingering his touch to his hand.

Phillip was unable to conceal his enthusiasm. "Great, I'll pick you up around seven."

As Phillip watched Jack leave, he grabbed his gym bag. *This day is beginning to look up,* he thought.

Chapter Twenty Seven

Clayton was a good two days behind the other men. As they rode back down, he was well aware that their clothes reeked of smoked beef; for a hungry bear, the potent scent would be truly enticing. Everyone knew that grizzlies in these parts were known to stalk, so the men kept constant guard. Clayton had the water sample safely tucked away in his saddlebag and planned to personally take it down and have it tested.

The men traveled quickly. Working their horses longer through the day, tiring them more than they liked, but returning home as quickly as possible had become top priority and Clayton knew that whoever was responsible for this could be ready to strike again. He had been provoked and wasn't about to pussyfoot around the matter. Someone was screwing with their livelihood; men were shot for a lot less.

As they neared the house and barn, the worn horses began to quickly trot with anticipation of stripping the heavy saddle off their backs and having a bucket of oats. Sedona barked with her oversized tail waving at the group of men in welcoming fashion.

Molly ran out to greet them. "Hey cowboy, nice to have you back."

Clayton looked worse for wear, but sturdy. "Howdy ma'am." He tipped the weather-beaten hat and dismounted his mare. His face was smudged with dirt, making his teeth appear snow white.

Not caring that he reeked or how much dust and soot covered his clothes, she wrapped her arms around his strapping body. "Boy, am I glad to see you."

Regaining her composure, to his disappointment she reluctantly released him and took the horse's reins from his grip so he could work on taking the saddle off.

She couldn't keep her eyes off his ass. "I called the sheriff and he sent someone over to write up a report. Did you get the water sample?"

"Yeah. I have it right here. Let me finish up here and wash some of this trail dust off and I'll take it down there myself."

"I don't think he's going to do much," Molly said doubtfully.

"You're probably right, but at least we're filing a report to cover our ass. In this country, we fight our own battles and believe me, there isn't a ranch owner out here that wouldn't hang or shoot the son of a bitch that killed their cattle. Sometimes you have to create justice on your own, Molly."

Molly was taken aback by Clayton's forward views. She had been the wife of an attorney who was strongly against vigilante justice and strongly believed in the court of law.

"Well before you do anything like that, don't forget I own this ranch and I'm not going to have a bunch of hot-headed cowboys stringing up the wrong person and causing me more grief. If you see anyone on this land that you don't know, you call me, and then we will handle it accordingly, by the law. I'll tell Rosie to fix you something to eat. It will be waiting for you in the house."

Molly turned, leaving the man dumbfounded with the sense of having just been scolded by their mother.

One of the men, who was near Clayton at the time, turned to him and spoke. "I miss the old man; he was one tough son of a bitch."

Clayton looked at the boys and said, "Yeah, we all do. Now finish up and feed these mares; we're burning daylight."

Clayton walked back to his bunkhouse with Sedona by his side. "Well old girl, we better not speak of the skeletons that her daddy buried in those hills."

Sedona tilted her head sideways in confirmation to Clayton's words.

After Clayton showered and ate, he jumped into his pickup truck and headed for town, the water sample tucked safely beside him. He would give the sheriff the sample and a statement and then head over to the Hard Saddle Saloon. He figured that he would have a few drinks and hang around and bullshit with some of the local cowboys.

They lived in a small town and Jack Daniels had a way of loosening lips.

Clayton knew that Molly wanted to believe in her false sense of trusting the law to handle this, but his views of handling this problem differed greatly from hers. She grew up out here and wasn't a stranger to how things worked, but moving away and living in the city disillusioned her. She believed that sticking by the book and following the law would end in justice. Out here, people believed in serving justice themselves in a swift and clean fashion. They didn't burden the sheriff with problems they could handle on their own, and in return, the sheriff appreciated the help and didn't ask questions. This was how it was done and

Molly was going to have to fully regain her roots or the men who desired to squeeze her out would feed her to the wolves.

The sheriff told Clayton that the sample should be back next week and then they would know what poison was used to contaminate the watering hole.

Clayton gave his statement to the sheriff even though both men knew that it was a waste of their time. Clayton then drove his trusty Ford to the local bar and parked it out front. The Hard Saddle Saloon was not a place for college kids to go. The men who frequented this place were whiskey drinking, tobacco spitting, bronco-riding sons of bitches who didn't give a rat's ass over proper introductions.

Clayton walked through the front doors and onto the sawdust covered wood floors. Several men were sitting at the bar on torn bar stools that had been repaired with duct tape, listening to Willie Nelson. Three pool tables sat in a row with a sign hanging on the wall that read: "Break a pool stick and it'll cost ya twenty bucks (Pay in Advance)." The sign was there so as to discourage the men from breaking them over each other's head.

Clayton sidestepped the chew spattered upon the floor and moseyed over to the bar and placed his order with his old friend. "Hey Buck, give me a Moose Drool."

Buck was the only man who could put these good old boys in their place. He was a lofty 6-5 and solid as a brick shit house. He wore a patch over his left eye; he'd lost it to some poor asshole, who had made the fatal mistake of trying to take him with a broken beer bottle. Buck broke the foolish man's neck as if it was a skinny chicken bone and then claimed it was self-defense. Case closed.

"Howdy Clay." Buck plopped the beer in front of him before he even finished asking. "Here you go."

Clayton leaned against the bar and scanned the dark room "Looks pretty tame tonight."

"Yeah, you know, same old shit. Give 'em a few hours, they're just starting," Buck spoke as he gave the men next to Clayton fresh bottles.

Clayton was smart enough to tread lightly and not ask questions too quickly. He had all night. He drummed up conversation with several of the men he knew and before he realized it, three hours had passed.

Things were picking up just as Buck predicted; voices and music were louder. Clayton began asking around to see if anyone had heard about the ranch's troubles. A couple of the guys who worked over at one of the neighboring ranches had said that they didn't know anything about it, but that there had been a lot of grumbling over Gavin's daughter running things.

"They're all scared she'll do something stupid like go against the grain and undersell her beef. You know those old ranchers stick together." The young cowboy slammed back another shot of whiskey. "Shit, it could have been anyone."

Clayton leaned back in his chair and shot one back. "Yeah, well you can also tell those old fuckers that I'm still there and they don't have anything to worry about. She's the seed of Gavin O'Malley."

An old dowdy woman sitting quietly in the corner was consuming her usual large amounts of poison as she overheard the men's rough talk.

"She's not the only seed of his. I knew Gavin O'Malley real well. You could say I knew every inch of him."

The men looked over at the wrinkled old hag slurring at them.

"Ma'am, I think anyone who ever lived here knew Gavin," Clayton spoke respectfully.

"Well!" (Hiccup) "Not like I knew him. And let me tell you something else. His little girl isn't the only one he had!" (Hiccup). The old woman then stood up with bottle in hand and yelled for everyone to hear. "That's right. Do you all hear that? I might as well spill the beans. After all he's six feet under and what do I care! I know secrets ... more than any of you here! I was real important and that's why he did what he did! Fuck you all!"

For the first time in the history of the Hard Saddle Saloon you could hear a pin drop. Every man in the place stared at the woman as she stumbled out the door while still ranting.

Clayton didn't know what to think; this wasn't the information he was looking for.

"Okay, she's gone. Show over. Get back to your drinking!" Buck yelled at the men and that was all the encouragement they needed. The music began to play and their voices were once again booming.

Clayton excused himself from the table of cowboys and rushed out the door. Putting the original inquiries on the back burner, he stood outside the seedy bar and searched for the strange old woman who had just caused a commotion then scurried out. But to his disappointment, she was nowhere to be found, so he decided to call it a night.

As he drove home the drunken words of the old lady repeated in his head like a broken record. "She's not the only seed of Gavin O'Malley. I know secrets ... lots of secrets."

Clayton spoke aloud to himself, as he drove down the deserted road, "Jesus, what the hell did she mean by that? What kind of mess did Gavin get himself into? Does Molly have a sister or brother that she doesn't know about? And worst of all, if she does, that means that they could show themselves and try to make a claim against the Ghost Bear!"

Chapter Twenty Eight

THE NEXT WEEK WHEN AMBERLY RAN INTO LEEZA AT THE COUNTRY CLUB, she gave her the play by play of her run in with Phillip. As soon as Leeza left the club she quickly had Molly on the other end of her cell phone, spilling all the juicy details.

"Chalk one up for the girls!" Leeza joyfully laughed at the thought of Phillip's embarrassment, as she finished recanting the whole story that was earlier told to her.

Molly listened to Leeza's detailed recital and couldn't help the smile that swept over her face. She felt a little guilty for not calling Leeza more often and keeping up with their daily talks.

"I wish I could have been a fly on the wall and seen his face," said Molly. "Hey Leeza, listen, I really appreciate you calling, and I'm sorry that I haven't called you. I've been so damn busy and a lot has been going on out here. I really miss you. Why don't you fly out and spend a couple of weeks? It would be great to have an old friend around and I can fill you in on what's been going on, and who knows, maybe you could help."

"You don't need to ask me twice! I'd love to, Molly, but let's get something straight right now. I don't clean horse stalls or have anything to do with cleaning up any type of shit. That includes horse shit, cow shit, or those cowboys' bull shit!"

Molly laughed until tears drizzled from the corner of her eyes. "Okay, I promise no shit. I can't wait to see you. Call me back with the dates. I have to run to town and take care of some business."

Leeza hung up with her friend. She was almost home. She was excited about visiting Molly and began planning her trip as she sat in her car waiting patiently for the light to change. But soon she had the sensation that someone was staring at her. She turned to look at the car next to her and there sitting in the passenger side was Sloan. Grateful the light changed as quickly as it did, she pushed her foot to the pedal and accelerated away.

Sloan had asked his friend to pick him up from the hospital and take him to the comfort of his own condo. He sat in the passenger side, looking and feeling a little better than he had on the first day that he'd been admitted. His doctor had started him right away on a large number of medications and told him that he would probably have to stay on them the rest of his life. He was still trying to adjust to the idea, and the affects of having so many pills in his system was making him feel a little loopy.

Sloan thanked his friend for driving and went inside his abandoned home. He opened the door, turned on the lights and looked around.

"Just the way I left it." He was disappointed that there was not a surprise arrangement of extravagant flowers waiting for him and a card with Phillip's name on it. He threw the large bag of pills on the kitchen table and slumped down in a chair.

"I know that the bastard was contacted by my doctor. You would think that he would at least come to see me in my room and apologize for giving me a death sentence!" He was once again complaining to himself and to the four walls that surrounded him.

As he had lay in the hospital bed over the past week with nothing to do, he kept going over and over how, when and where he could have contracted the diseases. When he had first met Phillip, they had both been tested and both were given a clean bill of health. Sloan knew that he had never been with anyone else, so Phillip had to have contracted it. Now Sloan had to figure out who gave it to Phillip. But when had Phillip had time to be with anyone else? Both he and Molly kept pretty good tabs on him.

"I guess it only takes one time," he thought. "I wonder if he was fucking around with that Frenchman when he was still with me? I should cut his balls off! What if the doc was right? What if Molly was screwing around behind Phillip's back? Phillip would never expect his perfect wife being a little whore and sleeping around on him! Great, she's probably laughing at herself right now! She figures she really stuck it to both of us! That sneaky, little bitch!"

Not wanting to concede to the idea that Phillip would ever cheat on him with another man, it was much easier to believe that Molly's infidelities were the cause. He had worked himself into mental derangement by giving in to his illogical thoughts of Molly purposely contracting the AIDS virus to pass it on to Phillip knowing that he would give it to Sloan.

Sloan's hair was as wild as his eyes as he spoke loudly and irrationally. "That damn bitch has been a pain in the ass ever since I hooked up with Phillip. She just couldn't let us be happy. She's such a selfish slut. Does she really think that I'm going to let her get away scot-free? That bitch is going to pay!"

He picked up the phone and dialed. "Reservations please. I would like a flight from Tampa, Florida to Bozeman, Montana."

Sloan knew what he must do, but first he had to get there.

Chapter Twenty Nine

She slowed things down after her last heroic act of injecting Sloan with the deadly mixture. She had somehow lost some of her passion and honestly felt like she needed to take a break from all of her good deeds. It was an endless battle. There were so many perverts out there. And when she heard or read a newspaper article, or news story of the abduction or molestation of another child, she felt overwhelmed and she couldn't kill them fast enough.

She had just gotten home and poured herself a glass of wine, sat down and put her feet up. She was ready for a well-deserved vacation, a self-reward for all of her hard work. She told herself that she was entitled to a little time off and when she returned she would feel rejuvenated and ready to get back to business. She closed her eyes and let her head fall upon the back of the chair. Her hum drum husband was gone for the week. She was used to being alone and actually enjoyed the time to herself.

The house was quiet and she was just about ready to fall asleep when a startling ring from the phone snapped her out of it. "Shit!" She jumped up, failed to look at the caller ID and answered.

Expecting the raspy old tone of her husband, she was disappointed when she heard the crackling voice of her drunken mother. "Hey, did you send my money?"

"Hello mother. Wouldn't it be nice if for just once you called me and asked how I was before asking me if I sent your check?"

"Okay, but why should I bother? I know you're doing a lot better than me!"

"Yes, I sent you the money just like I do every month." She rolled her eyes and plopped back down in the chair.

"You sent cash, right?"

"Mom, why do you ask me this every month when you know that I always send you cash? I honestly don't even know why I give you anything when you just blow it on booze. You're killing yourself."

"Now sweetie, we both know why you send me the money. It's because you feel guilty that you killed your daddy and left me to fend for myself. Besides, what do you care how much I pickle my liver? If I kick the bucket then you don't have to send me anything!"

She could picture the old woman, bottle in hand, sitting in her filthy house. No matter how much she hated her mother, she did feel responsible for her.

"First of all, he wasn't my daddy and we both know that! Second, don't assume that just because the son of a bitch raped me all those years that I did anything of the sort. I told you, if you want to keep getting your money, keep your mouth shut! You know I don't want my husband to know anything about those days!"

"Okay, okay. No need to get your panties in a knot. I've kept my mouth shut all these years about your real daddy, and baby I think I've really done you an injustice."

As she listened to the wickedly sweet tone of her mother's voice, she knew that the old woman was up to no good. "Really Mom, now why would you think that?" She asked, playing along.

"Well, I want to make it up to you, so I've been thinking that we should be honest about everything. I think we should hire ourselves one of those high-powered attorneys and make a claim against your daddy's will and that ranch. Do you have any idea how much that land is worth?"

"Mom, listen to me and I'm real serious about this. You are not going to do anything!"

"What the hell are you talking about? I'm your mother. You don't tell me what I'm going to do. I'm the one who had to put up with that son of a bitch running out on us, leaving me to raise you on my own! Do you know how hard it was?"

Her mother's words began to get under her skin. "I know. I was there. Do you remember where you were? Drunk off your ass, passed out while your poor choice of a husband was coming into my bed at night. You weren't any type of a mother. You and I both know that you tricked my father into sleeping with you, just so you could get pregnant and have a free ride. He paid you damn good. You were supposed to take care of me, but instead you used the money for your booze and drugs, and dressed me in rags and let me fend for myself."

Wounded by her daughter's words, the dilapidated woman began to sniffle. "I don't understand you. You should step up and claim a piece of what is rightfully yours. Then we can be happy and maybe you would come out here and see me. I haven't seen you since you ran away. I'm tired of living like this!"

"Oh Mother please, cry me a river! I'm not falling for that. But fine. I was planning to get away for a few days. I'll fly out and I'll come over and see you and then we can talk about this when I'm there. But in the meantime, I don't want you to say a word to anyone about anything, got it?"

The deceptive old lady crossed her fingers as she lied to her daughter. "Got it."

The dark haired woman hung up knowing that her mother would have a hard time keeping her mouth shut if she figured she could get something for nothing. She would have to work fast and that meant getting out there as soon as possible. She knew what she must do.

She picked up the receiver and dialed. "Reservations, please. I need a roundtrip leaving Tampa, Florida, to Bozeman, Montana."

Chapter Thirty

Phillip's navigation system led him to Jack's modest but lovely bungalow style home. He drove up the brick paved driveway and was pleased to see Jack waiting anxiously on his front porch. Jack jumped into Phillip's car and the two men put the top down and took off for dinner. It was a perfect fall evening; the temperature was 69 degrees with low humidity.

They arrived at the beach just in time to see the sun take its final bow and dive below the Gulf waters. Unable to contain themselves, the two men clapped their hands in full recognition of nature's spectacular ceremony, and then walked barefoot in the sand, carrying their shoes to the well-loved restaurant renowned for its succulent South African lobster tails. They ate by candlelight and toasted their newfound friendship.

"So Phillip, tell me, did you ever sign the papers and send them to Molly?" Jack dabbed at the butter that drizzled from the corner of his mouth with the linen napkin.

Molly was not the subject of conversation that Phillip wanted to have with Jack, but he replied politely. "Well honestly, I haven't really given it much thought. They're still in my desk." Phillip took a sip of his champagne and hoped that Jack would let the topic drop.

"Phillip, do you think that's fair to Molly?"

"Well, probably not, but I don't really see the rush. I'll sign them when I'm ready."

"When do you think you'll be ready?"

"I don't know when I'll be emotionally ready to let her go. We were married a long time and it's still hard to believe that she won't ever be a part of my life."

"Look Phillip, just because you sign those papers and you're legally divorced, doesn't mean she can't be a part of your life. It just allows both of you the freedom to find the right person to complete you."

"I know that." Feeling ashamed of his selfish behavior, he leaned across the table, peered into Jack's eyes and whispered, "Maybe after tonight I'll have found the reason to sign those papers."

Jack blushed, reached across the table and lightly placed his fingertips on Phillip's hand and spoke in his rich French accent. "Then I would be very happy for you, and we'll need another bottle of bubbly to celebrate." The waiter filled the men's glasses with the decadent liquid and Jack raised his glass to Phillip. "If there's delight in love, 'tis when I see that heart which others bleed for, bleed for me."

"Jack, that was beautiful. I have never heard anyone quote William Congreve. I'll toast to that!"

The clinking of the crystal glasses commemorated the love the two men were beginning to share.

They ate slowly, wanting to appreciate every bite and each other's company, and although they were both full, neither could resist the cherries jubilee and cappuccino. They lingered as long as they could, feeling secure and protected while sitting together in the shadows. Finally, they received the cue from the exhausted-looking waiter that they must leave.

They strolled together and took off their shoes to let their feet sink into the cool sand. The moon was high and hung perfectly in the night sky, illuminating the vast open waters. Waves splashed onto the seashore, spraying mist upon them as they walked hand and hand. The night air began to chill and they both decided they should head back. Within a short time Phillip was once again pulling into Jack's driveway.

"Phillip I really had a great time, and I just want to say thanks once more." Jack reached across the car and placed his hands on Phillip's face and his lips to Phillip's. They kissed tenderly.

"Maybe you should invite me in and thank me some more?" Phillip pulled himself away staring into Jack's large brown eyes.

"Well, I was thinking about that, Phillip. I really like you and I know you feel the same, but I think we should take our time with the intimacy. We already rushed into that and look what happened," Jack chuckled. "I want us to really get to know each other, take our time, fall in love and then make love, not fuck. Are you okay with that?"

"Of course I am. When I'm with you, I'm really happy and I feel complete, whole. I have nothing to hide. I know I shouldn't say it but I really could see me with you for the rest of my life. I hope that doesn't sound too strange. I know we really haven't known each other very long and I don't want to scare you off."

"Look, obviously I don't scare off easily. I have lost my heart to you." Jack pulled himself away from Phillip's car, waved and blew him one last goodnight kiss.

Phillip drove away with a mixture of strong feelings swarming inside for Jack. Once he was home, he took a shower and crawled into bed.

He looked over at the empty spot where Molly had once slept, picked up the phone and dialed. "Hello reservations. I need a flight from Tampa, Florida, to Bozeman, Montana. You do? Great, I need two seats." He then picked up the phone and called Jack. "Hello?" He could picture the cute Frenchman looking snuggly in his bed. "Jack, it's me Phillip. I was thinking about what you said earlier this evening, you know about the divorce papers. I'm ready to sign, but I need you to do one thing for me."

"Sure Phillip, name it. I would be happy to help you."

"Well, I made two reservations, one for you and me. You see, I want you to go with me. I want you to meet Molly. In my past, I hid so much. In my future I don't want to hide anything, especially you." There was silence on the other line and Phillip held his breath.

"Are you sure you know what you're doing?" Jack replied. "She might be really upset."

"I'm sure."

"Well okay, then I'll go with you."

Phillip went to sleep that night feeling happy and hopeful. He dreamt of living in Jack's little bungalow filled with happiness and love.

Chapter Thirty One

THE GIANT BERNESE MOUNTAIN DOG PERSISTENTLY PESTERED MOLLY TO go out, and no sooner had she opened the door than the massive dog flew out with tremendous speed, almost plowing her over. Sedona's black coat made her disappear into the night, but Molly could hear her threatening growl and then the deep bellow of what she believed was a man's voice. Sedona definitely had a hold of someone and by the sounds of it she wasn't letting go.

Molly grabbed her father's bullwhip. Although she hadn't applied her skill in years, she didn't think twice as she grabbed the weapon and flew out after her pet. She was running towards the commotion when she suddenly heard a loud shot echo in her ears. She could hear her beloved four-legged friend yelp as she witnessed the shadow of a tall man standing over her dog. Once again, the unknown assailant took aim. Without thinking, Molly cracked her whip and knocked the gun from the man's hand. He screamed in pain while recoiling his bloody fingers back to his chest. She didn't hesitate and pulled the whip back to spring it upon him once more, this time stinging him hard across his face. As the man fell to the ground Molly was ready to strike again. Letting her anger take control of her actions, she gave the man a whipping that he would never forget.

Clayton had heard Sedona and knew from her barking that she had a hold of something. He threw on his boots and was running to the door when he heard the loud gunshot and then the dog's whimpers. He ran to the commotion to find Molly whipping a man to death as he lay at her feet in excruciating pain. She was out of control. With each strike, she yelled at the man calling him various names.

Clayton grabbed her arm just as she was ready to strike yet another blow and pulled the bullwhip from her hands. "Molly, that's enough! You're going to kill him!"

She let Clayton take control of the whip and she ran over to where the man had dropped his gun and picked it up, aiming it at his head. "I should shoot you in the head, you lousy son of a bitch!"

The man, who was now lying on the ground in torn clothes, was crying like a little boy and begging for his life.

Clayton walked cautiously over to Molly and gently took the gun from her hands.

"Molly, give me the gun. It's okay. I have him. Let me handle it. You need to look after Sedona."

She came to her senses and ran over to her whimpering dog. She could see her black fur was matted and blood was flowing somewhere from her hindquarters. Molly took off the denim shirt she was wearing and applied pressure to her beloved dog's open wound. Several of the men, who had gathered to witness their boss deliver the beating to the intruder, gently picked the heavy dog up and carried her inside the main house. She would let Clayton worry about the man on the ground as she attended to Sedona.

She could see the shirt that she had covered Sedona in was now soaked in blood. "Someone call the vet and get him out here!" Molly was panic stricken at the thought of losing her companion.

One of her workers, Joe Pony, came into the room carrying a bowl full of a grayish-green substance. He asked everyone to give him some room and he knelt down by the dog. He inspected the wound and began cleaning it with the warm water and towels that Rosa had brought from the kitchen. The dark haired man began lightly chanting, soothing the gentle creature with his ceremonial songs.

"What the hell is he doing?" Molly asked one of the elderly workers who stood beside her.

"Joe is a Blackfoot. I've seen him do some incredible things. If he can't heal her then she can't be saved."

Molly and the men watched in silence as the Indian burned sage and began applying a mud-like substance over the dog's wound. He then applied fresh bandages and said a final prayer. As if Sedona knew he was finished with her she gently raised her head and gave her healer a lick.

Joe stood up, turned around and smiled at the group that had been watching him "She's a lucky dog. The bullet went clean through and I don't see any broken bones."

"Oh, thank God!" Molly bent down and kissed the dog, who was looking at her with her big brown eyes.

"If you don't mind ma'am, I would like to stay with her tonight to make sure she's going to be alright. She needs fluids."

"Oh absolutely, Joe. I can't thank you enough. I'll have Rosa prepare the room downstairs for you. Boys, make up a dog bed for Sedona and move her in there."

The men went to work. Molly then decided she had better check on Clayton and her unwanted visitor.

Clayton and a couple of the bigger men had the intruder gagged and tied up in one of the barn's feed rooms.

"We better talk about what the hell we are going to do with him," Clayton spoke with concern as Molly walked in.

She walked over to the man and looked him over. "Was he one of the men that killed my cattle?"

"Yep, he was one of them; there were two. That's all I could get out of him."

"Who do they work for?" She spoke to Clayton but kept staring at the man who had a blue bandana shoved in his mouth.

"He won't say."

Molly could see that she had given the man quite a beating. "Let him go."

"What?"

"Clayton, you heard me, let him go." Molly grabbed the man's face in her hand and made him stare directly in her eyes. "Listen to me, you bootlicker, go back and tell whoever sent you out here that you're through! If I catch anyone on my land I'll kill 'em!"

The weakened stranger stumbled out into the darkness.

Clayton looked at Molly in admiration. "Bootlicker? Jesus, Molly I think you're becoming more like your dad everyday!"

Chapter Thirty Two

Clayton was unable to get the old lady from the Hard Saddle out of his mind. It didn't matter if he lay quietly in his bed or was working the ranch; her drunken words kept nagging his brain. If what the old lady had said was true it could change a lot of people's lives, and he was sure it wouldn't be for the better. He needed to get inside the main house and have time to search. If there was anything at all to Gavin's secret, he hoped like hell that he could uncover it.

Several days had gone by since the unfortunate set of events with the intruder shooting Sedona had played out.

Molly thought that it would be a good idea to drive to town and do some shopping, eat at the local diner and attend church services. She was determined to let the group of men behind the recent incident know that she was a permanent fixture in the community and that no one could push her out. She informed Clayton that she would be gone for most of the day then drove away with determination written all over her face.

Clayton waited long enough for the dust of Molly's truck to clear and for her to be well on her way; the last thing he wanted was for her to forget something and have to come back to the house and find him rummaging through the office. She would surely ask questions and he didn't want to be stuck in a position to have to answer.

He quietly snuck into the house, looked around, and not seeing anyone, headed straight for his destination. He carefully opened the large wooden doors as if he was opening an ancient tomb.

To his surprise, the room that had once been dark and scented with cigars was now alive with a steady stream of sunshine bursting through the large glass windows. The intoxicating scent of Molly's perfume filled the air. He regained his focus and put his attention to the matter at hand. He started looking through the old ledger books, filled with Gavin's handwriting, that were now stacked neatly upon the library shelves. He wasn't sure what to look for so he began flipping through the leather-bound ledgers, searching for anything that might look peculiar. Page after page he kept an observant eye for some amount of money that was unaccountable for, or perhaps a letter, a picture or even a name he didn't recognize. He hoped that there would be nothing to find, but as he diligently searched every book and read every letter, the old woman's words echoed in his head.

The hours slipped by, and after finding nothing out of the ordinary, he was ready to give up. He plopped himself down upon the worn leather couch staring at the large desk that was across the room. His eyes admired the intricate design that had been expertly hand carved into the wood. The old man had exquisite taste. He stood up and walked over to it and ran the palm of his hand along the edge. The wood desk felt cool and smooth. He rolled the high back chair away, once again standing back and looking at it.

Suddenly it hit him; he wouldn't have noticed if he hadn't been looking closely. A carved scroll protruded and Clayton took his now-shaking hand and touched it lightly. A hidden drawer sprang open and he peered down, knowing its contents could be his worst nightmare. He reached down and pulled out the book hidden inside and pushed the drawer tightly shut, hiding it once more. He then tucked the book safely under his shirt and proceeded to leave the room that had once hid Gavin's secrets.

Clayton examined the long hallway. Rosa must have been occupying herself in another part of the house and quickly departed to the main entry hall and out the front doors. With no time to waste, he briskly walked to the small house where he resided. Once inside the privacy of his own home, he secured the dead bolt on the door and pulled the book out from under his shirt.

Clayton spoke to the man who no longer existed as he opened the book. "God damn it Gavin, what the hell did you do?"

The pages revealed the results of Gavin's transgressions, and by the numbers scrawled in his own handwriting, it looked like the man had paid generously. As Clayton studied the ledger he could see that Gavin had been dishing out huge amounts of cash for years, with the last amount dated the day before he left for Florida. All the amounts were payable to one woman and it didn't take a genius to figure out that the old woman from the bar was the one that Gavin had paid to keep quiet.

He leafed through the book once more, when suddenly a small picture of a little girl fell out and floated to his feet. He bent over and picked up the picture. The child was small, maybe three or four, with golden brown hair matted with tangles, her dark eyes pleading behind a dirty little face. She wore what looked more like a rag than a dress and her little feet were bare. Clayton stared at the pathetic creature, knowing she was of Gavin's blood. He just couldn't understand how the man he admired, so well respected by many, could hide his own flesh and blood. How could he have let his child live like this? Any money he had given was not used to benefit this little girl, but only to keep the woman's mouth shut.

Clayton had to sit down as reality came crashing down around him. Nothing could fully rectify Gavin's mistake. Clayton knew that he had to learn more.

"What could have happened to this child?" Clayton spoke to himself, letting his thoughts fall from his tongue to clear his mind to freely think of a solution.

"My God," Clayton thought to himself, "by the looks of this picture, this child would be in her forties by now. I wonder if she is even alive. I'm sure that Gavin would probably keep up paying this woman's blackmail demands even if the child had died; he couldn't risk losing his beloved Addie or Molly. His affair had to be kept quiet. If this child is a woman now, why hasn't she come forward? Was she ever told who her father was?"

Clayton tossed around every scenario he could think of in his head. He had to find out more. For Molly's sake and the sake of the ranch he needed to find out what the hell happened.

He returned the small tattered picture back to its original resting place and with one last glance, he shut the pages over the child's sad cherub face. He thought of Gavin, a father figure, the man he had admired so much and who had once taken him under his wing. He was angry that Gavin would leave them with this problem, but he also felt sympathy for the old man. He knew Gavin well enough that he was far from being an insensitive monster, but he also knew that Gavin was smart enough not to let his emotions rule him. There was no way while the old man was alive that this kind of news would get out and jeopardize his family or ranch, and Clayton knew that as long as he was still alive and kicking he would have done whatever he had to do to make sure Gavin's secret would stay hidden.

Clayton hid the book in a safe place. He would find the old lady; he needed more information to know how to proceed with this problem and he had to make sure that Molly never got wind of any of it.

Then suddenly it dawned on him that he had to get to the old woman before she approached Molly. He could picture the old woman in one of her drunken fits ranting at Molly about her father and revealing that he had another child out of wedlock. Clayton would have to act quickly before the careless woman would follow through with more demands. People who have nothing to lose could be dangerous.

Chapter Thirty Three

ONCE AGAIN, PHILLIP PHONED MOLLY. HE WANTED TO GIVE HER FAIR warning that he was flying out and would bring the divorce papers with him.

He chose his words carefully. If she still felt animosity towards him, she did not show it in her tone. After all the years that they had been together, Phillip knew her better than anyone. He could hear how tired she was. Their conversation was honest and calm, and they both knew that it had been a long time since they had been up front with one another.

"Phillip, are you still seeing Sloan?" She was glad that Phillip could not see her face as she winced just speaking the weasel's name.

"No, Molly that was over a long time ago. I'll always regret ever being with him, but I did want to let you know I met someone I really care about and I would like you to meet him and get your opinion." Phillip had hoped that Molly was ready for such a big step.

"Really? Sure. I mean, I'm not going to lie to you; it's still a little hard for me to grasp the idea that my husband had turned out to be gay, but knowing you and your family I know that you tried your best to be the person we wanted you to be. I want you to be happy, Phillip. I just wish that I didn't find out the way I did and that you would have told me years ago when I was much younger." Molly was gentle in her tone. She knew that Phillip really did feel sorry for everything and she didn't want him to become defensive.

"I know, Molly. I'm sorry. I need you to be a part of my life. Your friendship is important and I really want to be there for you and Savanna." Phillip's words were heartfelt.

"Okay, I'll tell you what, let's both try to move forward and build on this. What's this guy's name and how did you meet him?"

It seemed surreal that Phillip was even having this conversation with Molly, but he wanted to be as honest as possible. "I met him at Starbucks. And don't laugh, but he's French and his name is Jack."

"Do you like him?"

"Molly, he is really a great guy; he's intelligent, sweet, caring, and funny."

"He sounds great. Why do all the good ones have to be gay?" Molly laughed.

Phillip burst out laughing at his soon-to-be ex-wife. It felt good having her back in his life, and this time their relationship would be better than it had been.

"Okay Phillip, bring him along with you; the two of you can stay in one of the guest houses. That is, if you want to."

"Are you sure you are okay with that Molly? I mean, it's one thing to hear and know that I'm gay but when you see me with someone else, well ... I guess what I'm trying to ask is, can you handle it?"

"Phillip I'm not going to lie. It will be a little weird, but if we both want to move on yet still be a part of each other's lives I need to accept you for who you are. It's going to be okay."

"Okay, then I'll tell Jack to saddle up. We will be out next week."

The following week, Phillip was sitting next to Jack as the captain's voice boomed over the intercom. "Attendants prepare for landing."

Phillip had previously taken this flight with Molly in drudgery, but this time he was electrified with excitement. He was starting a new life. He had nothing to hide traveling with Jack and being with Jack made him happy.

They followed the line through the door of the plane, into the tiny terminal and headed down to the baggage claim when Phillip spotted Molly. He had wondered if she would send someone or if she would come to pick them up. He walked over to her, picked her up in his arms and gave her a hug. He was finally able to comprehend what he felt for her. She was a safe familiar friend and companion. Any straight man would have taken one look at her or smelled the sweet aroma of her scent and feel sexually charged. But Phillip didn't feel that at all.

He put Molly down and turned to his lover. "Jack, this is Molly." Phillip smiled at Molly while still holding her hand in both of his.

She pulled herself from Phillip and reached for Jack. "Jack, it's very nice to meet you. I'm very happy that you were able to make it." Molly looked straight into the Frenchman's eyes and could see they were filled with kindness and compassion, something that she had never seen in Sloan's.

Jack smiled and kissed the top of Molly's hand. "Madam, the pleasure is all mine. You are very gracious for inviting me to come along." He knew instantly that he would like her.

The three of them chatted as if they had all been old friends, while they waited for the conveyer belt to move and present the passengers with their luggage, then quickly gathered their belongings and left the airport.

As Molly drove them back to the ranch, they had no idea that a fourth acquaintance had been on that same flight. He did not fly first class as he once had. He had been slouched in the back stuck between a woman with her snotty-nosed brat, and a man so fat that he should have purchased two seats.

Sloan had not known that Phillip and his replacement were enjoying plenty of legroom in first class, feasting on filet mignon and drinking a bottle of wine, while he had to share his seat with the fat bastard who was spilling over into it. When the stewardess came around, he had to struggle just to reach into his pants pocket and retrieve five dollars to pay for the ludicrous offering the airlines called a snack box. His dinner consisted of stale crackers, string cheese that tasted like dirty feet, and M&M's all thrown back with a Coke.

The two men left the plane first. Sloan sat in the back and was last to get off. When he walked around the corner, to his surprise he spotted Phillip, Jack and Molly standing and babbling on like a bunch of sorority girls. It was more than he could handle and he just couldn't believe his eyes. Here Phillip was with his wife and the guy he was sleeping with, and she was talking to them like they were her best girl friends. He then watched the threesome leave the building together.

"Is there no fuckin' justice?" Sloan yelled, startling the few tired passengers that were getting their bags.

"Is there a problem sir?"

Sloan turned around to see a pleasantly plump, grey haired security guard.

"You're damn straight there's a problem, but I'll take care of it! Now get the fuck out of my face and lose some weight!"

Sloan turned on a dime and left the stunned guard and the small airport behind.

Chapter Thirty Four

SHE WAS ON THE LAST FLIGHT OF THE DAY. AFTER HER ARRIVAL SHE LOOKED forward to a nice dinner and hot bath. Her room was lavishly furnished and spacious. She didn't bother to unpack her suitcases, as she knew that she would only be there for one night. She drew a hot tub, threw in some shower gel to make her own bubbles and while soaking her tired body, toyed with the idea of going out somewhere to have a stiff drink and dinner.

"A nice stiff drink does sound yummy." She spoke to no one but herself and blew the self-created bubbles from the palm of her hand. She closed her eyes, allowing herself to revel in the moment; but that damn persistent little snit of her alter ego kept nagging her, and her tranquil state was short lived.

"Jesus, nag, nag, nag. That's all you do!" She spoke to her own reflection, only what she saw was not the grown woman who sat surrounded in a tub full of bubbles but a little girl of eight, with matted hair and a dirty face.

"I do all the work and you just whine and bitch all the time!" She was now yelling at the little girl, though her voice wasn't her own, but her mother's. "I would think that you would give a little bit of appreciation for everything that I have done for you! Is that too much to ask for?"

The women's reflection put her head down and she spoke timidly with the voice of a scared little girl. "I'm sssssoory," she stuttered.

"I just think that you should have a plan for tomorrow," she spoke in her mother's stern voice. "You know how she makes you feel when you see her in person. You can't think straight, you need a plan."

The grown woman's body began quivering as she spoke in the childish tone. "I know, I'm sorry. I'll take care of her. I will work on a plan. Don't worry, everything will be fine. Don't I always take care of everything?"

The woman smiled chillingly at her reflection and this time the reflection of the small child raised her head and smiled back. "Yes, you have always taken good care of me."

Now satisfied, the reflection was once again that of her mature body. She drained the water, dried off, draped herself in the lush chenille robe that was a gift from her husband and ordered room service.

"Well I guess tonight I'll have it mini-bar style. I had better keep a low profile. I'd hate to run into someone from the past." She opened the fridge, pulled out two small bottles of Absolute and cracked open the tops. "Straight up please." She poured the bottle down the back of her throat. "Thank you. I think I'll have another." Again, without hesitation, she gulped down the smooth alcohol. She always became more creative after she had a couple of drinks in her.

Maybe it was something in her genes, she thought to herself as she lay on her bed while flipping thru the menu. Choosing pasta and salad, she called in her order.

She pondered over the woman who brought her into the world. "Decisions, decisions, life is full of them. Now mother, what am I going to do with you? "You really weren't a very good mother, now were you? But, then again I did okay for myself, didn't I?"

She was in a definite quandary. Her mother had backed her into a corner.

She walked to the window and noticed the snow falling. It had come early. She loved the snow but hated the cold. Icicles had formed from the roof into gigantic proportions, and hung down like deadly daggers, ready to break and impale themselves upon some poor unsuspecting victim who might happen to be walking under them.

"Nature can be so deadly." Her problem was solved.

Later that night she cuddled into the big down comforter and slept soundly without even one dream. At daybreak, she showered, gathered her belongings and headed down to the front desk to check out.

"Checking out so early?" The young man smiled as he printed out her receipt. "I hope you had a pleasant stay."

"Yes, thank you. Your property is lovely." She spoke in a thick southern accent. "Oh just one thing. I would get rid of those icicles hanging from your roof. You would hate to kill one of your guests." She headed out the door to her rental car, ready to pay her mother a long-awaited visit.

The drive was roughly an hour, and even though she hadn't seen her old house in years, she knew the way with her eyes closed. Each mile marker was a reminder of her revolting up-bringing. Memories of the abuse she had to live with for so many years made her inner child start to whimper.

"Stop it! You're not a child anymore," she spoke sternly to herself. "You are in control and she's just an old drunk trying to get what she can."

Just like Popeye eating his spinach, listening to her own words gave her the power and strength she needed.

She turned onto the dirt road that led to the secluded drive. Everything was overgrown and the path leading to the old farmhouse was barely drivable as it had snowed all night. Tree limbs reached out and scratched the surface of the rental car like nails on a chalkboard. She crept along until the path had widened, exposing the dilapidated dump where she had been raised. The paint had faded leaving the wooden exterior exposed to the elements. The front porch was falling in and her mother had taken cardboard to cover the hole in the broken side window.

"All that money that she got and look at this dump!" It disgusted her as she pulled the car around the back of the house to see her mother's personal dumping grounds. Trash was everywhere; even the snow on the ground didn't cover it up. She parked her car far removed from the front drive and hid it behind the house, then trudged through the snow. She knew the back door would be open; her mother never worried about locking the doors. As she walked up the cement blocks that were used as stairs, she looked up to see perilous icicles clinging to the roof. She remembered as a child that sometimes they would get so big that they would almost reach the ground.

She opened the door, announced her presence and walked into the filthy kitchen. The house was dimly lit as the sunshine diffused the dirt that blanketed the windows. Empty bottles of cheap wine were tossed about like bowling pins. There sitting at the table was her mother, nursing her daily hangover.

"Well would you look at what the cat dragged in. If it isn't my fancy-pantsy, long lost little girl."

"Don't you mean your meal ticket?" She walked over to her mother and kissed her greasy head. "Hello mother. You really need to clean up a little. Is this what you've been doing with the money I send you?"

The old woman picked up the wine bottles that were scattered at her feet. "You know I have a problem. Why should I bother cleaning? Who do I have to impress? No one ever comes out here. But let's not talk about me. Let me get a good look at you. My goodness, look how pretty you are! I guess you grew out of your ugly stage. You used to look like a little rag doll."

"Thanks Mom, you have such a way with words." She hated the old bitch. "We need to talk. This thing about my father and you wanting to..." She barely got the words out when she heard a pound at the front door.

"Who the hell could that possibly be?" Shrieked the old woman. "I haven't had anyone give a rat's ass about my well being since Old Gavin croaked, and now I have two visitors in one day. Don't move, I'll be right back."

"Don't worry I'm not going anywhere, Mom, but whatever you do, don't mention to anyone that I'm here, okay?"

"Yeah, yeah, I know. Mums the word."

The old woman raised her dirty finger to her mouth and then left her daughter safely behind the kitchen door while she scuffled her way through the piles of papers strewn about her living room. Once at the door, she stretched to her tip-toes to get a better look through the peephole. She recognized the man.

As she opened the door, she thought to herself, "Son of a bitch, do I have bad timing."

Chapter Thirty Five

After finding out about Gavin's secret ledger, Clayton had been determined to learn all he could about the woman who was the sole beneficiary of Gavin's pay offs. He spent his spare time behind his computer and hung out at the Hard Saddle so as to coyly pry information from some of the locals who knew people from years back.

One particular old timer who would have roughly been the same age as Gavin had known the old woman named Beverly since their school days. "Yup, I know who you're talking about. When she was younger, she was a real looker and she liked to give it out freely. You know what I mean by that, don't you, son?" The old man laughed and slapped Clayton's back.

"I know exactly what you mean," Clayton laughed as he poured both of them another shot out of the bottle of Jim Beam, hoping to loosen his lips a little more.

"Anyway, where was I? Oh yeah. So Beverly, that's her name. I just remembered that. Isn't it funny how things just come to you like that? She liked the boys and she especially liked her drink. We would get her drinking and then she always loosened up. She was a wild cat! Yes siree bob, a real wild cat. Now mind you, that's not the kind of girl you marry. You keep that in mind, Boy, when you find yourself a filly to settle down with. Those kinds of girls are just trouble. So, where was I?"

"You were telling me about Beverly."

"Oh that's right. Now back then everyone knew her, and let me tell you the other girls hated her! Whew wee! The girls would call her names and then she would let them have it. She could fight like a man. Hair would be flying. They'd try to scratch each other's eyes out. Boy, you don't want to be stuck in the middle of two girls fighting. They don't have any rules. It's kinda like a couple of wild mountain lions going at it."

"Don't worry about me. I don't want any part of a woman's fury. Now, what about Beverly?" Clayton wanted to keep the old timer on subject.

"Oh right, right. I was a year or two older, but rumor had it that she got herself knocked up and dropped out of school. She was gone for some time, but when she came back, she had paid cash for that old farmhouse on Boy Scott Road. She married some bum and kept that daughter of hers under lock and key. You'd never see her with the kid in hand, only a bottle of booze. I could understand her not being much of a mother because of the way she was brought up. Her parents were pretty trashy and didn't care much about what she did. She never worked a day in her life, but she always had plenty of cash."

Clayton listened intently to every word that the old man said. His heart was pounding as he asked, "What ever happened to the little girl? Did anyone know who the father was?"

"Oh hell, that's the funny thing; no one knows. She just up and vanished. As for who the hell the dad was, it could have been any one of a half a dozen guys. One day, Beverly's got a bum of a husband and some kid she could care less about and the next thing you know the husband's brakes go out, sending him flying off a mountain top. And who the hell knows what she did with the girl. Everyone just suspected maybe she sent her away; figured it was too much for her to handle. Some people say she went in a drunken rage and killed her daughter and buried her somewhere out under a tree. Other people say the little girl was as wild as a pack of wolves and took off to live in the woods. The kids in school say she's crazy and still out there. You never heard that rumor, Clayton?"

Clayton couldn't believe what he was hearing. "You mean the little girl just up and disappeared and no one asked the mother what happened?"

"Oh sure people asked. The sheriff even went out there and checked things out. I guess he got the answer because we never heard another word. Back then the sheriff was old Pat. You remember him? He had that heart attack. The next morning his wife looks out the window and old Pat is frozen solid right outside the front door. Poor old son of a bitch didn't even make it in the house."

Clayton politely listened to the old man's ramblings. He had hoped Beverly would walk through the doors of the saloon and he would have the chance to get her alone and talk with her, but she never came and no one had seen her for weeks.

He decided he would drive out to her place and take a look around.

Winter had arrived a few days earlier and the plows were having a hard time keeping up with the daily snow. Clayton was familiar with the road that Beverly lived on and knew there was not much traffic that went down it, so he was surprised to see a set of fresh tracks cutting a path through the hidden drive and around behind the old house.

Clayton slowly pulled his truck in front of the house. It looked abandoned except for a dim light that found its way through a pair of tattered old curtains. He walked cautiously onto the rotted porch not wanting to fall through. As he stood at the door, he listened carefully. He thought he heard voices inside and knocked loudly.

It was Beverly who came to the door looking haggard, her youth and beauty stolen years ago by all the bottles of booze she drank. "What do you want?"

Clayton could tell that Beverly didn't recognize him from her drunken fit at the Hard Saddle. "Beverly Fletcher, I'm Clayton Leatherbe. I think we had a mutual friend by the name of Gavin O'Malley."

Clayton then edged his way through the open door and into what was the woman's main living area.

"Yeah, I knew Gavin. Who didn't in this town, but what I want to know is how do you know me?"

Clayton turned and faced the woman. "Beverly let's cut to the chase. I was at the Hard Saddle the other night when you were shooting your mouth off. I worked for Gavin and I know that he had been paying you off to keep your mouth shut about the girl. I just want to know what the hell your intentions are and where your daughter is." He was firm and threatening, hoping to intimidate the old lady into submissiveness.

Forgetting that her daughter was in the kitchen, the old woman went off on the young man. "Don't you try and intimidate me, you son of a bitch! I've been playing this game since before you were born. So you know that the great Gavin O'Malley went and had himself a little bastard brat! Well, I'm going to tell you what I'm going to do! I know how much that ranch and property are worth and my daughter is going to get her share! I'm all done with getting measly payoffs to keep my mouth shut while everyone else is getting rich! Fuck you! I know that big land developer wants that ranch and I'm going to call on him tomorrow, and by the time I get done the whole damn world will know the truth!" She pushed at Clayton to move him toward the door. "Now get the fuck out of my house!"

Clayton turned around and grabbed both of the woman's brittle arms; he squeezed them with brute force, causing her to cry out in pain. "You, listen to me, you old bitch, your blackmailing days are over! If you even think about telling anyone or doing anything, I'll personally hunt you down and kill you! Do you understand? You live a long way from town and no one gives a shit about you! Your body will be out here rotting for months before anyone even thinks about looking! I'm not Gavin! I'm your worst nightmare!" And with those threatening words, he slammed the door behind him.

Beverly stood rubbing her arms and stared at the door in shock until the voice of her daughter brought her out of her daze. "Mom, who was that? Are you okay?"

Coming to her senses, Beverly turned around and headed back to where she'd left her daughter. "What kind of daughter are you? Didn't you hear him threaten me? A little help…"

When Beverly opened the door of the kitchen she was met with a fatal surprise; her only daughter thrust a massive icicle into her chest. She fell instantly and was unable to catch her breath.

As Beverly lay dying, she heard her daughter's voice. "Oh yes, Mother, I heard him, but I must say I have to agree with him. No one will find you for months!"

The young woman then left her unfit mother and the home she had been raised in for the last time. As she drove away she couldn't help but think of her mother's body alone on the dirty floor, the giant piece of ice stuck in her chest slowly melting.

"I just don't know how I come up with these things." She laughed aloud and began singing her favorite childhood song. "Ding dong, the witch is dead."

Chapter Thirty Six

Since Sloan's finances had been restricted down to near poverty levels, he had to stay in what he called a "down and out". Definitely not his style, but it was clean and came with a bed and shower. After unpacking his clothes, he lined up the bottles of pills that he now had to take on a daily basis.

He looked at his miserable surroundings. He hated the snow, the room and all the dirt roads that led to nowhere. He already missed the palm trees that swayed in the breeze and the air thickly scented of jasmine and magnolias. Winters in Florida were the best, but here he sat in a drafty old room, right in the middle of the cow shit capital.

"God, maybe I am nuts! No, I'm just scorned and want some justice; I need some sort of compensation for all I have been through."

After he finished giving himself his pep talk Sloan decided he had better find a place to eat. He left his room behind and at the suggestion of the girl at the front desk in the lobby, he made his way to a local steak house. He wasn't really a big meat eater, but he thought he'd give it a try.

Maybe if I'm lucky, I can find myself a big strong cowboy, he thought.

He followed the waitress who was nothing but skin and bones and looked as if she desperately needed to eat a rack of beef herself. She smiled at Sloan and batted her fake eyelashes at him. "Here you go honey, what can I get ya to drink?"

Sloan watched her desperate attempt at picking him up and thought about smashing her hopes, but decided he better get his food first. He smiled back at her and complimented her on her hair, even though it looked like it had been cut by a three-year-old with a pair of safety scissors.

She excitedly took his order, ran to the kitchen and dashed back with a bottle of Bud in her hand. "Here you go baby. You look like you could use this. My name is Colorado. If you need anything, and I mean anything!" She smiled wide to reveal a missing tooth.

"Are you serious? Your name is Colorado and you live in Montana?" Sloan couldn't help but sound condescending. After all, it was his nature.

"Well sure. Ain't ya ever heard anyone named Colorado before?" The girl was looking at him as if he had just landed from another planet. "Where are you from? Wait let me guess. With that accent I'd say you're from the South."

"Why, Colorado they must have some pretty good schools out here, because you are absolutely right! I'm from Florida."

The naive waif had not picked up on the fact that Sloan was making fun of her.

"Well there you go! That's why you ain't ever heard of anyone being called Colorado, 'cause you live in Florida! Who on earth would name their daughter Colorado when they live in Florida?"

Sloan couldn't believe he was having this conversation. He thought that she had to be the dumbest person he had ever met. How the hell could he respond to that?

"Well Colorado, I guess you're right, that's probably why I never heard the name Colorado before. Everyone in Florida names their children names like Georgia or Alabama, and let's not forget Mississippi; that's a big one. Now Colorado, I think I'm going to need another bottle of Bud."

Sloan watched the young girl turn and bounce to fetch his beer. She then handed it to him and stared while he took a sip. Within minutes, the cook appeared with a plate of a big T-bone thrown upon it. He took the plate and thanked the large hairy man.

The chef raised his head and winked at him. "No problem, big guy!" He turned and headed back to the kitchen.

Not sure of what he had just seen, Sloan had to ask Colorado, "Was the chef wearing mascara?"

She responded in a hushed voice. "You mean Bruce? He's one of those, you know what I mean? Today he went light on the eye shadow. He's an only child. His mom wanted a girl; you know the story. He's a little sensitive and has one hell of a temper, so I wouldn't say anything if I was you."

Sloan broke out in laughter. "Oh sweetie, I know that story real well."

The steak that Bruce prepared was the best tasting piece of meat Sloan had ever laid his teeth into. He gobbled it with gusto and even splurged on desert.

With a full stomach and his head a little tipsy, Sloan decided to check out the ranch that he had hated so much, despite having never been there. He let his headlights lead the path while he kept his eyes alert at all times waiting for a suicidal deer to leap from the side of the road into the path of his SUV. He eventually came to the massive log gate, which was closed, as luck would have it. He had two choices: he could drive five miles down to the other entrance that was located on the east side of the property or he could get out of the safety of his car and open the gate.

"Shit, there are wild animals out here!" He thought.

He turned his car off but kept his headlights pointing in the direction of the gate. Squinting to see better, he surveyed the area. Tiny little eyes were peered back at him.

"Shit, shit, shit! Oh hell, Sloan, just get your little pansy ass out there and open the damn thing already," he yelled at himself. He opened the door and flew out of his car, sinking his thousand dollar Gucci shoes into a pile of horse manure. "Son of a bitch!" He shrieked, scattering the deer and nearby small animals into all directions.

He darted as quickly as he could to open the large gate and while gagging, jumped back into his Envoy, foolishly smearing the shit onto the floorboard. It was more than the city boy could bear. Not one but both of his designer shoes were covered and the smell was repugnant.

Whimpering, but not slackening in determination, he drove through the gate and down the snow-covered road. He wasn't sure where he was going, but he figured he should follow the main road and it would lead him to Phillip.

He allowed his unbridled sense of justice to press him on. Phillip, Molly, everyone was going to pay for the monstrosities that they brought on him!

Spotting lights in the distance, Sloan slowed to a snail's pace and turned off his headlights. He drove a little further and decided he had better stop. He pulled a pair of binoculars to his eyes and was able to quickly spot Phillip through the large picture window of what must have been the main house. There were several people gathered by a warm fire drinking, laughing and enjoying each other's company.

The more he observed them the lonelier and segregated he felt. "This is torture! Why am I putting myself through this?" He didn't know why but he felt compelled to make them feel as miserable as he had become.

Shivering and stinky, he watched the happy people until late into the night, getting more pissed off with each hour. Finally, having had enough he turned his SUV around and drove back to the gate and to his secluded room.

Chapter Thirty Seven

MOLLY WOKE WITH A SLIGHT HEADACHE FROM THE LARGE AMOUNT OF wine she had drunk the night before.

But she was feeling surprisingly happy. When Phillip had called and asked if he could come to make amends, she was less than excited about it at first. Then, when he asked if he could bring his new lover, she almost laughed out loud. But she kept her feelings inside as she wanted those divorce papers signed, sealed and safely delivered in her hands without any monetary attachments. So for one last time she put on her happy face and found some leftover southern hospitality and opened her home to her soon-to-be ex-husband and his new companion.

Molly had forewarned all of her men, as she knew that they would rather string him up and drag him behind one of their old bulls than have to look at him. But after some strong talk with the boys and dire warning she made them promise to be on their best behavior.

What had started out as a simple quiet dinner for the two men wound up being a full-blown party. The men were in rare form, and surprising to all, everyone had a good time.

Molly had found Jack irresistibly charming, and at times actually forgot that he was Phillip's new boyfriend. Phillip was relaxed, like a new man; he really seemed happy, and the funny thing was that Molly didn't feel anything for Phillip other than friendship.

Clayton, on the other hand, was something else. When Molly got near that man, she couldn't help but feel the electric charge in the pit of her stomach, and the more she drank the more she wanted to saddle him up and ride him all the way home. As she lay in bed, she hoped her feelings weren't too obvious. She would have hated for the other men to pick up on anything. She wasn't sure if Clayton shared her feelings, but then she remembered the special moment that the two of them had shared together a few months before, how he had surprised her by whisking her away to a romantic dinner and an unforgettable night.

It was early and as she allowed herself to linger alone under her covers she suddenly had a vivid vision of Phillip spooning Jack in the bed of the guest house. She burst out in an uncontrollable fit of laughter. "All those years, who the hell would have imagined?" Molly spoke to her dog, Sedona, who was healing nicely from her wound.

She thought of how different Phillip and Clayton were. Such complete opposites. Then the phone rang.

"Hey girlfriend!" Leeza's cheerful voice sang into Molly's ear. "Guess what, I'm here!"

"What do you mean you're here?" Molly tried to hide the panic in her voice. "Are you at the airport? I thought you weren't supposed to be here until next week."

"Oh, I know, but I was bored and missing my favorite girl-friend, so walla! Here I am. You're okay with this, aren't you?"

"Okay? I'm thrilled," Molly lied. "Just give me a little time. You hang out there and I'll jump in the shower and head on over. It's close to an hour drive."

"No problem, there is the cutest restaurant here at the airport. I'll get some breakfast and maybe a Bloody Mary. See you when you get here!"

With her tranquil morning abruptly ended Molly jumped out of bed and rushed to the shower.

She had thoughts that her ranch may not be big enough to keep Phillip and Leeza together without one of them killing the other. "Well, they are just going to have to deal with it. Phillip has Jack so I'm sure the two boys can find lots to do to entertain each other. And as for Leeza, I'm sure I can get one of the better-looking ranch hands to amuse her."

Molly was well aware that even though Leeza was married, when a hot looking guy came around that she found enticing, she couldn't help but have a taste of the forbidden fruit. She may be a lousy wife but she was a good friend.

By the time Molly finished dressing and made it downstairs, Phillip and Jack were in the kitchen having breakfast with Rosa.

"Miss Molly, I like your husband better now that he is gay."

Phillip chuckled as he tried to look surprised.

"So do I, Rosa," Molly laughed as she grabbed her purse.

"Hey, where are you going?" Phillip asked.

"Well, you're not going to be happy about this, but Leeza called and she's at the airport. I have to go pick her up. Before you say anything, I'll have a talk with her and keep her on her best behavior."

Phillip had terror in his eyes. "And you really think she's going to listen to you? That woman is a pain in the ass! Maybe Jack and I should just get a room in town."

"Don't be silly, Phillip. She'll be fine. Once I have a talk with her and she understands that we're okay, she'll back off." Molly looked at Phillip with a pleading face. "Besides, I know you and I know those rooms. You wouldn't be happy."

Jack reached over and lovingly touched Phillip's hand. "Come on, Phillip, there's a lot to do around here and we'll keep ourselves busy, so you'll hardly see her."

"Okay, I'll try my best at being civil."

"Great! That's all I can ask for." With that Molly flew out the door as Clayton was coming in.

"Hey sunshine, where you off to?"

"To the airport. I have to pick up my girlfriend. You're looking mighty dapper this morning. Trying to impress Phillip?" Molly grinned as she teased her ranch manager.

"Now, you know he's already taken, and besides he couldn't handle all of this!" Clayton playfully responded.

You're probably right, but I sure would like a try, she thought as she drove away.

Molly parked her truck in short-term parking and went into the small airport. Leeza spotted Molly and squealed with delight. The two women wrapped their arms around each other while rejoicing like schoolgirls.

"Oh my God, you look great!" Leeza spoke with sincerity as she held Molly back away from her so she could get a better look.

"So do you! God I've missed you. Being around all these cowboys I'm starting to feel like one of the guys. I need some girl time!" Molly held her friend's hand and led her out the door.

"Oh, I'm sure it's been just hell, being around all of those handsome rugged cowboys." Molly's friend rolled her eyes as she laughed.

As Molly drove, the two women chatted. "Okay Leeza, I have to warn you. Phillip is here and he is with someone, and they will be staying with us." She looked over at her friend.

"What? Are you serious? Please don't tell me he is here with that infinitesimal piece of shit! Because if he is I will…"

Molly stopped her friend before she could say anymore.

"No, no, he is not with that little ass! He actually found someone who is really nice. He's French and charming; nothing at all like Sloan." Molly's voice was soothing and relaxed while she spoke of Phillip.

"You mean you don't have a problem with this?" Leeza sounded skeptical.

"Nope, not at all. He brought the divorce papers signed, and he's not asking for any part of the ranch." Molly spoke with enthusiasm and sincerity. "What more could I hope for? I would rather end on good terms and try and stay friends. We were a part of each other's lives for a long time."

"Well you definitely don't sound like a woman scorned! I don't know if I can behave as nicely as you, but I'll try and be civil and maybe even friendly just for you, because I love you!" Leeza looked over at her friend with admiration.

"I love you, too, Leeza." Molly smiled as the two women pulled down the driveway of Molly's little piece of heaven.

Chapter Thirty Eight

Clayton decided to head into the main house to be sociable and enjoy a little breakfast with Molly and her soon-to-be ex. This whole new friendly relationship was difficult for the cowhands who lived and worked on the Ghost Bear to understand and they had enjoyed making Phillip the butt of all their jokes. But Clayton was thrilled to see Molly's marriage coming to an end on good terms; Molly would soon be free and Clayton was delighted. He decided to make a sincere attempt to make Phillip and his new friend feel comfortable.

Clayton had spent the previous evening with the men and Molly and they had all enjoyed each other's company. As the night had progressed, he could not help but find himself captivated by Molly's beauty. So at the break of day he jumped out of bed, enthusiastic to partake in the glorious morning with her. He showered, dressed and shaved, and as he journeyed to the house, he was only to be left in the lurch, as she ran from the main house shouting at him that she was in a rush to get to the airport to pick up her close friend. He was disappointed but continued to the main house to join the others who were happily eating Rosie's breakfast creations.

"Morning men. I see everyone survived their first night here." Clayton reached for the pot of steaming coffee.

"We did indeed and I slept like a baby," Jack spoke, his mouth filled with pancakes and warm maple syrup. "Rosie, these pancakes are the best!"

Clayton took a seat next to Phillip, and Rosie piled some eggs and sausage on his plate.

Phillip stopped filling his mouth to admit his wrong doings. "Clayton, I really wanted to apologize to you."

"Really? About what?" Although he had an idea, Clayton played dumb.

"Well, the last time I was here, I behaved like an ass and I'm sorry about that. I had been under a lot of stress," Phillip said.

"Hey, no problem. I owe you one, too. What do you say we let bygones be bygones?" Clayton spoke honestly, wanting to let Phillip off the hook.

"Sounds great," Phillip agreed.

"So, what's the plan for today?" Clayton asked while sitting back and enjoying another sip of Rosa's fresh brew.

"Well I think we might head in town. Jack would like to do a little shopping and I would love to get the hell out of here before Leeza gets here!"

Phillip pulled himself away from the table and took Jack's empty plate over to the sink.

Suddenly, there was a pounding on the front door. Sedona, still healing from her wound, leapt to all fours and with her vicious bark ran to the door, startling all three men and Rosa.

Regaining his composure, Clayton went to see who was at the door. Tail wagging but still barking, Sedona stared at the door.

"It's okay. Back off. Let's see who it is," Clayton spoke to the massive pet while opening the door. There standing in front of him was the sheriff..

"Hey Bill, how are you?" Clayton asked. "Have you found out who's been causing all the trouble?"

"No. We are still working on it, but that's not why I'm here." The rugged sheriff looked very serious. "Clayton I'm going to have to ask you to come down to the station with me. I have some questions that I need to ask you about old Beverly."

Clayton had figured that she would call the police on him and inform them of his threats.

"Look Bill, there is no need for me to go down there. I went over to her house to tie up some loose ends that pertained to Gavin. I know I was a little harsh on the old woman but no need to worry, it's all been sorted out."

"Clayton, when did you go over there? Do you know the approximate time?"

"It was yesterday. Oh I don't know; around three or three-thirty."

"Was anyone with you?" Bill was very somber.

"No. Why? What the hell is the problem? I told you everything is fine." Clayton was becoming agitated.

"Beverly was found dead on her kitchen floor. You are going to have to come with me for questioning. Do you have an attorney?" Bill put his hand on Clayton's shoulder to lead him out of the house.

Clayton couldn't believe Bill's words. "What the hell is this, Bill? You know me. When I left that old woman's house she was alive and just as nasty as ever. I would never do something like that!"

Phillip, Jack and Rosa could hear Clayton's rising voice and walked into the living room just in time to see the sheriff lead Clayton out of the house.

"Clayton, don't say another word. Sheriff, I am this man's attorney and I will be right behind you." Phillip grabbed his coat and keys and headed for the door. "Rosa, when Molly gets back you tell her that we are down at the police station. Don't worry; we'll be back in no time at all."

"Oh, my God. Clayton would never hurt a soul!" Rosa exclaimed. "Mr. Phillip, you take good care of him!"

"Don't worry about a thing. I promise he'll be fine." And with those words of encouragement Phillip left Rosa and Jack behind.

"Wait up one second. Sheriff, would it be possible for Clayton to ride with me? You know how people in this town talk; we don't need them to see Clayton sitting in the car with you, I'll take full responsibility and you can follow us in."

Phillip hoped that Bill would be reasonable with his request, as he needed some time to talk with Clayton before he was questioned.

"I suppose that would be alright. I'll follow you." Bill let a stunned Clayton get into the truck with Phillip.

"I'll drive, you talk," Phillip said as he jumped into the driver's seat.

The two men pulled out with the sheriff close behind.

"Okay Clayton, tell me everything." Phillip coolly spoke.

"What's there to tell? I went over to her house, we talked and I left," Clayton said.

"That's not going to fly. What did you talk about and why did you go over there? How do you know her?" Phillip tried to stay level-headed, sensing that there might be more to this than what Clayton was saying.

"Okay, I was at the Hard Saddle the other night having a few beers. We had some trouble at the ranch that I'm sure you've heard about, and I went there to see if someone may have heard something or knew who was behind this. So I went there, and towards the end of the night, Beverly was sitting in a corner pretty loaded; according to all the locals, she's usually that way. She started yelling something about Gavin. Then she ran out of the bar so fast that I didn't have time to talk to her. I went back to the Hard Saddle and hoped to see her again, but no one had seen her around. I didn't even know who the hell she was until one of the old timers told me where she lived, so I drove out there."

"Okay, so you were there by yourself?" Phillip asked.

"Yup," Clayton replied.

"Was anyone else there with her? Did you notice if anyone was around?"

The questions triggered Clayton's memory. "Yes. I do remember something. It had been snowing real hard and when I drove down her road, I did notice a set of fresh tracks. I also remember right before I knocked on the door I thought I could hear her talking to someone, you know, voices."

"Okay, this is good. Did you actually see anyone?" Phillip asked as they neared the town.

"No, I didn't see anyone, but when I was standing on the front porch I thought I could hear voices coming from inside. When I went in, I didn't see anyone and I assumed it was her TV or maybe she was talking to her cat." Clayton was beginning to see the gravity of the situation. "Shit, my fingerprints are in that house!"

"Okay, listen to me. No matter what, you are going to have to tell me the truth. You should never lie to your lawyer or doctor. Did you kill her?"

"Hell no! I didn't kill her. Why should I? I don't have a motive. Why would I want some poor old woman who I didn't even know dead?" As he spoke, he thought of the hidden journal that the police could use as a motive. He hoped to God that while he was gone they would not search his house; he would have to convince them he was telling them the truth.

"Okay, I believe you. What do you say we go in together and see what they have?" The two men pulled into the station with the sheriff right behind.

Chapter Thirty Nine

WHEN SLOAN AWOKE FROM HIS SLUMBER, HE HAD FORGOTTEN THAT HE was not in the comfort and warmth of his own bed, snuggled in Egyptian cotton, but was instead lying upon a hard mattress that was barely covered with a worn, thin Kmart sheet. He rubbed the sleep from his eyes, rose to his feet and waddled over to the bathroom. Glancing down and remembering the night before, he rolled his eyes at the once-favorite pair of shoes that were now soiled and discarded in the corner. He inspected his pale reflection in the tiny mirror that hung on the wall. Sighing loudly, he began his daily grind of opening the bottles lined up like little soldiers that contained a battlefield of pills and ready to perform their duty of fighting the vicious viruses that filled his body. While he showered, he thought of Phillip, his body aching for him; and as he dressed, he allowed visions of Molly to fill his heart with malice.

After a light breakfast, he was ready to plot his day. He thought he would check out the small western town he knew Molly and Phillip had frequented in the past. He wore a large down jacket and a hat that covered his head and nestled over his ears. His winter attire kept him warm as he emerged from his modest hotel and into the brisk morning air. Snow crunched beneath his feet as he walked to where he had parked his car the night before, only to become discouraged as fresh snow had blanketed the car.

"Son of a bitch!" The Southerner whined as he opened the back of his rental SUV and pulled out the scraper. He brushed the car off with vigorous detail, jumped inside and started the engine, allowing the car to warm before heading off.

Sloan drove one time through the old town incognito before parking on a side street near the small police station. He wanted to get a better feel for the town, talk to some of the locals and find out as much as he could about the layout of that ranch.

He was ready to get out of his car when suddenly a large Ford pickup pulled into the nearby parking lot at the station with a sheriff's car close behind. He caught a quick glimpse of the two men inside the pickup and saw that Phillip was undeniably driving while a man Sloan did not recognize sat in the passenger's seat. Not wanting Phillip to see him, he slumped down into the seat as far as he could, while still being able to observe Phillip and the stranger.

The two men looked serious as they left their vehicle and walked side-by-side allowing the sheriff to lead the way. A lightning bolt of panic struck Sloan hard in the chest and he swallowed hard, trying to gulp down the lump that had magically formed in his throat. Sloan's thoughts scrambled as he tried to come up with a rational reason for Phillip to be at the police station, only to conclude that Phillip must have discovered that he was stalking him and had gone to the police for their help. As he sat in his vehicle, Sloan grew increasingly apprehensive over the idea of not being able to execute his ruthless retribution. He could no longer see the men, as they had walked inside.

After a few minutes, Sloan thought it might be a good idea to get the hell out of there. He started the car and so as to not draw attention to himself, slowly maneuvered it from where it was parked. He once again drove along the one-lane road that went through the western town. The palms of his hands had become slippery with perspiration and he held the steering wheel tightly so his hands would not slide down the leather wheel. He had almost made it out of the small town when another truck, similar to the one that Phillip had been driving in, flew past him. He was sure that Molly had been driving with a woman who looked vaguely familiar. He prayed that Molly had not seen him, and he quickly accelerated to a higher speed, wanting to create as much of a distance between himself and the town he despised.

His head now filled with illusions that his enemies had known of his presence, that he had been on the ranch the night before and was now occupying their sleepy little town. He drove the car erratically as he kept his eyes fixed on the rearview mirror expecting to see them chasing behind him in a hot pursuit. He was so worried about who was behind him that he scarcely paid attention to the road that was in front of him.

As the road curved to the right Sloan continued straight, thrusting his SUV onto a large wooden wagon that was parked in front of a weathered barn. It was full of garbage and various wastes that were soon to be taken to the local dump. He had plowed through the wooden planks of the trailer, sending the garbage spewing into the sky and avalanching upon his car. Stunned and not sure of what had just happened, with shaking hands he turned off the engine. He could not see out of any of the windows as the vehicle was wedged beneath the rotting trash. Unable to withstand the incarceration, he gathered his wits, turned the key in the ignition and with a thud backed down off from the trailer. Once off the trailer, he made a failed attempt to turn on the windshield wipers and clear a path in the glass so he could see. He strained his eyes as he squinted through the smeared rubbish that refused to wash off with his squirters, and with his tires grasping for traction in the snow he sped away, leaving behind an angry farmer who was now running from his farmhouse yelling profanity to clean up Sloan's deplorable mess.

Originally wanting to appear inconspicuous in his getaway, Sloan now created a trail of garbage that flew from his mishandled auto, extending through the air and floating to the ground. He couldn't believe his luck. Had karma raised its ugly head to bite him in the ass? The thought blew through his conscious like a summer squall, only to leave him further provoked and tormented.

He drove back to the dumpy hotel, where he stayed hidden for the rest of the day, peeking out from behind the curtains whenever he heard a car's engine.

Chapter Forty

Returning from the airport, Molly proudly drove down the long drive to the main house. She was aware that she had changed and she appreciated that her good friend had noticed and credited her on her inner strength.

"Out here the mountain air toughens you up. You really don't have a choice," Molly explained with a grin.

"Well that's for sure." Leeza didn't look at her friend, but instead she gazed out the window at the barren snow piled along the road.

As Molly drove up to the house, she felt a twinge of disappointment in noticing that Clayton's truck was gone. She parked the truck and pulled Leeza's luggage from the extended cab while Sedona performed her meet and greet with her new guest.

"My God, I think your dog is still growing!" Leeza laughed while she put her face down next to the dog's enormous head letting the beast smother her face with wet kisses. "Every time

I see her, she's bigger and bigger. Look when she wags her tail her whole butt moves back and forth."

"No, she's still steady at 150 pounds. You just don't get to see her that often. You've become used to all the little purse puppies that live down South." Molly smiled as she watched her friend's interaction with her beloved pet.

"Hey, don't make fun of our purse puppies. I'm sure there are some cowboys out here that have some."

The women struggled to carry the heavy cases into the house.

"Speaking of cowboys, where the hell are they when you need them?" Leeza huffed as she climbed the front steps of the enormous porch.

"Well, yes there are purse puppies out here, but they are all over a hundred pounds, and they don't sit in your purse, they protect your purse! You're right, where the hell is everyone? We could use a little help here!" Molly yelled out as they entered the large log home.

Rosa and Jack emerged from the kitchen to help.

"Here, here let me help you with those." Jack relieved the two women from their heavy burden. "Where shall I take them?"

"What a gentleman." Leeza cooed.

"Cool down; he's taken." Molly smiled at Jack. "Rosa, will you show him…"

Molly removed her coat, looked at Rosa and instantly knew something was wrong.

"Okay, what happened?" Molly looked around the room and down the hall towards the kitchen. "Where is Phillip?"

Knowing that Rosa was slightly panicked and not wanting to needlessly frighten Molly, Jack spoke up. "Oh, Clayton and he went down to the sheriff's station."

"Really? Did they get a tip on who has been behind all the trouble around here?" Molly asked.

"What trouble? You didn't mention any trouble." Leeza asked.

"Oh, it's nothing," Molly replied brushing Leeza off.

"No, no, I don't believe it's related," Jack spoke casually in his French accent.

"Well, then why did they go down there?" Noticing Jack's hesitation, Molly was becoming slightly impatient. "Rosa?"

Molly's housekeeper broke down. In between bouts of sobbing and broken English Molly was able to get the gist of what happened.

"So let me get this straight; the sheriff was out here to take our Clayton in for questioning over some old woman's death that we don't even know? And Phillip went with him?"

Molly looked at Rosa and then Jack as the two nodded in agreement.

"How long have they been gone?" Molly asked.

"Not very long," Jack replied while still holding onto Leeza's bags.

"Okay, I'm out of here. Rosa, show Jack where to put those. Leeza, if you want you can freshen up. I'm going to town to see what the hell is going on." Molly grabbed her coat and threw it back on.

"Screw freshening up. I can take a shower anytime. I'm going with you. Jesus, I never knew it was so exciting around here!" Leeza yelled at Molly as she flew out the door. "Hey, wait up!"

Leeza had barely jumped into the seat next to her friend when Molly threw the gearshift into reverse and at a great rate of speed took off in the direction of town. As Molly's foot hit heavy on the gas, the back end of the truck fishtailed. Unlike Leeza, Molly was an expert driver on icy roads and effortlessly corrected the steering wheel to maintain the vehicle on the road instead of plowing in a snow bank.

"Fuck me! Molly, slow it down before you kill both of us!" Leeza bellowed while her knuckles turned white as she grasped tightly onto the bolted handle that was above her head, trying to keep her small-framed body from bouncing around in her seat belt. "They aren't going anywhere and I'm sure Phillip is totally capable of getting to the bottom of this. They're grown men, Molly, not little boys."

Molly shot her a death glare.

"Okay, sorry."

Leeza had known Molly long enough to know that she knew better than to say another word.

At the speed they were traveling, it did not take long before they neared town and Molly finally began to slow down. Knowing that she was possibly overreacting, Molly turned to her friend who now had a slightly green twinge about her. "Hey, are you okay? I'm so sorry; I just really wanted to get here as fast as I could. Lately there's been so much stuff going on. I sort of caught a guy doing some stuff that he shouldn't have been and I sort of whipped the son-of-a-bitch with my bullwhip. Anyway, I think this guy might have killed that woman and is trying to frame it on Clayton."

Molly was talking so fast and paying attention to the road that she failed to notice Leeza's mouth was wide open. "What did you do to some guy?" Leeza wasn't sure she'd heard Molly correctly.

"I whipped him, you know with my bullwhip. Hell, he shot my dog and I would have shot him back if Clayton hadn't stopped me!"

"That's what I thought you said," a stunned Leeza replied.

The two women marched into the tiny sheriff's office defiant and ready for a challenge. Molly had imagined Clayton's interrogation within a small room with bright lights or possibly stuck in a nasty little cell with only a dirty mattress and a disease-ridden urinal. But when they walked into the pleasant small town police station, she was relieved to find Phillip and Clayton sitting behind the sheriff's desk with coffees in hand, the three men chatting like old friends.

"Molly, what are you doing here?" Her presence surprised Clayton.

"I'm here for you! What are you doing here?" Molly asked, while nodding at the sheriff who was leaning back in his chair.

"Listen, there's nothing to worry about," Phillip spoke with a cool voice that showed his years of legal expertise. "Clayton came down to give a statement and tell what he knows. I just came along in case he needed a hand."

"Well men, I guess that answers the questions I had," the sheriff broke in. "Clayton I'm going to have to ask you to stay around town while we get to the bottom of this, and ma'am, keep an eye out at your ranch for anything unusual and call us immediately. I don't want you taking the law in your own hands or giving out your own justice; that's my job. We have a killer amongst us in this town and I don't take it lightly." The sheriff's voice was deep and stern.

"Yes sir, I understand." Molly knew the sheriff was well aware of the troubles upon her ranch.

Acting on the sheriff's offer the two men stood at attention and put on their jackets.

Clayton reached his hand out to the lawman. "Bill, if you need me for anything just give me a shout. I hope you find out who is behind this, and if I think of anything else that will help I'll call."

Clayton raised his hat and the rest of them followed him.

Just as they were almost out the door, Bill shouted out to Clayton, "Oh Clayton, one more thing. Did Beverly ever say anything to you about her daughter or where she might be? She's the only family the old lady had and no one has a clue as to where she is."

That was not the question Clayton wanted. He turned to face the officer he had known for most of his life and looked him square in his eyes. "I have no clue, Bill; she never mentioned her."

The four friends left the station and headed to their trucks.

"Okay, we will meet you boys at home and then Clayton, you can fill me in," Molly said as she jumped back into her Ford.

"Yeah! I can't wait to hear this story." Leeza spoke in the voice that Phillip despised. "Oh by the way, hello Phillip. Who knew I'd see you out here?"

"Nice to see you too, Leeza. Try not to annoy me while you're here." Phillip rolled his eyes and jumped in Clayton's truck. "She's a perpetual bitch," he muttered to Clayton.

They followed each other out of town.

As they drove back to the sanctuary of the Ghost Bear, Clayton replayed his statement over in his mind, surprising himself at how capable he was at lying.

Chapter Forty One

Clayton was the first to walk through the door and Rosa was there to greet him. The Spanish woman smothered him like he was her lost child.

"Rosa, it's okay, really I'm fine." Clayton spoke affectionately, but wanted the woman to stop treating him as if he was five.

"I know, I know, but get in here and sit down. I'll get you all some coffee. I was so worried!" The plump mother hen pushed them all into the large living area.

Leeza plunged herself down upon the couch. "Rosa skip the coffee for me and make it a martini. I'm still on Eastern time and it just hit cocktail hour!"

"I'll make it, Rosa," Phillip offered. "Sit down. I think we all could use a drink." He began to expertly mix the concoctions behind the hand carved bar, which had been one of Gavin's favorite pieces of furniture.

Molly scooted Leeza's legs aside and perched herself upon the leather couch. "Clayton, why did the police want to question you over that lady's death?"

"Well, when I was hanging out in the Hard Saddle Saloon trying to see if anyone had heard or known anything about the trouble that we had out here, she was really drunk, made a scene and ran out. I asked around and was told that she had been a regular for years, so I kept going back there hoping that she would come back so I could talk with her; but she never did. So I found out where she lived and drove out to her place. I specifically inquired if she had ever heard anyone talking about the Ghost Bear or Molly on one of her frequent haunts to the saloon. She wasn't any help so I left. End of story." Clayton hated lying to Molly.

"Well then, you don't have anything to worry about. That explains why you were out there and I feel certain the sheriff will find out who did it. Hell, it was probably a drug addict who knew she lived out there alone and she caught them in her house looking for money or jewelry." Phillip mused, while carrying two martinis for Leeza and Jack. He smiled at Leeza, who was now sitting attentively and staring at Clayton.

Without even a glance, she carefully took the peace offering from Phillip's slender hands.

"Mmmm, just the way I like it; cold and wet. I should have known you were gay, Phillip. You can make a hell of a martini."

"Thanks asshole." Phillip winked at Jack as he gave him his drink, then sat and put his arm around him.

Phillip's outward affection towards Jack still took Molly by surprise, as she had been married to this man for so many years without any inkling of his preferred sexual habits.

"What if it wasn't some druggie, Phillip? What if it was someone trying to set Clayton up?" Molly asked.

"How'd the old bag die anyway?" Leeza asked.

"They're not sure. From what I could gather they didn't find a murder weapon and the sheriff isn't offering up a lot of details," Phillip replied.

Not wanting to appear ungrateful or spawn any speculation, Clayton remained amongst them and poured himself a shot of whiskey. As he listened to everyone and their various theories on the murder mystery he felt as if he was one of the characters in Clue. Could it have been Scarlet with the candlestick? Or was it Mr. Watson with the knife in the library? I know. Yes, definitely the butler in the kitchen or the ranch foreman at the old lady's house?

Clayton appeared to be part of their conversation but he was in the midst of his own train of thought. *I didn't kill the old woman and the more I think about that day, I'm sure I heard her talking to someone just before I knocked. There is a chance that whoever else was in that house was the murderer and if they were there, then they had to have overheard our conversation and my threats. Did they intentionally want to set me up? No way; no one knew I was going over there. Did my beef with the old lady provide them with the perfect opportunity to get away with murder? If they were in that house, they know about Gavin and the real reason I went over there. Shit, I just gave someone the opportunity to blackmail me.*

Clayton had to get out of there and head back to his own house. He had to get rid of the ledger and the picture of Beverly's little girl. Those things were all the police would need to arrest him on suspicion of murder.

The conversation had finally moved off the subject of the police and onto making plans for dinner.

"Well everyone, I need to go check on the men," Clayton broke in. "I can't let them think I've been sloughing off from my share of the work around here. I'm going to pass on dinner tonight." He slung back one last shot of whiskey, shook Phillip's hand one last time and headed to his house. He had things to do and he had wasted enough time.

Clayton walked swiftly home and securely locked the door behind him. He had to get that damn ledger out of the house and destroy it. With Beverly dead what was the use of keeping it? He closed his blinds and pulled the leather bound book from its hiding place. It was the only tangible piece of evidence that Gavin and this ranch had any type of connection to Beverly. He decided he would burn it.

As he built the fire, he thought of the unusual group gathered in the house. He had only met Leeza one other time at Gavin and Addie's funeral. After they had come back from the sheriff's office, even though Molly's friend enjoyed verbally sparing with Phillip, he sensed that she did not care for him and might have suspected him.

Once the fire was burning strong, Clayton took one last look at the book and tossed it in. He watched the flames engulf the book, the pages burning as the leather melted into the logs. The small picture fell from the burning contents and the heat made the edges of the photograph curl.

Clayton felt sympathetic for the child, but then it hit him. There was something very familiar about her. He searched the depths of his mind trying to put a finger on it; something about her eyes. He concluded that he would find something familiar in the little girl, since she was Molly's half sister, and Gavin's other daughter.

He stayed by the fire long after the book was gone and the picture had dissolved to ash. He lost track of time until a knock at the door snapped him back to reality. The visitor knocked a second time. When a woman's voice called out, Clayton recognized it to be Leeza. She was the last person he cared to talk with. He sat quietly waiting for her to leave.

Although Leeza was a close friend to Molly, Clayton did not particularly care for her. He had noticed that she enthusiastically enjoyed belittling Phillip. He couldn't question the woman's loyalty to Molly, as they had been friends longer than Clayton had even known her. Now with his character up for question and the penetrating looks that Leeza had earlier shot his way, he was not surprised that the woman would leave the comforts of the warm house and tromp through the snow and pound on his door. He did not want any more questions or confrontations from a woman that he barely knew.

Clayton stayed in the house for the rest of the night. While everyone else on the Ghost Bear Ranch slept like babies, he lay awake with unsettling speculation and concern as to who had killed Beverly and whether their sinister actions would affect him. He knew it was just a matter of time that whoever had been in that house would be calling on him. He was determined not to be taken by surprise. He would be ready and waiting.

Chapter Forty Two

THE NEWS OF BEVERLY'S DEATH SPREAD THROUGH THE TOWN LIKE AN infectious disease. No matter how much of a bother the old woman had become, she was a constant fixture in the town and it didn't sit well with the locals that she had been brutally murdered.

Evin's office was buzzing over the details, and when someone had seen Clayton walking into the police station with Molly's husband, and the sheriff in lead, the rumors began flying. Even though Evin did not know the woman personally nor had he ever cared to get to know her, he did find the whole matter quite interesting and was sure that he could use it to his advantage.

The beating that Molly had given out to one of Evin's hired hands had cost him quite a penny. He was not happy about having to shell out the cash to get the idiot out of town and keep his mouth shut. The stall in acquiring the ranch frustrated him, but now it looked like lady luck was smiling down on him.

If he could make sure Molly's precious foreman was charged with murder, he was sure she would crumble and just want to get out from under it.

God, if I knew that Clayton was going out to that old lady's house, I might have even considered killing her myself, just to set his ass up, Evin thought to himself with a large smirk resting upon his face.

Thanks to the actions of a stranger, a delightful scheme was forming inside his devious brain. Even though he knew that Clayton didn't have it in him to commit the act, Evin was clever enough to plant the seed of doubt inside the feeble minds of most of the townspeople. He would add to the various rumors in order to sow that seed of doubt, and within no time that little seed would be rooted like a nasty weed, entangled deep within their thoughts, feeding heavy upon their fear and producing a need for vigilante justice. Yes, it would only be a short time before he began reaping his rewards.

Evin walked from the secluded privacy of his office to mingle and plant the rumors amongst his agents. He had learned this trick early on when he'd opened his first real estate agency. To leak a tidbit of information, he strategically picked those individuals in his office that he knew had loose tongues. He began by saying he knew that what he was about to tell them would be kept in the greatest confidence, and once he had their full attention he would whisper the intimate gossip, filling their ears with the lies. Then once the scuttlebutts were free from restraint they would blab all the details.

Evin's treachery was already taking a toll on Clayton Leatherbe's character. People had begun questioning who he was, where he came from and how long he had worked for the Ghost Bear. The more people talked, the more questions they had for which they wanted some answers.

Clayton had never shared any details about his past with anyone, and before the murder no one had really cared. They knew that he was Gavin's number one man and no one ever questioned Gavin O'Malley's judgment of character, let alone get into his business. In other words, if Gavin said Clayton Leatherbe was okay, then he was okay. But that was then and this was now, and Gavin was dead.

For all the locals knew, Clayton could be a wolf hiding in sheep's clothing. So they began fostering their own false opinions and harboring ill feelings towards the Ghost Bear Ranch and its new owner. People figured that the only reason Clayton hadn't been thrown in jail wasn't due to lack of evidence, but due to Molly O'Malley's power and money.

But money didn't mean a hill of beans; it was about character. One's character told a person the type of man you were and most importantly, a man's word meant more than anything money could buy. The men lived their lives true to this western code that had been established generations before them. So Evin shot holes into Clayton's character by spreading lies about him.

Soon the sheriff's office was fatigued with repeated visits and phone calls of citizens demanding the arrest of Clayton Leatherbe. They called the sheriff a coward and accused him of being on the take by Molly. They did not care that he had searched Molly's home as well as Clayton's and came up with absolutely nothing. The locals were creating such a fuss, and even though he was impassive to their demands, he was quickly becoming concerned for the safety of those who worked and lived at the Ghost Bear.

The sheriff was familiar with the recent damage that someone had caused on the ranch and he couldn't help feel that this murder and that damage were somehow linked. Bill suspected Evin and his men were behind Molly's worries and were likely the ones that had killed off some of her cattle. A person would have to be blind or a complete fool not to see how badly that man wanted to get his hands on that land. But he couldn't prove it and he knew that a man like Evin would stop at nothing to get what he wanted. But was he capable of murder?

Bill let the thought bounce around as he picked up the paper that sat on his desk. "Well at least one mystery is solved: a phone number for the mythical daughter of the departed."

Chapter Forty Three

Molly had moved back to the ranch wishing for a peaceful life, but instead it was becoming increasingly problematic. The day after Clayton's trip to the police station, the sheriff stood at her doorstep, along with a posse of men with a warrant in hand. They ransacked every building, leaving no stone unturned as they searched for the murder weapon or evidence of Clayton's guilt. To no avail, their search ended well after dark and the defeated men left the premises empty handed.

Molly's problems were mounting and she was becoming increasingly tired of listening to Leeza and Phillip's squabbles. She was finding it more difficult to get a good night's sleep and she found herself becoming increasingly aggravated. She wasn't sure how much more she could take and she needed some time to herself to clear her head.

The day was warm for winter and Molly was increasingly becoming bored with the company of her visitors. She told her friends that she was leaving them to squabble amongst themselves, packed a sandwich and headed off in her daddy's old Jeep.

With the heater cranked up, she drove the Jeep around her property. The land was so vast that she could get lost for days out there and no one would be able to find her. It was just what she needed.

Leeza not only continually complained about Phillip, but she was hypercritical of Clayton. Every time Molly heard her friend scrutinize his actions, she could hear a growing contempt in her words. She was aware that Leeza didn't have many friends and always had been overprotective of their friendship. She could understand that Leeza had been witness to Clayton's questioning by the police, which would in turn lead to Leeza's distrust of the man.

The snow was melting rapidly due to the warmth of the day and the sun's full strength, leaving the trees light and bare. The white snow that had once blanketed the branches had transformed into small droplets of water that slowly fell to the ground.

Molly moved the Jeep forward, following the trails she assumed her workers had made. She looped along the path slowly as cattle had appeared on both sides of her while acknowledging her presence with an occasional lopsided glance and a moo. As she drove in the warmth of the sun, she allowed her mind to push away her cluttered thoughts.

She thought of the discussions she'd had with her best friend. Although Leeza's words had been filled with speculation, she had a point. Molly really didn't know much about Clayton's past. Her father had hired him years before she came along and there was never a reason to doubt her father's judgment. Her dad had grown to love Clayton like the son he never had, and since Molly had come back to the ranch, she could understand why. Molly knew without any question that he would never kill anyone, but she was falling in love with a man that she really didn't know much about. Why had he been so tight-lipped about his past? Where and when did he learn to fly aircrafts? She told herself that she would have to find out more about him.

Molly continued her drive and enjoyed the time to her own thoughts. She was well past the area where a large number of her cattle spent time. She had always admired the variance in the terrain of the Ghost Bear. She drove upon a remote path that led further amongst the giant Ponderosas. As she looked ahead, she became suddenly puzzled. Up ahead of her was Clayton who was in a heavy-hearted conversation. As Molly grew closer, she clearly saw a flustered look on Clayton's face as he realized she was approaching them. He handed over a piece of paper to the men and it seemed as if they had been quickly dismissed, as they jumped into their truck and dispersed. Clayton waved at Molly. She was curious as to who the men were and why they were with Clayton.

"Clayton, what the hell's going on?" Molly wasn't going to beat around the bush and she asked him straight up, hoping for an honest answer.

"Molly," Clayton tipped his hat at his boss. "I was meeting up with some old friends. I asked them to help me out and do a little investigating for me."

"Well, why in the world would you meet them out here?" Molly asked with doubt in her voice. "There sure does seem to be a lot I don't know about you."

"I figured it would be best not to give anyone more reason to question my motives or overhear our conversation. And as far as my background, your dad had known enough about me to know I'm a man to be trusted. I will explain everything to you. It's a long story and I promise I will tell you all of my chapters, but that is meant for another day."

Clayton was beginning to tire of the constant scrutiny; he was only trying to protect her.

"Molly, it's my head on the chopping block and I need some help. I need to find out who is behind all the problems we've been having. I have a clue, but I need to know for sure. They could also have killed Beverly."

Although Clayton was being honest, he failed to mention that he also wanted those men to find out who and where the old woman's and Gavin's daughter was.

Molly felt ashamed. *Jesus, I'm spending too much time around Leeza and she's getting into my head*, she thought to herself. She walked closer to Clayton, took his hat from atop of his messed hair, gazed into his eyes and with a heavy remorseful voice, apologized for doubting him.

She was only a few inches from his face and he could feel the passion radiating from her. He grabbed her tightly in his arms and with deep affection and a kindred heart he kissed her mouth hard, taking her breath away. The intoxication of the kiss took them both by surprise.

Holding the back of his thick blond hair she feverishly welcomed his lips on hers when he suddenly and without reason pulled himself from her.

"I'm sorry Molly, I shouldn't have done that," he spoke as he let go of her and stepped back trying to put some distance between them.

Trying to catch her breath and confused by his reaction she replied, "I don't understand, Clayton."

"I'm sorry. There has been so much shit lately and I don't want to make things worse." As soon as Clayton spoke, he felt as if someone had just kicked him in the stomach.

Searching his eyes with hers, Molly once again felt rejected by a man. "You're right, you shouldn't have done that." Then she turned around, walked back to her Jeep and drove off.

Her forwardness embarrassed her and she felt stupid. With tear-filled eyes, she refused to look back at the man she had left alone with the remnant of her kiss upon his lips.

Clayton felt the sting of her words and the pain of remorse. The kiss between them had contained such passion that it left him weak. He wanted a relationship with Molly. He wanted a lifetime of those kisses, having her next to him in his bed so he could awake the rest of his mornings and watch the dawn light illuminate her flawless features. He knew that they would eventually be together, but not under these circumstances. She deserved more than that.

Chapter Forty Four

Evin believed in the old saying, "Kick 'em when they're down." And that was exactly what he planned to do. His whole life he had kept company with questionable characters and he had a long list of contacts, the types of men who would commit crimes for the right price. Personally, he never liked getting his hands dirty. He preferred to be the Rembrandt behind the masterpiece. He enjoyed playing the game, but when he played, it was for high stakes. He used hired men like game pieces, wagered on each move and then put it all in. He was now on the verge of putting it all in and he was ready to take the pot.

Evin had found out about a rancher who had the bad fortune of having a couple of his cattle contract mad cow disease. The ravaged beasts were roaming and living amongst hundreds of other unsuspecting heifers. Tests proved that the cows were definitely infected. The FDA had stepped in and ordered the whole herd destroyed. It was the worst nightmare for a cattle-man; or in Molly's case, cattlewoman.

As soon as Evin heard the story, the wheels began to turn. He made the necessary phone calls to implement his wrath upon the woman. He was able to pay off those he needed and got his hands on some of the sick cows. The hired men whom he'd flown in from New Jersey took a trailer, picked up the sickly cows, then scorched the cows' hides with the Ghost Bear brand and tagged their large ears with tags stolen from the ears of the prime cattle that thrived upon Molly's land.

The men drove the afflicted beasts onto the ranch and under the calm night sky unloaded the disease-ridden cows into Molly's herd.

SLOAN HAD WAITED long enough; he was ready to carry out his revenge and then get the hell out of the cold. He cared about nothing in this state. As he drove to the Ghost Bear, he stopped at several different gas stations, filled up cans of gasoline and put them in the back of his SUV.

He drove with the windows down, but the fumes overpowered him and gave him one of the best highs he had in years. Since it was late at night, he was able to sneak onto the ranch without too much worry. He drove quietly and left the main entrance to ride down a secondary road towards the house. He felt comfortable as he crept slowly along with his headlights off, as the sky was clear and the stars and moon lit a path. As he inched closer to his destination an image of himself played out like a movie reel inside his head. He was able to visualize the act of pouring the flammable liquid upon the houses and buildings. Striking a match, he would light up the night sky with a flame so large it would reach out and singe the stars while reducing every building to ash.

As Sloan neared the house he came upon a large herd of cattle. The gas fumes were becoming increasingly intoxicating inside the confinement of his car and he thought it might be best to stop and get out and breathe some fresh air. As he stepped out of the car, cattle surrounded him and provided excellent camouflage from anyone who might have been looking his way. The herd was so big it looked like a sea of black cows. A small calf approached. He stuck out his hand and the calf took its large tongue, wrapped it around his fingers, and began to suck.

"Are you hungry?" He asked the large brown-eyed creature.

As the cow suckled upon his hand, he suddenly began to get aroused. The calf continued its determined sucking. Sloan unzipped his pants and spoke to the unsuspecting animal. "It's been a long time since anyone has given me one of these."

While looking around he allowed his organ to hang from the front of his pants and led the animal's mouth to his erect member. The hungry calf sucked upon it as if it was her own mother's tit. Sloan had never felt anything like it. He was enjoying the pleasure that the poor creature was providing and failed to notice the large truck and trailer that had snuck up on him. He was quickly ready to fill the calf when voices with a New Jersey accent rang in his ears.

"Yo, Johnny, look what we found. It's a cow fucker. Can you believe this sick mother fucker?"

Johnny had walked around the truck, followed his friend's voice through the cows and stood next to his partner, who was a few feet from a man who had his dick shoved in a cow's mouth.

"You got that wrong, Tony. That ain't a cow fucker; this here is a cow sucker. What the fuck are you doing? Are you raping that cow?"

"Hell no, Johnny. He ain't raping that cow; that cow wants to suck on his little pecker. I heard about these cowboys. Don't you remember *Outback Mountain*? They fuck all sorts of things with each other: cows, sheep, pigs. You know, it doesn't matter to them; they just stick their pecker in it!"

Sloan was now trying to pull away from the calf, but she had such a tight hold on him that he was unable to free himself.

"Hey cow fucker, don't stop on our account! We'll just stand here and wait for you to finish up, then we'll kick your ass!"

In one last ditch effort to free himself, Sloan punched the little calf in the head and when it opened its mouth, he yanked himself away. In great pain, he yelped and zipped up his pants.

"Hey, I didn't mean any harm to your cows, I was just driving by." As Sloan slowly backed up to his car so he could try to make his escape the brawly men were on to him.

"Oh yeah? Well we don't like grown men taking advantage of God's creatures."

Sloan couldn't help but smirk as he heard those words coming from the three-hundred-pound Italian.

"What the hell are you smirking about, you little queer?"

Sloan didn't have time to respond, as Johnny reached out and with extraordinary agility for a man his size, grabbed a hold of Sloan's neck and snapped it like it was a small chicken bone. He then shook Sloan and watched as his lifeless head swung around.

"He looks like a damn bobble head," Johnny laughed as he let Sloan fall to the ground.

"Little bastard was trying to get his rocks off on the wrong night," said Eddie. "Since you killed him, Johnny, you take care of it. I'll let the cattle out."

Johnnie shrugged in agreement, picked up Sloan's dead body and carried him over to his SUV. He opened up the door to stuff Sloan behind the wheel when the strong mixture of gas fumes and horse shit about knocked him over. The smell was so bad that it kicked in his gag reflex.

"Fuck Eddie, get over here. Jesus, the car is loaded down with gas cans and there's animal shit all over the floor."

"What the fuck? Do I have to do everything? Go puke your goddamn brains out away from here. Hey, why did this guy have so much gas in his car anyway?"

Eddie unloaded the cans out of Sloan's car and began dousing the vehicle and Sloan's body.

"Hey dumb ass, you don't suppose the boss hired someone to torch the place up? Shit, I bet he did and you just took the fucker out!"

Johnnie stood next to Eddie dumbfounded. "How was I to know? He didn't say anything."

"Just help me get the rest of these cows out and then we'll light him up on the way out. Keep your fat mouth shut, and if the boss asks us, we'll tell him we don't know a thing. He'll think he hired a dumb ass who had an accident and burnt himself up, but in the meantime, we did our job."

Within minutes, the hired thugs had mixed the cows into the herd and thrown their burning cigarettes upon Sloan and the SUV.

They left feeling no remorse; they had done their job.

Chapter Forty Five

A SUBSTANTIAL BLACK SMOKE THAT REEKED WITH A MIXTURE OF BURNT rubber and burnt flesh strangled the fresh mountain air. The cattle had moved on to leave the car with Sloan's body to burn alone in the vast snowy field. Clayton and several of the men had woken early to begin their daily chores of feeding the livestock and running the ranch.

As soon as they stepped out into the cold morning air, they began to choke.

"Clay, what the hell is that?" One of the men shouted as he pointed towards one of the pastures. "Jesus, that smells awful!"

"I don't know. The field is covered with snow. There's nothing out there to burn like that except cattle."

Panic stricken, the men jumped to action and wildly drove towards the site.

Upon arrival, they were flabbergasted to find the burning remains of a torched vehicle. The stench of charred skin was overpowering and the men tied their bandanas around their heads to cover their noses.

"Oh my God, Clay, is that a human body behind the wheel of that car?"

"Yeah, I think it is!" Clayton had seen enough. He took his cell phone out of his pocket and called the sheriff, then Molly.

The shrill ring of the telephone abruptly awakened Molly. She had sensed something was wrong, jumped out of bed and answered it on the first ring. "What is it?"

"We've got a big problem. Have you been outside?" Surprised by her tone, Clayton assumed she had been awake for a while.

"No, you just woke me. What is it?"

"Get dressed and come outside. I'll be there in a minute. The sheriff's on his way. There is a car out in the front pasture and it looks like it has been burning pretty much most of the night; and it looks like there are human remains in the front seat."

Molly panicked. "What the hell? Who is it? Are all our workers accounted for? What sick person would do something like this to me after both my parents burned to death in a car crash?"

"I know, Molly. I did a headcount and all of the men are accounted for. Check to see if your guests are in the house and then come out."

Molly hung up the receiver. She pulled on a pair of sweatpants and the dirty sweatshirt that she had worked out in the night before and ran down the hall, knocking on each door checking to see if everyone was safely in their room. Relieved to hear their responses, she then ran downstairs and was ecstatic to see the motherly housekeeper in the kitchen.

"Miss Molly, I didn't want to wake you but there is a terrible smell outside. Are they burning something?" Rosie asked as she poured Molly some coffee.

"Yeah, something's burning, but it's okay. Clayton's aware of it and he has it under control. Thanks for the coffee, but I don't have time to drink it right now. Clayton is on his way and I need to get out there."

"Okay. Oh, looks like he's already here." Rosa threw Molly her coat. "It's cold out there; throw this on."

Molly ran out the door and jumped into the truck next to Clayton. "Everyone in the house is safe and sound. Who the hell do you think it is?"

"I don't know," Clayton replied. "The car is all burnt and there's not a whole hell of a lot left to the poor son of a bitch. Listen, this is not something I think you should see. I picked you up to drive you to town. I know the sheriff is going to ask us a lot of questions and I think it would be best if you weren't around here when they investigate."

Molly agreed with him; she wasn't sure how she would react seeing the burnt automobile and charred human remains. Just knowing it had happened on her ranch was horrible enough.

They drove through the gate as the fire trucks with sirens followed by police squad cars flew past them. As they drove to the police station, she thought it would be best to call the house and inform Phillip what was happening. She trusted him to inform everyone and asked him if he could go out and assist the police with anything they might need.

Clayton and Molly drank coffee and gave their statements to the police while forensic crews and the fire department were busy on the ranch looking for clues and hauling off the body and car. They had asked Phillip and some of the men who worked for Molly to keep the cattle out of that area and used yellow crime scene tape to mark off a large section of the field. Phillip observed the area closely and quickly spotted the tire tracks in the snow along with what looked like several cans that had contained gasoline.

"By the looks of these tire tracks it appears to me there was more than one car out here," Phillip spoke to Jack who was standing beside him looking nauseated. "Are you alright, Jack? Would you like to go back to the house?"

"No, no, I'm fine. When I agreed to come, I never expected so much." Jack replied in his thick French accent.

Phillip was surprised to see such a thorough investigation team for such a small town. He watched with increasing interest as they carefully searched the car and removed the melted body of the victim. It was the most ghastly thing he had ever seen. Jack could not stand to watch and turned his head.

The men put the crispy remains on the gurney when suddenly a charcoaled arm with a boney hand attached to it fell free. Around what was left of the person's wrist was a bracelet.

A shiver went down Phillip's spine all the way to his feet. "Wait. The item around the wrist, is it a bracelet?"

One of the men who wore protective clothing and rubber gloves replied. "It appears to be just that." He began to remove the bracelet and put it in a plastic bag.

Phillip held his breath as he spoke. "Will you look at the back of it; is there an inscription on it?"

The investigator turned it over and sure enough found the engraved inscription that read: *To Sloan, forever my love P.*

As the man read the words Phillip's face turned pale white as his knees buckled. "I might know who this is."

Everyone turned in shock and looked at Phillip. Seeing his response, Jack didn't even need to ask, as he too had a strong hunch as to the body's identity.

"I believe you'll find the car to be a rental registered to a Sloan Davis," said Phillip.

One of the detectives walked over to Phillip. "Mr. Madison, I will need you to come with me. I need to ask you more questions."

Phillip knew the routine all too well. With a shaken voice he replied, "I would be happy to help in any way, Officer." He turned to Jack. "Jack, could you please take the car back to the house. I will go with the officer and after I'm done I'll catch a ride back with Molly and Clayton.

"But Phillip, are you sure you wouldn't like me to come with you?" Jack spoke sympathetically. "I know you must be in shock."

"I'll be fine. I promise. Don't worry, I don't even know for sure that it's him. We won't know until they get the dental records." Phillip forced a smile and gave Jack a hug. "Now go on back to the house. I won't be too late."

Phillip sat next to the police officer with tear-filled eyes. He kept trying to tell himself that there was no way it could have been Sloan in that car, but he also knew that Sloan never took that bracelet off. The odds of someone stealing the bracelet and driving out to the Ghost Bear were slim to none. But even so, Phillip said a silent prayer to God that Sloan hadn't been stupid enough to compromise his life.

Molly and Clayton had been sitting in separate rooms recounting the morning's events when Phillip walked in and sat down with another detective.

Molly noticed that Phillip was visibly upset and she was finding it very difficult to give the police officer her full attention. "Excuse me, Officer, but why is my husband here? He seems to be really upset. Could you just check and see what's going on?" She tilted her head in a pleading look.

"Molly you know I wouldn't even be doing this if it weren't for your dad." The officer got up and shut the door behind him. He walked over and sat on the edge of the desk. His back facing her, she was unable to read his lips as she anxiously awaited his return.

"Molly, I'm going to be honest with you," said the sheriff, "A lot of shit has been happening around here since you came back."

Molly tried desperately to keep her cool, but she was starting to get pissed. "I know. There are a lot of people who haven't given me a warm welcome. So what is going on?"

"Your husband gave us a name on who was in the car. They're running a check and it looks like it could be the guy."

"What? Who the hell could it be? Phillip doesn't know anyone who lives out here."

"The guy isn't from here. He's from Tampa, Florida. His name is Sloan Davis."

Molly almost fell out of her seat as soon as the officer said Sloan's name. "Oh my God! I don't believe it. Are they sure?"

"Well we won't be positive until the dental records come back, but it looks like he flew in a week ago and was staying at one of the hotels in the next town over. Molly, I need to know how you know this man and what type of relationship did you have with him?"

Molly was stunned and didn't like where this was going. "He worked for my husband and I didn't have any relationship with the man."

"Do you have any idea what he was doing out at your place? Were you expecting him?"

"No, I didn't even know that he was in town."

Molly's answers were brief. She was scared that if she told the police the truth they'd arrest her on suspicion of murder, as she did have a motive to kill him.

After Molly, Clayton and Phillip finished their inquisitions, they walked out of the station in a daze. None of them had any idea what to expect next.

As they drove home Molly looked at Phillip and asked, "Phillip, do you think that Sloan did that to himself?"

Phillip put his arm around Molly. "I don't know, Molly, but I'm really sorry that I was ever mixed up with that man."

Chapter Forty Six

THE NEXT DAY WHEN EVIN CAME INTO HIS OFFICE THERE WAS SUCH A BUZZ that all of his agents were unable to concentrate on their work.

"What the hell is going on?" He asked.

One of his agents was sitting like a peacock grinning from ear to ear. "Haven't you heard?"

"No, so spill the beans." He knew that wouldn't be a problem for her as she was ready to explode.

"Well yesterday I got this call and you know I'm not suppose to talk about it, but anyway the whole town is going to know soon enough."

Evin could not keep his eyes off her turkey neck as it jiggled when she talked and resembled a second mouth.

"You all know that my brother works for the force, right?"

"God yes, we all know it; you like to remind us daily." Evin rolled his eyes as he kept staring at her double chin. "Get on with it. I have shit to do."

"Okay, Okay. Anyway, my brother got called out to the Ghost Bear and you will never believe what they found when they got there." She stopped with her eyes and mouth wide. "Well guess."

"Oh for Christ's sake, I have no idea. Tell us already."

"Well, it was a car planted right in the middle of one of their pastures and it was on fire."

Evin and the group began booing and hissing, disappointed by her boorish babble. "Oh big shit. Who the hell cares if one of their cars was on fire."

"No, no, I didn't tell you the best part," she said, gloating that she had their undivided attention. "There was a body that was burnt up inside the car!"

The crowd in the room went wild. People throughout the room were throwing out questions faster than the woman could respond.

"Holly shit, are you serious?"

"Oh my God, who was it? Was it anyone we know?"

"Jesus, isn't that how Gavin and Addie died?"

"Yes, that's right. Holy shit. Did Molly see the body?"

"Well I don't think it's anyone we know," the chubby woman replied. "Everyone who lives out there was accounted for, but Molly's husband. You know who he is, right? The one that is staying out there and rumor has it he's gay. Well he was standing there when suddenly he stepped up and out of the blue announced he thought he knew who it was!"

Evin couldn't believe what he was hearing. "That's unbeliev-able. I hope those people finally get what they deserve and the sheriff locks the bunch of them up! Now everyone, get back to selling houses!"

Evin felt like he was walking on air as he went back to his office. "Damn! I can't believe my luck! Enough shit happens to that woman on her own. Just wait until all her cattle are gone. Hell, I'll be able to low ball her even more. She'll be begging me to take that land off her hands."

He decided he'd do some early celebrating. Even though it was only ten a.m., he decided it wouldn't hurt to have a drink. He took the key out of his pocket and unlocked the bottom drawer of his filing cabinet where he kept his favorite bottle of scotch hidden. He removed the bottle along with a short glass. After he filled the glass he took a long sip taking his time to enjoy the flavor of his drink.

Suddenly a woman with a sexy southern drawl opened the door and stepped into the room. "Buy me a drink handsome?"

"Well that depends. Are you staying long?" Evin replied.

"Long enough to join you. You know, you should never drink alone; you could develop a bad habit."

"Well then, please by all means."

Evin went to the cabinet and pulled out another glass. He sat it in front of the southern dame. She held the crystal glass in her hand while she swirled her finger in her drink. She then removed her long finger and placed it to her lips while suggestively sucking the beverage from it.

"Are you going to drink it or play with it?" He asked, leaning forward and resting his elbows on his desk.

"I like to savor my scotch and my men."

While staring directly into Evin's eyes, she took a large gulp of the golden liquid, then set the glass down as she licked her lips.

Wanting to get to business, Evin regained his composure and sat up straight. "Okay, as much as I like the show, would you like to tell me who you are and what I can do for you?"

"At this point and time I'd prefer not to use names. I am interested in possibly making an investment in some land and

I heard you're the man. And from where I'm sitting I'd have to say you certainly are." She smiled seductively at the handsome man.

Evin pointed at the large rock sitting on her ring finger. "Well, who prefers to be nameless and who is obviously very married, what and where are you exactly looking for?"

"A man who is observant as well as handsome. Let's not focus on the married part, shall we? And as far as what I'm looking for, I think I might have found it. Or are you talking about what I want to buy?"

She stood up, walked over to Evin and leaned against his desk. She reached down and plucked a piece of lint from the crotch of his pants. "You had a piece of lint." She could see the rise she was getting and she smiled.

Evin wasn't sure who she was or where this woman had come from but he liked what he was seeing and he privately thanked God for sending her his way. He tried to play it cool as he was enjoying their little cat and mouse game. "Well, my mysterious woman, I understand you're in a quandary and obviously your needs are not being met. You've found the perfect man for the job." He boldly moved his hand to her leg and rubbed the top of her thigh.

She jumped to attention. "Sir what kind of woman do you take me for!" She spoke loudly and moved back to her seat.

Evin was dumbfounded. "Excuse me. I have quite a few tracts of land for sale. How large of a piece were you wanting?"

Enjoying the game she raised an eyebrow. "I was thinking a large piece. Why don't you show me what you have."

Evin was confused but intrigued by the woman who sat across from him. "Finish your drink. Let me grab my coat and let's go for a drive. I can't wait to show you what I have."

"Bring the bottle," she replied.

Chapter Forty Seven

CLAYTON HAD NEVER ASKED MOLLY AS TO HOW SHE HAD LEARNED THE truth about Phillip's sexuality and freed herself from the illusion that he had been a loyal husband; he figured that if she needed to talk about it, she would have elaborated on the details. Since she didn't and he didn't ask, naturally he was surprised when he found out that the sick bastard cremated inside the rental car was the evasive answer to Molly's disintegrated marriage.

But Clayton was not the only one stunned by the discovery. Phillip had sobbed uncontrollably as Jack tried to do his best at consoling him. Molly's nerves were shot from listening to Phillip's remorse over a man who in her mind was equivocal to a home-wrecking whore who rejoiced over telling her that her husband was gay and that he had been the one having an illicit affair with him. Hadn't Sloan harmed her enough? Had he flown all the way out to Montana and deliberately driven to her ranch to further torture her?

Clayton could see that Molly was trying her best to hold it together, but he was concerned that she might break. He was also surprised that even Molly's opinionated friend Leeza had been somewhat sullen over the news. Although she made it known that she had hated Sloan, Leeza was very concerned over the fact that the man who had burned up in a vehicle mocked the tragic accident of Molly's parents.

Clayton spoke to Leeza of the problems the ranch had been having before she arrived. He gave her all the details except about Gavin's affair and the possible harm that could come from the foolish man's actions.

It appeared to Clayton that unfortunate events were occurring daily and he was finding it harder to protect Molly. He knew he couldn't do anything to make her feel better or change what had happened, but he could keep working on finding out the identity of Beverly's daughter so as to prevent a cataclysm of disaster. It was apparent to him that if Gavin's illegitimate child were to raise her ugly head now, it could be the final blow for Molly. The poor woman had been through more than anyone should have to go through and he would make it his mission to ensure that the truth never came out.

Clayton was fortunate to have kept his past behind him. He knew what it meant to have secrets; everyone had secrets. Over the years of living on the ranch, he never had to use any of his resources. He had always enjoyed the serenity and seclusion that the Ghost Bear had offered, but now with so much suspicion by the police focused on him, he needed quick answers and he didn't have the time nor did he dare to play the detective.

He called his contacts, the men whom he had sworn he would never see again, and they rushed to his aid without question. It would be no problem for them to trace the whereabouts of the elusive girl. His prior associates had resources that he did not have. He knew it would take them only a couple of days to give him a heads up on whether the girl was still alive and if so, where she was.

He knew the woman would be grown and close to Molly's age, but the image of the small tattered child left an impression in his head. He pulled out the untraceable cell phone that he had asked his associates to bring with them at the meeting that Molly had interrupted. He was not about to take any chances, as he knew that he was the number one suspect for many of the recent crimes. The odds that they would run a trace on his cell records as well as tap his home phone were more than likely. He dialed the number that he had memorized years before.

An Arabic-accented voice answered.

"Do you have it?" Clayton asked.

"Of course we have it. Are you ready?"

"Go ahead."

"She changed her identity; new name; lives in Tampa, Florida. I'll text you what we have on her. Now, we did what you asked. Are you ready to do what we've asked of you?"

"Tell him not to worry. I'll do it, but I need you to do one more thing for me."

Clayton relayed the specifics to his foreign associate then hung up the phone. He waited a minute before the cell phone informed him that he had a closed text.

"Okay, let's find out where you live and who the hell you are." He opened the text to anxiously read the information for which he had traded. "Jesus, help us!" The surprising news socked him in the gut and nearly knocked him over.

Clayton knew that they were all in grave danger. He would have to handle the situation very carefully as it could be a matter of life or death.

Chapter Forty Eight

THE WOMAN JUMPED IN THE TRUCK NEXT TO EVIN. HE PULLED OUT OF THE parking lot and headed out of town.

"So, I'm thinking I would like a large parcel, remote with maybe a small cabin on it," she said as she looked through the papers that contained written addresses.

"Well, you came to the right place, because that pretty much describes every listing I have. What price range?"

"Oh, I hate to limit myself by putting a price on anything, don't you agree?" She smiled. "If it's what you like then the price of something shouldn't stop you from getting it."

"At least it doesn't stop me."

"I'm sure it doesn't."

Evin wasn't quite sure what to think of this woman, but he was intrigued and distracted. "I have a couple of places in mind I would like to take you to, on a secluded mountain lake, gorgeous views and extremely remote."

"Are they currently occupied?"

"The owner uses the place in the summer; he lives out East. Typical story. Husband buys it and the wife hates it, so he's selling. So to answer your question, it's vacant."

"Good. Is it furnished?" She asked.

"Fully furnished."

"How's the bed?" She asked, turning to look at him.

Evin tried to keep his eyes on the road. Keeping his composure and playing along, he answered, "I'm not sure. Like I said it's very remote and I've never been on the bed. But I think it's a good idea that you try it out before you make an offer."

She took hold of Evin's free hand and placed it inside her shirt upon her bare breast. "Oh, I'm a firm believer in testing it out," she swooned.

"You are firm."

She paid close attention to where the man was driving, though unbeknownst to him, she was already familiar with the area. The cabin was set back off from the main road, hidden amongst giant pine trees. He parked the car and with a skip in his step, he opened her car door, allowing her to emerge and join him. Even though the weather had once again turned cold, Evin was beginning to perspire from the building passion that was erupting inside of him.

After fiddling with the lock box and retrieving the key, he opened the door allowing his temptress to go before him.

"It's freezing in here." She wrapped her arms around herself as she watched him flick on the light switches.

Evin turned on a dime, grabbed her into his arms and pried her mouth open with his tongue. "I'll warm you."

She pulled herself away. "Hey, slow down. Who's rushing? Show me that bed."

Feeling victorious Evin grabbed her hand, turned his back and began to lead her to their final rendezvous. He hadn't gone but a half of step when she tugged at his arm.

"Hey, come on." He turned towards her only to realize that she held a lamp in her free hand, just before she smashed it over his head.

Evin awoke abruptly as water was being doused in his face, completely confused as to why he was handcuffed to the bed frame. "What the hell?" He sputtered. "Why am I tied to this headboard?"

"Don't worry. We are going to play a little game," she chanted.

His checks were red with anger. "Oh yeah, well I'm not playing, so untie me."

"You're a very naughty boy, aren't you Evin?"

"Fuck you! Who the hell are you?"

"Now see here asshole, you don't get it do you? I ask the questions and you answer. It's very simple, but I think I have to show you what happens when you don't answer."

She put the towel that she had found in the small linen closet over Evin's face.

"You know, lately there has been such controversy over water boarding. I really don't see what the big deal is, do you?" She retrieved the garden hose that she now had hooked to the bathroom facet. She kinked the hose in her right hand and turned the cold water on as high as it would go with her left. "Sometimes drastic events call for drastic action, don't you agree?"

"Screw you lady!" He screamed out, unable to see where she stood.

"Some assholes just deserve what they get!" She unkinked the hose and let the water flow freely over Evin's face. She kept the water running for several minutes, letting Evin feel the full effects of drowning.

"Now," she spoke again, "I think I asked you if you've been a naughty boy?" She kinked the hose to stop the flow of water.

Choking and coughing Evin replied, "Who the fuck are you? Do you think I'm going to let you get away with this shit!"

She once again unkinked the hose and began soaking his covered face. "Wrong answer. So as I was saying, I personally feel water boarding is a much better form of torture than, oh I don't know, like maybe pulling someone's finger nails out with pliers."

In between choking and crying Evin begged her to stop, but she kept on.

"Well, I don't know about you but I hope you…" The cell phone in her purse began to ring. "Hold on. I need to get this." While holding the hose in one hand, she flipped open her phone with the other. "Hello?" She sweetly spoke. "Hey, it's okay. You can bother me anytime. What's up?" She looked down at Evin who now wasn't moving.

Holding the cell phone against her neck, she again kinked the hose, and peeked under the soaking towel to discover her victim had passed out. "Oh you know honey, I've been so busy. I'm sorry I haven't called to check in." While talking to her husband on the phone, she began slapping Evin hard in the face trying to revive him.

"Listen love, I'm in the middle of something right now, let me give you a call later, okay?"

Evin awoke and began yelling. Once again she covered his face and turned the water on him.

"Kiss, kiss. Love you, too."

Aggravated by her husband's call, the woman was no longer in the mood, and she became bored of her game. She once again kinked the hose and went into the bathroom to shut the water off. When she returned to the bedroom she observed the full-grown, six-foot bully, lying on the soaked bed. She removed the heavy towel from his face. He was fully awake and gasping for breath, whimpering and sniveling like a baby.

"Okay, I'm going to tell you what I think. You're an asshole through and through. You see, you do terrible things to people, and yes, I know what you're thinking. So do I. But you see there is a big difference between us. You do it for the money and I do it because they deserve it! Ever hear the saying you reap what you sow?"

Evin didn't answer. He was completely terrified of this woman.

"Well anyway, I think you get the idea." The woman put her face only inches from his. As she spoke her southern accent vanished. "And one last thing; as to who I am? Just call me your worst nightmare and I'm the one who will hunt you down and cut your nuts off if you ever tell anyone of our little game!"

She reached inside Evin's pocket and pulled out his keys and cell phone. "Here is your cell. You figure out how to use it." She laid his cell on his chest. "I'll leave your truck at the agency. I'm driving it back."

"Bitch, you can't just leave me like this. It's freezing. When I get loose I'm coming for you!" Evin snarled.

"If you value any part of your pathetic life, I wouldn't make threats to a crazy woman while handcuffed to a bed and in such a vulnerable position."

She wasn't worried that Evin would contact the police, as she knew that his ego was too big to let anyone know that a woman could put him in such a compromising situation. She walked out of the house, put the key back in the lock box and drove off to retrieve her car.

Chapter Forty Nine

MOLLY WAS HOME WITH PHILLIP AND JACK WHEN THE SHERIFF CALLED with the news and had asked that everyone stay in the area. There were too many unanswered questions in the murder of Sloan Davis. Molly felt that Sloan was reaching out from beyond and selfishly manipulating their lives with his revenge one last time.

The police had raided the room in which Sloan had been staying and confiscated all of his personal belongings for evidence. It appeared that he had kept a small diary documenting his habitual hostility and animosity towards Phillip and Molly. He had flown all the way from Florida to Montana to execute his revenge and now his victim's characters were under suspicion.

"His neck was broken. Someone had to have killed him," Phillip spoke as he sat next to Jack and Molly at dinner. "I feel that this is entirely my fault."

"Why? Did you break his neck?" Molly scornfully asked.

"No, I didn't break his neck! Did you?" Phillip defensively replied.

"Well after he spilled the beans that he was screwing my husband, believe me, I fantasized about breaking more than his neck, but no, I didn't do it and I definitely would not be stupid enough to set his car on fire while it was parked on my land! Phillip, someone is trying to set us up, just like they did with Clayton"

Clayton then walked into the room. "What did someone do to me? Sorry I'm late." He sat down at the table and began to pile up his plate.

"The sheriff called," Molly snarled. "Seems that he thinks one of us broke Sloan's neck and set his car on fire."

Clayton stopped scooping the potatoes while holding the spoon in mid-air. "Did he say that?"

"No, he didn't say that, only that he suggests that we stay around," Phillip replied glaring at Molly.

"So, his neck was broken. Was he dead before the fire?" Clayton asked.

"Dead as a door knob," Rosa spoke up as she sat down. "If you ask me, he got what he deserved. What was he doing out here?"

"Maybe he came to apologize," Phillip piped up.

"Phillip, you know that wasn't the case," Molly protested. "The police found his journal. He wanted revenge. He was a conniving asshole, and I'm sorry, but I really can't feel sorry for the man."

Clayton glanced around the table. "Well, I think the big concern for all of us is what the hell happened to him? It doesn't make any of us look good."

Jack had been sitting quietly, taking stock over the dinner conversation, then finally spoke up. "Phillip, I know that right now you feel guilty and keep thinking that if you would have handled things differently none of this would have happened. The fact is that Sloan had many problems and it isn't going to help or change anything by you beating yourself up over it. What you did or didn't do doesn't matter. We need to stick together."

"Speaking of sticking together, where is Leeza?" Clayton asked.

"Oh, she's on her way back," Molly spoke. "I called her earlier and told her the latest news."

"How did she react?" Clayton asked.

"Just as surprised as the rest of us? Molly had picked up on something in Clayton's tone. "Why?"

"Just curious," Clayton replied. His cell phone rang. "Excuse me. It's one of the hands."

Clayton removed himself from the table and proceeded to the kitchen. Molly could hear bits and pieces of the conversation and it didn't sound good. Clayton then returned and apologized that he needed to go and check on the cattle.

"God, now what?" Molly's eyes followed Clayton as he put his hat on and headed to the door.

"One of the men thought a couple of the cows were acting funny. I'm sure it's nothing. Finish your dinner and I'll let you know if we have any reason for concern." He said his goodnights and ventured out.

"Molly, you really are lucky to have that man working for you," Phillip said. "I sure am."

CLAYTON TOOK ONE look at the sick cows and knew instantly that they would have to be put down. He took the revolver from his holster and shot the suffering beasts square in the eyes.

"Clay, is it what I think it is?" Asked one of the old timers. He already knew the answer to the question before he had even asked it.

"Could be." Clayton's nerves were shot. "I don't want anyone to say anything to Molly, got it? Check the feed. We grow and process our own feed. If those cows have the disease they didn't catch it from eating the grain we gave them. I also want the rest of the cattle checked out. Get rid of these two."

"Shouldn't we call someone out here and check them out?" Asked one of the younger cowhands.

"No. I'm not about to let the whole herd be destroyed until I know for sure if the food was contaminated or if it's spread to the other cows. If more come down sick then we have a problem."

Clayton handed out the orders then drove back to his house. He knew that he didn't have a choice but to contact the law. He pulled his truck in front of his house, opened his window and dialed the sheriff. "Bill, it's Clayton. Hey I wanted to let you know that we had some sick cows out here. It looks like it could be mad cow, but the funny thing is that they were in the pasture where Sloan was found."

Clayton knew Bill was a reasonable man who did not like trouble in his town. Yet lately there had been a hell of a lot of it. "Really. That's interesting. It may not be anything but bad luck, and let me tell you lately it seems that anyone who comes in contact with that ranch has had their share of it. But we definitely had a second set of tracks out by Sloan Davis's car. We already checked out the tracks on all of the vehicles out at your place and none of them matched. It also looked like it was a truck with a large trailer behind it. Clayton, I'm starting to think that you guys are being set up out there. Could have been that the poor son of a bitch was out there on the wrong night and was a witness." Bill felt relieved. He felt that finally the puzzle pieces were falling into place.

"That's what I'm thinking, Bill. I think you need to go out to Evin's office and give him a talk. He's been really hounding Molly to sell out to him and he actually had the deal lined up with her husband until she left him and came back. I have a strong hunch that he might be behind all this. There's also one more thing. I need to talk to you about Beverly's daughter. She's alive and we may have another big problem."

Clayton knew that time was running out and he would have to come clean with everything he knew, otherwise Molly's life could be at risk.

"Do you think Phillip Madison could be in on this whole thing?" Bill mused. "He sure had a reason to kill Sloan; the man cost him his wife and the profit from that ranch. He doesn't seem like the type of guy to roll over so quickly."

"I know that it seems like he would be a suspect, but I've been around the man, and he is pretty shaken up. I don't believe he's acting. Phillip signed the divorce papers. He's not fighting anything, and doesn't seem to want any part of the ranch or Molly's money. I think he's on the up and up. He's in a new relationship and wants a fresh start. He's not stupid enough to risk what he has left; but I do have a clue who might. How about I come in and we can talk privately sometime tomorrow afternoon. It's been awhile since I've flown over the ranch and gotten a good look at the whole place. I want to make sure everything looks okay. I've got the plane tied down in one of the barns. I'll leave at daybreak and be back by noon."

"Sounds good; it should be a nice day. Be careful up there."

Clayton had just hung the phone up and shut the door to his truck, when out of nowhere Leeza appeared with Molly's dog. "My God, Leeza, you scared the shit out of me! Where the hell did you come from?" He asked as he stepped back from her.

"Oh sorry, Clayton. I just thought I'd take the dog for a walk. I didn't want to interrupt your conversation. So I missed all the excitement today?" She asked as she placed her hand on the neck of Clayton's coat and gently rubbed the collar.

He reached out for Leeza's hand and removed it. "I guess you did. Molly told me that she filled you in on all the details. Where were you today?"

She cocked her head to one side. "Why? Did you miss me?"

Clayton rolled his eyes and didn't respond. He walked into his house, leaving her standing alone with Sedona.

Leeza looked up at the sky, then down at the large dog, its ears raised with an inquisitive expression upon its furry face.

"Come on Sedona, let's take our walk."

Chapter Fifty

CLAYTON STEPPED OUTSIDE, BREATHING THE FRESH MOUNTAIN AIR INTO his expanding lungs. He raised his favorite mug full of strong coffee to his lips and while appreciating its aroma slowly sipped at the dark liquid. He loved to fly and it was a perfect morning for it. The air was brisk and clear, making the visibility very good; he would have no problem inspecting the property.

Sedona lazily lay upon the porch and Clayton said his good mornings to the slumbering pet. "What's wrong, girl, are you still worn from your walk last night?"

Clayton lovingly patted the top of her head and Sedona responded in agreement by a brief wag of her enormous tail.

Leaving Sedona to continue her nap, Clayton jumped into his truck and drove over to the large barn-like structure where he currently stored his plane. Retrieving his Thermos and placing it inside the aircraft, he untied the aircraft and did his safety inspection. All looked good and he jumped inside and revved up the engine. Within no time, he was accelerating down the private runway and lifting up in the air. Just for fun, he buzzed past the house, giving everyone their morning wakeup call and then zipping on to the back half of the ranch, which entailed navigating some treacherous mountain terrain.

Molly heard the buzzing of a plane over the house and smiled, as she knew that it was Clayton doing what he loved to do best. She was still embarrassed over the fact that she had foolishly come on to him only for them to passionately kiss and then have him coldly reject her. The feelings she had for him were obviously much stronger than his were and whenever she saw him, she had wished that she could taste his lips again. She sighed as she couldn't help but wonder if she would ever find a man who would fall madly in love with her, as the chances were slim finding that man living on the Ghost Bear.

"Maybe I'm destined for heartache and I'm romantically twisted!" She sighed as she tidied up her room.

"Oh yeah? Well, girlfriend, join the club." Leeza stood in her doorway with her hands upon her hips. "Was that your cowboy who buzzed the house and woke me up?"

"Well, I wouldn't call him my cowboy, but I do pay him, and yes it was him." Feeling depressed, Molly plopped down upon her bed and started to cry.

Leeza walked over to her friend, put her arms around her and pulled her next to her. "Hey, what are you crying for?"

"That's a silly question to ask me, don't you think? Look at the mess my life is in. I came out here to give myself a fresh start and look at what has happened!" Molly took the tissue that Leeza held out for her and blew her nose.

"Oh come on, Molly, I know everything seems bad right now, but I promise it's going to get better. You just have to hang in there. Don't give up. Fight!" Leeza held Molly's face in her hands as she talked. "I'm here for you, aren't I?" She asked her friend as she pulled another tissue out of the box and handed it to her.

Molly took the offering. "Thanks Leeza. You really have been great and I'm sorry that your vacation had to turn out like this. You know, I really don't know if I'm capable of running this ranch. And I really miss my daughter."

"Don't be silly. It's in your blood. This ranch is a part of you. If you miss Savanna, fly back to Florida and visit or have her come out here. Isn't she coming out with her husband at Christmas?

"That's the plan," Molly smiled slightly.

"Okay. What else is it?" Leeza asked.

"It's Clayton. Leeza, I really like him. God, I sound like I'm ten." Molly clasped her hands in her lap and lowered her head.

"Well I can certainly understand what you like about him. He's completely scrumptious. But Molly, he's not the one," Leeza said bluntly.

Molly lifted her head and looked at her friend. "Really? Why do you say that?"

"He's a player."

"Clayton? Clayton Leatherbe, a player?" Molly's tears had dried and now she was leaning away from her friend as if she had no idea who she was.

Leeza looked at Molly as if she couldn't believe that she didn't already know this. "Yup. That is what I said, a player, a man who is a habitual womanizer."

Molly squinted her eyes as she leaned farther away from her friend. "Now what on earth did he do to make you think that?"

"He made a pass at me. Why are you looking at me that way?"

Molly's mouth hung open and repeated the words as if she had not heard correctly. "Clayton Leatherbe made a pass at you?"

"That's what I said," Leeza spoke as she pretended to remove lint from Molly's bedspread.

"When?" Molly asked skeptically.

"Last night."

"How?"

"He kissed me when I took the dog for a walk," Leeza stated without giving any details.

"You took the dog for a walk and you're telling me that Clayton just grabbed a hold of you and kissed you?" Molly asked dumbfounded.

"Well not like that. He was on the phone and I sort of startled him, and we were talking and he made a pass at me. Next thing I know he's got his tongue down my throat," Leeza boldly embellished.

"Are you sure? I mean, it just doesn't sound like Clayton." Molly was shocked by what she was hearing.

"Of course I'm sure. I wasn't going to say anything, but I just don't want you falling for a man that is obviously not the right one. Well, I had better go take my shower. Molly, don't worry. Give yourself some time and the right man will eventually come around."

Leeza gave her friend a kiss on the cheek and left her room.

The inconceivable notion that Clayton would have the slightest sexual interest in her friend stunned Molly. She had recalled Clayton asking about Leeza's whereabouts the night before at dinner. The more Molly reflected on Clayton's actions towards Leeza, the more it made sense that he would have rebutted their own kiss. It was becoming more clear that she was not a good judge of character when it came to the men in her life and she had better just keep them at arm's length.

Chapter Fifty One

Clayton felt free as he flew over the mountaintops; he didn't get to fly as often as he liked these days, but when he did, it was the perfect remedy to cure whatever was ailing him. As he soared through the air, he beheld the stunning landscape that lay below. Everything looked good so he decided to venture a little further out towards the more rugged peaks. A blanket of snow covered the giant mountains, making the large herds of migrating elk easier to spot. He followed the herd with enthusiasm.

Suddenly his small aircraft began to sputter. He had glanced down at his fuel gage to discover that it read empty. "What the hell?"

He knew instantly that he must have had a ruptured line and he was in deep trouble. He didn't have much time so he began scaling the area for a place to bring the plane down when suddenly the roar of the engines went eerily silent. He was out of time. There was nothing he could do except hold onto the steering column and fiercely try to glide the plane down. The treetops flew past him, their branches grabbing hold of his plane, shredding it to pieces as he plunged to the ground with compelling force, jolting every bone in his body. He had hit his head, which knocked him unconscious, as his craft had disintegrated around him only to leave a trail of metal debris.

Clayton abruptly awoke from his unconscious state with confusion. He did not know where he was or how he had gotten there. He tried to move his arm to unbuckle the seat that held him captive, when he felt excruciating pain shoot down his arm. With his right arm crippled he used his left arm to do the job of releasing himself from the seat. He kicked what was left of the door, allowing himself to fall out of the wreckage and into the snow. He quickly regained his wits as the details of the crash replayed in his mind. He slowly tried to stand only to fall forward in tormenting pain, passing out once again.

THE MORNING SUN had risen high in the sky and turned into a spectacular afternoon. Unfortunately, Molly had spent most of it speculating over Leeza's comments about Clayton. No matter how hard she tried to picture him being the dog that her friend claimed he was, it was just inconceivable. After long consideration, she decided that when Clayton got home she would confront him and ask if Leeza's claims were substantiated or just fabrication. She knew that whether she wanted to hear it or not he would tell her the truth.

Molly glanced at the clock. "Where the heck is he?"

The clock claimed that it was one o'clock in the afternoon. Clayton had been gone since daybreak. It wasn't like him to be gone so long and not to call in.

She was beginning to worry when the phone rang. *Thank God*, she thought as she picked up the phone, expecting to hear Clayton's voice.

"Mrs. Madison?"

"Yes, this is she." She was disappointed that it wasn't Clayton, but alarmed as she recognized the sheriff's voice.

"This is Sheriff Bill. Is Clayton there?"

"No, I'm sorry Bill, he's not back yet." She was unable to hide the growing concern in her voice. "I was getting a little worried about him. He's usually back by now and he usually checks in."

"I understand. He said that he would be back by noon. He was supposed to meet me at the station so we could talk. I understand that you had found a couple of diseased cows."

Molly was taken by surprise being that Clayton hadn't mentioned anything of the kind. "He told you that we had some cows with mad disease? Do you mean mad cow disease?"

She hoped she had misunderstood him.

"Yes. Didn't you know? I'm surprised that he didn't say anything to you about it," the sheriff replied.

"Me, too, especially since it's my ranch and that is something I should definitely be aware of." Molly began to think that maybe Clayton wasn't as honest as she had hoped that he was.

"He called me yesterday evening informing me that they found the sick cows in with the herd that was near where the fire was. He thought it appeared suspicious because there were only two that had been sick out of the whole herd. We found a second set of tracks in that field that likely belonged to a heavy pickup truck towing a large trailer behind it. We suspect that someone had brought the sick cows in hoping to mix them with the rest of the herd and cause you a few more headaches."

"Like I need any more headaches," Molly complained.

"I'm sure he was going to say something to you, but he probably wanted to talk to me first. The bright side out of this is that we finally have an answer as to how Mr. Davis got his neck broke." The sheriff was trying to give Molly some good news.

"And how do you think that happened?" Molly asked.

"Well, we think that by the looks of it, he could have just been at the wrong place at the wrong time. Also, Clayton had mentioned something about finding Beverly's daughter. By any chance did he mention anything to you?"

"No, not a word. I'm really starting to feel a little embarrassed that an employee of mine is more informed of pertinent details than I am," Molly remarked.

"It seems to me that Clayton Leatherbe might be a little more than just some hired hand of yours, the way he's running around and watching out after your wellbeing. I think he views you as more than just his boss. I wouldn't be so hard on the man until you get all the details from him."

The fatherly advice from the sheriff touched Molly's heart, as she had given up on the hope that Clayton did have stronger feelings than he had led her to believe. "I'm sure you're right, Sheriff. I shouldn't be so hard on him, but I am concerned that he isn't back yet."

"Let's give it another hour, Molly. If we don't hear from him, I'll send a search plane out. Don't worry. I'm sure he's on his way back in."

Bill tried to quiet the poor woman's fears, although he felt she was right to be worried. As soon as he hung up, he made some phone calls ordering up a couple of planes to begin searching.

THE WARMTH OF the afternoon glow was now making a downward descent, causing the temperature to drop. Clayton had again awoke from his unconscious state and shivered uncontrollably from the rapid loss of his inner body heat due to being unconscious for hours in the snow and being exposed to the elements.

He knew by the sun's placement above him and the dark shadows that had fallen on the thick forest floor that he had to begin preparations for surviving the night. He slowly moved his body. He knew that his left arm had been busted up, but, although bruised, the rest of his limbs were in working condition. He removed the belt from around his waist, and making a sling for his broken arm, he searched around the wreckage to see what he could salvage and be able to utilize for the night.

"Okay, Clayton, you only need to make it through tonight and tomorrow morning. Then you can start to hike down," he cheered himself on.

He had a pretty good idea where he had crashed and knew that he would be spending the night barricading himself inside what was left of the cockpit of his plane. He was not about to become the tasty dinner of a hungry mountain lion.

Clayton inspected the wreckage and found his Thermos, which still contained his morning coffee, and close by he found his compass and map. He then gathered up some sticks to build a warm fire. He needed to regain his body temperature if he expected to have any chance of surviving the frigid night.

The forest was quickly becoming dark and within no time Clayton was warming his battered body by the flames of the fire's warmth. The night air was frigid. He kept his back pressed against the plane wreckage where he would be sleeping. Wolf packs had always been a big nuisance and now as he sat quietly he could hear their harrowing cries.

He warmed the coffee and sipped it gratefully, thanking God for making it through the crash. By the light of the fire, he pulled his map from his coat pocket and with his trusty compass he plotted his course down the mountain. He was fairly high up and the snow was deep, but with the help from the pair of snowshoes that he always kept in his plane, he knew that he could make it down the mountain. He folded the map and tucked it safely back in his pocket.

The ritual howls of the wolves grew closer. He stoked the fire higher, unable to see through the blanket of black that surrounded him. Although the broken bones in his arm throbbed, he would have to try and get some rest as he would need all of his strength in the morning.

Molly spent the rest of the afternoon planted in front of the window of the house desperately hoping to hear the roar of Clayton's plane heading to the landing strip, but the day ended and night fell upon them with no trace of him.

She could wait no longer and picked up the phone. "Bill, something terrible had to have happened; he still is not back." The anguish in Molly's voice was like no other.

"Molly, I've had search planes out all afternoon, and they just came back in. They haven't seen anything. Keep the faith; they're heading back out at first light."

She hung up the phone and with her head raised high she prayed for God to bring Clayton Leatherbe back to her.

Chapter Fifty Two

CLAYTON HAD SURVIVED THE BITTER COLD AND THE SUN'S RAYS WERE NOW peeking through the trees. The pain in his arm was excruciating and he had slept very little. He gathered up what little supplies he was able to salvage and strapped the snowshoes upon his feet. He looked back one final time and bowed his head in a sympathetic gesture to his dead aircraft. He then took a symbolic piece of metal and strapped it to his back; he thought he might put it to good use by utilizing it for a sled. He then began the perilous journey.

For Molly, sleep was unattainable. She couldn't imagine anyone surviving a night alone out in Montana's bitter cold, especially if they were hurt. She called the sheriff at the first sign of light and received confirmation that the search was already underway. Bill told Molly to stay put. He had his best men out and he was sure that they would find Clayton.

She was sure that he would be found, but in what tormented state?

Phillip and Jack tried their best to comfort her but their efforts were fruitless. She had relayed the detective's earlier news that it had appeared that they had been cleared from the suspicion of Sloan's murder and Phillip was free to make the necessary arrangements to fly the incinerated body of his friend back to Florida for a proper burial. Phillip and Jack were thrilled with the good news but abstained from reacting too ecstatically, as Phillip was well aware that Molly was afflicted with the added anxiety over Clayton's disappearance.

"Molly, maybe I should stay here with you," said Phillip. "I can make the arrangements for Sloan by phone. I'm sure that Jack wouldn't mind going back home by himself, would you Jack?"

"No, I will be happy to assist in any way." Jack walked over to Molly and put his hand on her shoulder, then sat down in front of her and held her hands in his. "Phillip, would you mind if I talk with Molly alone?"

Phillip who was more than happy to oblige and retreated to the kitchen to see what Rosa was up to.

Molly felt exhausted as Jack held her hands. She fixed her eyes on his when he spoke.

"Molly, you have had a tough road and I have never known a woman to be as strong and kind-hearted as you." Jack spoke the words with compassion and love for his new friend and he meant everything he said. "I have noticed the affection you feel for Clayton and I have seen how that man has looked at you. He cares very deeply, and he is very intelligent. Whether you believe in God or a higher spirit, you need to know that something has brought you two together. He will be back, you will be with him, and you will both be the happiest you've ever been."

Molly tightened her grip around Jack's hand. "Jack, the odds are not good; it's really rugged territory. If he does make it home, I just don't think that I can go on with this."

"Go on?" Jack repeated her words with concern.

"I mean, running this ranch. I feel that I'm failing. I'm tired of fighting. I just want my life to be easier. I'm really considering selling out and going somewhere that is completely fresh, somewhere no one knows who I am. I know it sounds like the old cliché, like I'm running away, but I just don't care anymore."

"Listen Molly, I am not the expert at what's right or wrong, but I do think you need to be honest to yourself before you can make anyone else happy. Isn't that the lesson in life? You're a nice person. Don't stay here because you think it's expected of you; stay and fight because it's something you feel strongly about. It's what you want. To hell with everyone else. They can figure it out on their own." Jack gave Molly a big friendly hug. "Listen, I am going to have to go back home because I need to get back to work. I don't mind if you would like Phillip to stay here with you."

"No, God bless him, but he's all yours. Please take him with you."

Molly and Jack broke out in a fit of laughter as Molly wiped the tears from her eyes.

"Hey what's so funny?" Phillip asked as he returned with pastries in hand. He set the homemade sweets and a cup of coffee in front of Molly.

Molly sipped her drink and passed over the sticky roll. "Thank you, Phillip. I was just talking with Jack and I really think that I'll be fine. You go back home. You have your practice and I'm sure you will feel much better when you know that Sloan is taken care of."

"Well, if you're sure. I just feel terrible…"

Leeza had walked into the room and cut Phillip off mid-sentence. "She'll be fine. I'm staying." She walked over to where Molly was sitting and plopped down in the chair next to her.

"Well then, I guess that settles it. I better get on the phone and find out when the next flight is available," Phillip concluded.

Phillip and Jack left the two women alone as they went to prepare for their departure.

"Any word?" Leeza asked as she leaned back in her chair.

"Nothing yet," Molly replied, looking out the window. "I feel so damn helpless sitting here on my ass and waiting for everyone else to look for him."

"Well there isn't anything you can do." Leeza replied as she picked up a magazine. "You're much better off waiting here in case he calls."

CLAYTON HAD BEEN making good time and on several occasions he had utilized the large piece of wreckage that he had salvaged as a sled to speed up his descent. Several times, he heard the planes that he was sure had been sent out in search of him, but he knew that his strenuous efforts in attracting their attention had been wasted, and he could not afford to waste any more time.

Daylight during the winter months was very scarce and he knew that not much farther down there was a remote lake with many seasonal cabins. He would much rather spend a night in the comfort of a log cabin than another sleepless night exposed to the elements and the wild animals. He was unfazed by his hunger or the fatigue he felt from his exceedingly brisk pace. He no longer felt the cold but had worked up a sweat under the down of his jacket; he did not rest nor falter and kept going.

The day was once again quickly disappearing. Clayton knew that he must be close and as he began to quicken his steps. "I know I should be coming up on the lake. It should be right around here," Clayton spoke loudly to himself as his own voice echoed back at him.

He had finished walking through one last stand of Ponderosa pines when he came across one of the most beautiful sights that he had ever seen. It was a small lake that was frozen over and sitting alone nestled in the forest with the lake as its backdrop was a tiny cabin. He had made it, and he allowed himself to rest upon the boulder that was perched just above the spectacular spot. He could tell that the place had been closed for the winter.

His adrenaline was no longer pumping and as he slowly stood to his feet, his knees almost buckled. "Come on Clayton, look how close you are. For God's sake man, it's just right in front of you. Get going; there is still a lot of work to be done."

After cheering himself on, he mustered all of his strength to finish the last part of his horrific journey and was soon standing at the doorstep of the house, removing the well needed snowshoes.

"A lock box. Well I guess I'm just going to have to go through the window."

He grabbed a nearby rock with his free hand and smashed the glass of the window. He was halfway in when he had heard the unyielding cries.

"Hey, I'm in here! I'm in here, damn it!" The man's voice sounded very familiar to Clayton.

"I'm coming; just hold on." Clayton pushed himself through the rest of the small window, tearing his jacket on a piece of the jagged glass. He then proceeded to follow the fervent yells to a back bedroom. Unsure what to expect he thrust open the closed door.

"Clayton Leatherbe?" Evin still lay tied to the four-poster bed and was astounded to see the man he had been plotting against standing in the doorway as his savior. "What the hell happened to you? You look like shit."

"I think I should be asking you that question," Clayton replied as he hobbled over to the naked man.

"Long story; just untie me."

Evin was naked as he lay upon the covers and fully exposed.

"I guess you're cold?" Clayton stated as he nodded to Evin's shriveled man pickle.

"What the hell do you think? I've been tied to this damn thing for two days now and I'm in no mood for your sense of humor."

Using the hand on his good arm, Clayton struggled with untying the knot that securely held the naked man in bondage. "Well I'm sure that you can't tell by the way I look, but I've had my own damn problems."

After a determined attempt on Clayton's behalf, Evin jumped to his feet and grabbed his clothes. "Thank God you came along!"

Evin picked up the cell phone that had fallen to the floor and started dialing. "I suppose you don't have a car?"

"Do you think I would have broken into this place if I had a car? My plane went down last night on top of the mountain. I hiked down this morning, and by the looks of it you're damn lucky I came along." Clayton observed the soiled bedclothes. "How many days have you been here?"

"Damn thing is dead." Evin threw the phone against the wall. "Too many. I'm starving." He proceeded to head into the kitchen.

Clayton rummaged through the bathroom medicine cabinet looking for any available pain reliever. "Advil will do." He downed three of the pills and retreated to the other room to find Evin with a can of soup in one hand and a can opener in the other. He quickly observed logs sitting neatly inside the river rock fireplace. "We need to turn the heat up in this place."

"I hope you like chicken noodle," Evin called out. "Because it looks like we have a hell of a lot of it."

Clayton was preparing the loose kindling by crumpling the newspaper around it when Evin walked into the room offering him a hot bowl of chicken soup. Clayton lit the match, setting the fire ablaze and took the bowl of soup. "Thanks."

The two men both ate like savages, filling their bellies with seconds and then thirds. The fire was stoked and Clayton, content, for the time being, laid his bruised body across the couch. "I hope you don't mind," he asked as he wrapped the homemade quilt that he found around him comfortably.

"No, please do. I've been lying down for days." Evin thought of the woman who had brazenly betrayed his trust.

Clayton couldn't help but think of how the man had looked tied naked to the bed and cracked a smile. "So, why don't you tell me how you got into such a predicament. I'm assuming that there was a woman involved."

"I'm glad you find it so amusing and I'm sure you love to see me like this. Some out-of-town bitch, who you probably hired," Evin furiously retorted.

Evin's remark confirmed Clayton's suspicions that he had been the master behind the problems at the ranch, so he decided to play along, although he was confused about who the woman was.

"We thought we'd give you a little taste of your own medicine," Clayton sarcastically replied. "You've caused us enough headaches."

Evin intently fixed his eyes upon Clayton. "Fine, let's cut through the shit. I want that land. How much is it going to cost me?"

Clayton was now sitting fully upright. "Well, it's been pretty obvious that you've been intent on getting it and I can see that you are willing to do whatever it takes. I guess you were never taught what the word "no" means."

"It's not in my vocabulary; there's too much at stake," Evin spoke as his eyes narrowed.

"Like murder?" Clayton asked.

"I didn't murder anyone," Evin retorted.

"The police found a second pair of tire tracks near Sloan Davis's car. The tracks were of a truck and a large trailer. Probably the same trailer you brought the sick cows in."

Evin smiled deviously. "The mad cow was an ingenious plan, but I didn't order a hit on anyone."

Clayton lay back down on the couch. "I never said you ordered it; the poor guy just happened to be in the wrong place and was a witness. There is no doubt that your men knocked him off. You, my friend, are in a shit load of trouble."

"Oh yeah? Well if I go to jail you can be my cell mate, convicted of conspiracy of kidnapping and torture."

"I don't know what the hell you're talking about. My plane crashed and I just happened to find you in the first cabin I came across," Clayton replied.

"At least I'm man enough to admit what I've done. No one else is around. I know that the three of you were out to try and break me down into talking by having that woman play me."

"Really? And who might this woman be?" Clayton asked.

"She spoke with a pretty good southern drawl. I'm sure it was one of Molly's friends. The way that bitch acted, it was a total set up. I'm sure you filled her in on all the details, from your bitch's dog being shot, the poisonous water holes, all the way to the mad cows." Evin had revealed the truth of his schemes.

"I don't owe you anything, but here it is. Molly nor I had anything to do with what happened to you, but I'd have to say you got damn well what you deserved!"

Chapter Fifty Three

Pʜɪʟʟɪᴘ ᴀɴᴅ Jᴀᴄᴋ ᴡᴇʀᴇ ᴀʙʟᴇ ᴛᴏ ɢᴇᴛ ᴛʜᴇ ʟᴀsᴛ ꜰʟɪɢʜᴛ ᴏᴜᴛ ᴏꜰ Bᴏᴢᴇᴍᴀɴ and Phillip made the necessary arrangements for Sloan's body to be flown back to Florida the following day. Phillip made sure that Molly had all the necessary paperwork for a clean divorce. The two men reluctantly said their farewells and one of the ranch hands took them to the airport. As Molly watched Phillip and his new love drive away she sighed with relief that she was finally able to close the door on her past.

Molly still had not heard a word from Clayton. The sun was descending in the sky and she knew that they would soon call the search off and restart tomorrow.

Leeza had stayed near Molly throughout the day and tried her best to divert her friend's worries with idle chit chat, but Molly had a hard time focusing on anything but Clayton's whereabouts. She was mentally preparing herself for the worse.

The phone rang but she could not bring herself to pick up the receiver, scared of what she might hear.

"Molly, aren't you going to pick it up?' Leeza asked as she walked over to the phone and placed it to her ear. "Hello? She's right here." She put the receiver in Molly's hand.

"Molly, this is Bill. We have some news. They found the plane, it had gone down in a heavily wooded area."

"Clayton? Please tell me he's not..." Molly began to choke up.

"Molly, he's not there. There were a set of tracks leading out. It looks like he survived and headed down. I'm sure he's going to be fine. There is a private lake roughly a day's hike away with some seasonal vacation homes. Clayton is familiar with the area. My guess is that he headed for the cabins. A storm is heading in, so I'm going to go ahead and send someone up to the lake and check on the cabins and see if he's out there."

"God, that's great news. Can I go with you guys?"

"No, I'd prefer if you stayed at the house. If he can get a hold of a phone he'll be calling through to you."

Molly hung up and with her face lit up like a beacon, turned to her friend who had been anxiously awaiting the news.

"Well, did they find him?" Leeza asked.

"They found the wreckage. Clayton was nowhere to be found, but the good news is that they found tracks leading down the mountain. They think he hiked down to where there is a lake with some cabins." Molly repeated what Bill had told her and noticed a look of surprise on Leeza's face. "Isn't that great news?" Molly asked.

"Yes, that's great, but how do they know for sure that he made it? How far are these cabins?"

"The sheriff said going down hill, he could have made it in a day's hike."

"That's great news," Leeza responded with a smile.

ALTHOUGH BOTH MEN were physically deprived of their strength and sleep, neither one trusted the other enough to let their eyes fall shut and get the rest that their bodies needed. Clayton knew that since Evin had blatantly admitted his crimes, he would be capable of anything, and that would include murder. He was smart enough to know that he was now a threat to Evin and he knew that it was very likely that the man was not about to let him leave that cabin alive.

They were both silent. Evin sat in the chair and kept intently focused upon his adversary, patiently waiting for the man to close his eyes. The room was quiet, except for the hypnotic crackling of the fire as it burned. Clayton glanced at the flames, keeping vigilant as to Evin's whereabouts. He had just placed a piece of wood on and had stoked the fire when in less than a blink of an eye the six-foot menace leapt from his chair in a single bound to use his fists to pummel Clayton to death.

Although Evin clearly had the advantage with the use of both of his hands, he did not expect Clayton's light-footed response. With incredible agility and strength the bronco buster ducked the developer's attempted blows and with one severe punch to the gut, sent Evin flying backwards, toppling across the floor temporarily knocking the wind out of him. But he wasn't down for long. The malicious man rose to his full height and with unflinching determination waged war against Clayton.

The two men battled endlessly, crashing into tables and splintering the wooden furniture. Clayton fought back feverishly, not just for himself but for Molly, and for the future of the Ghost Bear. But with only the use of his one arm Evin was getting the better of him.

Evin finally got Clayton down on the floor, striking blow after blow to his head. Clayton was helpless and the room began to close in around him as he struggled to stay conscious. He could no longer hear the gentle crackling of the fire as his head

filled with a loud ringing caused by the frenzy of punches landing upon him. Suddenly a loud shot echoed through the air and
unprompted by Clayton, Evin fell lifeless, crashing down upon
Clayton's broken arm. Men in uniform had burst through the
front door and surrounded Clayton and the deceased developer.
The officers pulled Evin's dead weight off the trapped man and
found who they had been searching for.

Clayton was bruised and bloody, his eyes were swelling shut,
and his bone was now protruding from his arm as he cried out
in torment. The sheriff cleared a path for the needed emergency
workers to assist him as they gently lifted him upon the stretcher
and placed him inside the waiting ambulance.

Molly received the call informing her that they had found
Clayton. She yelled to Rosa and Leeza letting them know that he
had been found alive, although in critical condition, and he was
being taken to the emergency room. She asked Rosa to inform
the men that she was heading to the hospital.

"I'm coming with you," Leeza yelled as she ran after her
friend.

The two women jumped into the truck and headed off to the
hospital.

Once on the road Leeza turned to her friend and asked,
"Okay, give me details; where did they find him?"

"He made it to one of the deserted cabins on the lake that
had been for sale." Molly's eyes were wide as she recounted the
traumatic details. "According to Bill they got there just in time,
because that awful man who has been trying to get me to sell the
ranch tried to kill him."

"Are you serious? What the hell was he doing out there?"
Leeza asked.

"Who the hell knows. The sheriff believes that it was Evin
who killed Sloan, and that he was the one behind all of the

problems we've been having out at the Ghost Bear. When the police arrived at the cabin, everything happened so quickly and the police didn't have a choice but to shoot him." Molly shook her head at the thought. "I'm glad that man is dead."

"I don't blame you, Molly I'm glad he's dead too. Everything is going to be alright."

Leeza smiled contently as she leaned her head back.

Chapter Fifty Four

A WEEK HAD GONE BY SINCE THEY HAD FOUND CLAYTON AND TAKEN HIM to the hospital and Molly had stayed diligently by his side. She had lots of time to dwell intently on her future and that of the ranch. She had not forgotten what Leeza had told her about the night that Clayton had tried to kiss her and Molly had decided that she had probably been foolish to think that she would ever be able to tie him down.

Clayton healed relatively well throughout the week until the doctors concluded that he was strong enough to go home.

As Molly helped him into her truck she decided to break the news. "Clayton, I've been thinking a lot about my future."

"I can certainly understand why you would," Clayton replied.

"I don't want to be alone the rest of my life out on some God forsaken ranch; there is always going to be someone who is trying to get me to sell."

"Do you view yourself as alone, when you have all of us living out there?" Clayton asked. He looked out his window and thought to himself how ironic it was that Evin had wanted the land so bad that he was willing to break the law and then pay with his life, and now Molly wanted to sell out.

"Clayton I don't always want to sleep alone. I want a husband, someone with whom I can experience love."

Clayton was silent as Molly spoke. Thoughts raced through his head. Even though they had rid themselves of Evin, there was still a perilous threat that lurked amongst them.

"Do you have any buyers?" Clayton asked.

"No, I wanted to talk to you first."

She longed for Clayton to beg her to stay. "Well, if you feel that strongly, then I guess I understand."

Those were not the words Molly wanted to hear. Disappointed, she kept her tongue still and drove in silence until they were home.

Clayton thanked Molly for her watchful eye and continued support while he healed in the hospital and then headed for his house.

"Clayton, don't you want to come over? Rosa would love to see you and Leeza has been waiting all day for your arrival."

"I'll be over in a little while. I have a few things to take care of."

The evening had come and gone and after no sign of Clayton, Molly had given up. She headed out the door and yelled to Leeza that she was going to the corral and stables. The night was cold and the air was brisk. As she walked past Clayton's house, she could see the flicker of shadows from the fireplace and the warm glow within. She wrapped her arms around herself and continued on to the corral.

Clayton had taken care of all the necessities needed to move ahead with his plan. Time had run out and the situation was becoming increasingly dangerous. He was left with no other choice but to disclose the shocking truth to Molly that she had a sister.

He left the warmth of his small cabin to clear his head and try to find the right words to tell her. He wandered over to the stables and barn to check on the horses when he was startled by Molly's presence.

"Clayton, what on earth are you doing out this late at night?" She walked over to Clayton and, as if he was a small boy, buttoned his shearing jacket tight around his neck. He took her securely by the arm and with his good hand, pulled her to him.

Molly felt herself go limp as Clayton firmly held her with his strong callused hands, the same powerful hands that she watched lustfully as they roped Angus cattle, broke prized stallions and fixed miles of old fence post. She watched these same hands perform their daily duties and would daydream of the sensation of his touch on her skin. She had admired their strength and had become intoxicated by them.

Clayton gazed down into the depths of Molly's blue eyes with such intensity that he was able to reach in and pluck out her soul. All of her desires were mounting and taking over and she knew that she had lost control of the lust that was building inside her.

Neither one of them had any control over the passion they felt for each other. As her body quivered under his touch, Molly reached up for Clayton's lips, parting them ever so gently with her moist tongue. From the first moment that Clayton pressed his lips to her, Molly knew that they were destined for each other and she would never let him go. She loved this man, and for the first time in her life, she felt whole and complete.

As Molly inhaled heavily, the aroma of spice and leather swirled off from Clayton's masculine skin and filled her nostrils with delight. He enthralled her. He had heightened her senses to a level beyond her wildest dreams.

Clayton could not contain the burning passion he felt for Molly. He slowly unzipped her coat and reached under her denim shirt, longing to feel her swollen breast. Even though Molly was in her forties her breasts were firm and ample and seemed to reach out with anticipation for his touch, as if they were aware of the great pleasure that awaited them. As he gently caressed her peaks he looked again into her spectacular eyes, blue as the glacier lakes that lay amongst the surrounding mountains. His emotions were soaring to new heights and he felt drunk with lust.

They used the blackness of the night as if it was a blanket to conceal their intertwined bodies. As they kissed, Clayton could hear the snorting from the stud that they used for breeding earlier that day. It was as if the giant stallion was observing Clayton's actions with his gentle black eyes and giving approval for Clayton to give in to his fleshly desire for Molly.

Although Clayton had been with many women in the past, Molly had stirred up something that had been hidden deep inside his soul. At first, he had tried to disregard the feelings that he had towards her, knowing that nothing could become of this relationship. He was her ranch foreman.

Molly was such a beautiful woman, her softness mixed with an incredible strength. As each sunrise woke the Montana skies, Clayton rose with the eagerness of a new colt, knowing he would get to spend some time with this lovely creature. She had changed him in more ways than he ever thought possible.

With an undeniable sense of urgency, Clayton picked her up, set her on the wooden fence and began to slide her skirt up. He brushed his long fingers against her thighs as if she was his canvas. Her body quivered with each stroke.

"Yes, Clayton let me feel all of you inside me!" Molly gasped.

She grabbed hold of her muscular cowboy's tight rear and tugged at his zipper in feverish desperation to free his manhood from its tight confinement. Clayton felt the heat rising from between Molly's legs. He moved forward almost touching the warm, wet invite.

The full moon moved out from behind the clouds where it had been hiding in order to take a peak and shine its bright beam down as a spotlight upon the two lovers. The emotion between them was of such a compelling force that neither one had heard the twig break under the heavy footstep.

Just when Clayton was ready to feel the undeniable pleasure of Molly's inner flesh, he heard a thud and then felt a huge pressure on the top of his skull.

Crimson blood drizzled down through his blond hair and he gazed at Molly just in time to see her widen her eyes with terror as she stared at him in horror.

All went silent; all was black.

Chapter Fifty Five

Too heavy to hold, Clayton slipped from Molly's grasp and crumbled to the ground. Molly was not sure as to what had just happened and dumbfounded by the deranged appearance of the woman with the long dark hair who was standing behind the crumpled man with a large rock in hand.

"Leeza, is that you?" Molly stammered as she knelt beside Clayton and lifted his bleeding head into her lap. "What did you do? Jesus, don't just stand there! Go and get some help!" Molly screamed.

Suddenly and without cause, Leeza reached down and grabbed a fistful of Molly's blond hair and with incredible strength, dragged her through the snow towards the raging waters of the icy river.

"I didn't want it to turn out like this. I really didn't, but that stupid son of a bitch left me no choice." Leeza no longer spoke with her southern accent but now sounded like a complete stranger to Molly.

Molly struggled against the woman who had been her closest friend throughout the years, wildly flailing her arms in desperation and trying to scramble to her feet.

Leeza kicked Molly in the rib cage, knocking the wind out of her. "Goddamn it, stop struggling you sniveling little bitch. You are so fucking naive; and weak! You were married all of those years to a damn queer and your best friend was your sister and you had no idea. Fuck, Leeza isn't even my real name." She laughed out loud in her crazy cackle.

The deranged woman had now managed to drag Molly to the edge of the frozen river bank.

"What? I don't understand. Talk to me, Leeza. I'm your friend. Whatever it is I can help you."

Molly was in a state of shock, her mind unable to process what was happening. She lay in the snow as she tried to talk some sense into her friend.

"What? You think you can help me? What a fucking joke. You can't even help yourself, you weak, stupid girl. You still don't get it, do you? Well I'll fill you in on some of the details before I end your pathetic existence."

Softening her voice, Leeza reached down and stroked the side of Molly's face.

"I never wanted to hurt you. Well okay, maybe that was the plan at first. When I first stalked you down and befriended you, do you remember the day we first met? I approached you at the club.

"I knew who you were. I've known you my whole life. My momma would always tell me how my daddy loved you more. You got the fancy house, the nice clothes while I got rags and grew up in a rat infested shit hole. I always knew that you were the special one. Daddy loved you. I was just the mistake he had to pay for. I would stare out the window for hours praying he would come down that drive and save me from her. She was nothing but an old drunk and I was nothing but her meal ticket. He could have saved me, let me grow up with you and with a loving mother like yours. But fine, whatever. I got dealt the shitty hand and I dealt with it.

"I kept close tabs on you for years, and when we met, I was happy to have you. We had a bond. I fell in love with you. You were my sister and I would do anything for you, Molly. I've always been there on the sidelines for you. Jesus, I even got back at Sloan. I wanted him to suffer for what he did to you. Don't you see how much I loved you?

"That son of a bitch deserved a slow painful death for his crimes. But the little twit had to come out here and get himself killed by that damn money-hungry, skanky land developer. Oh, by the way, I even gave that asshole a taste of his own medicine. If it wasn't for your lover boy there, Evin would still be tied to that bed and no one would have found him until the spring.

"Damn it, I've been the one to protect you, Molly. I even killed my own mother when she was ready to spill the beans. I never wanted you to find out. Things were good between us! Clayton is the one who had to go sniffing around and find out all of our family's dirty little secrets. He ruined everything. He knew everything, and now you do, too. I can't leave anything to chance." Leeza was now screaming hysterically at Molly. "This is where I draw the line. You have to go. I'm sick of taking care of you!"

Molly couldn't believe her ears. She was paralyzed with horror as she listened to the woman's rant. "Leeza, I never knew. I never had any idea. You could have told me. We could have had a sisterly relationship. I love you. I won't say a word," Molly begged in desperation.

Leeza paused for a moment and tilted her head to the side, as if to consider a truce. "Times up, bitch; you got to go!"

Leeza abruptly lifted the large rock over her head, building momentum to slam the boulder down upon Molly's face.

Molly reacted at the precise moment and rolled out of the way while jumping to her feet, and with true grit and speed of a race horse, charged head first, knocking the mad woman backwards. Leeza, flew off her feet and Molly jumped on top of her chest, pinning her to the ground, throwing blow after blow smashing her friend's face in. Molly fought ferociously, for her life, but Leeza was not about to let her sister get the best of her. She was able to get one of her arms out from under Molly's leg and jammed her fingers into Molly's wind pipe.

Unable to breath, Molly jumped off from Leeza and while gasping for air walked backwards nearing the large cliff.

This gave Leeza the ability to now charge after Molly and she jumped from the ground. "You fucking bitch!" She screamed like a wild banshee running towards Molly.

Just as Leeza approached her target, Molly moved to the right, sending Leeza over the edge to plunge into the river. Instinctively and with incredible reflexes Molly reached out and grabbed hold of the woman as she fell.

"Hang on, Leeza, I have you." Molly had Leeza, but by the hair. "Give me your hand. I can't hang on."

Leeza reached out for Molly but it was too late. She was falling, leaving only her black wig in Molly's grasp as she fell backwards into the water. The current of the icy river quickly swallowed the woman down, as she held her white ghastly hand out for her sister's help. Molly frantically cried out for her, only to see the hand completely disappear beneath the black waters. Beyond hope, Molly was inconsolable as she scanned the waters.

Molly's screams had awakened Clayton and he descended from behind her and pulled her to him, wrapping his arms tightly around her.

"Honey, she's gone, she's gone. It's going to be alright." Clayton stroked Molly's blond hair as she cried uncontrollably.

Through the flood of tears, Molly could see the blood flowing over his face. "Clayton, your head, oh my God, we need to get you some help."

"I'm okay." He took a bandana out of his pocket and wiped his stained face, then pressed the cloth to his head. He grabbed the back of Molly's head and pulled her lips to his, giving her the most passionate kiss of her life and only pulling himself away long enough to ask, "Molly O'Malley, will you marry me?" Without giving her time to reply he finished the kiss that he'd started.

Chapter Fifty Six

IT HAD BEEN ONE OF THE LONGEST WINTERS FOR MOLLY, CLAYTON AND the history of the Ghost Bear Ranch. The snow had finally melted and been replaced with a sea of green grass with white lilies and tulips sprinkled amongst them. The waters of the river now flowed freely and contained lively trout just waiting to be caught upon the line of a determined fly fisherman and fried for dinner.

The Ghost Bear Ranch teemed with new life, as on this particular day great preparations were being made for the joyous event of Clayton and Molly's wedding. People from miles around were arriving and Molly was nervously in her room getting dressed in a long flowing gown with the help of her daughter.

"Savanna, I'm so nervous. I hope I'm not making a mistake," Molly whispered as her daughter placed the veil upon her mother's head.

"Mom, you know that you're not making a mistake. I've never seen you so happy."

Savanna kissed her mother's cheek.

"He does make me happy," Molly beamed. "And so does this ranch."

Molly stood up and walked over to her window while looking out at the crowd of family and friends who were sitting in their perfectly aligned chairs amongst rows of white lilies.

Molly sadly turned from the window and sat down on her bed. "Savanna, I keep looking out at everyone arriving expecting to see Leeza's face beaming up at me."

Savannah sat next to her mother and dabbed the tear that fell from her eye. "I know. It was such a shock, but she really was troubled. You were so lucky. Don't cry. We don't have time to do your makeup all over," Savannah spoke gently.

"They never found her body, only her tattered clothes. I just cringe at the thought of a pack of wolves pulling her from that river and feasting upon her frozen remains. She was my friend for so long; and then to find out she was the sister I always wanted. Things should have been so different. I would have shared all of this with her."

"Mom, I think a part of her knew that you would. Try to hang on to the good memories and forget the rest."

Savannah pulled her mother to her feet. They could hear the band signal the cue for them to leave and for Molly to make her appearance.

Molly took one last glance out her window, seeing Clayton handsomely dressed in a black western tuxedo with Sedona patiently sitting next to him, a small barrel tied to her neck that hid Molly's diamond wedding band.

Molly let out a giggle, turned around to her daughter and grinned. "I'm ready."

Epilogue

THE WOMAN SAT IN THE SMALL CAFÉ ON THE OUTSKIRTS OF QUÉBEC patiently waiting for her newest victim. He was a registered sex offender who normally liked little girls and had hired her for a couple hundred dollars to play the part. She was early, so she ordered a cup of coffee and pulled out the paper that she had neatly tucked under her purse.

Inhaling the dark aroma of her coffee, she opened the *Montana Gazette* and flipped directly to the wedding announcements. Under her breath, she read the details of the happily married couple, Mr. and Mrs. Clayton Leatherbe. She sighed, spotting her little fly who was now walking through the door. She left the paper on the table and approached him,

"Hey, Daddy, ready to play house?"

Taking him by the hand, she led him out the door.

Author's Notes

I WOULD LIKE TO TAKE THIS MOMENT TO THANK ALL OF MY READERS. Without you I would not be able to do what I love the most. I am always happy to hear from you. So if you have access to the Internet you may contact me at my website, www.TmarieBench ley.com. I do try my best to respond to everyone, but please be patient as it seems that there are many people with so many questions. Please do not send any attachments, as I do not open them, and please, no more marriage proposals. I am happily married and in complete bliss!

I work with several charities worldwide by doing live as well as virtual book signings, in which I donate a portion of my books' sales. If you are interested in attending a book signing, please visit my website to find updated lists as to my tour schedule.

For those of you who wish to make offers for rights of a literary nature or to schedule a book signing, please contact my agent or publisher at their website MmwePublish@aol.com.